EDEN MINE

EDEN

FARRAR, STRAUS AND GIROUX   NEW YORK

MINE

S. M. HULSE

Farrar, Straus and Giroux
120 Broadway, New York 10271

Copyright © 2020 by Sarah M. Hulse
All rights reserved
Printed in the United States of America
First edition, 2020

Permissions Acknowledgments tk

Library of Congress Cataloging-in-Publication Data
ISBN: 978-0-374-14647-4

Designed by Abby Kagan

Our books may be purchased in bulk for promotional, educational, or business
use. Please contact your local bookseller or the Macmillan Corporate and
Premium Sales Department at 1-800-221-7945, extension 5442, or by e-mail at
MacmillanSpecialMarkets@macmillan.com.

www.fsgbooks.com
www.twitter.com/fsgbooks · www.facebook.com/fsgbooks

1   3   5   7   9   10   8   6   4   2

[dedication tk]

EDEN MINE

My brother's bomb explodes at 10:16 on a late April Sunday morning.

I don't know. I'm a hundred and fifty miles northwest, in the house he and I share. I've just taped together the first cardboard moving box, and it sits on the hardwood before me, yawning empty.

Later, I'll imagine the explosion with such regularity and intensity the details become etched in my mind alongside my own memories, sharp-edged and indelible. I'll be hounded by those details, haunted. The shattering glass, thousands of jagged pieces slicing the air, capturing and fracturing the light. The enormity of the sound, the brute physicality of it, and then its numbing absence. The clouding dust, the crumbling rubble. The blood.

But at 10:16, I know nothing. Packing my biggest problem.

Twelve injured, one critically. A child, the daughter of the pastor of the church across the street from the bomb. Services barely begun, only the first hymn sung, the first reading spoken. The child's father prays over her for the three minutes it takes her to lose consciousness, for the four minutes more it takes the paramedics to arrive. He cradles her as he prays, and he'll find flecks of red on his skin and under his nails for days afterward. *So much blood*, he will say. *So fast.*

I don't know any of this. There's no tingle at the back of my neck, no sudden catch of breath at the moment of detonation. I have no idea. None, until the radio cuts off the newest country star in the midst of his climb up the weekly countdown, replaces his easy twang with the clipped voice of a reporter. If my gut contracts when I hear the word *courthouse*, it is only because we got bad news there not long ago. If I try calling Samuel's cell phone, and then try again, and again, it is simply because a person wants to talk to family after a disaster like this, and he is the only family I have. And if what I feel when the knock comes and I open the door to the sheriff is not exactly surprise . . . well, that's just the shock.

———

Jo, what can I say to you?

———

"You heard about what happened down in Elk Fork?"

I've known Sheriff Cody Hawkins all my life. His son was Samuel's best friend when they were young, and for that reason Hawkins has always seemed as much a family friend as an agent of the law. When I was a girl, he was the first to confirm my mother's death, to say aloud what I already knew.

"The radio said there was an explosion." The final word a whisper, the syllables reluctant to leave my lips. I swallow. "A bomb."

Hawkins nods. He's still on the porch; past him, a young deputy stands near the truck, a hand on the butt of his gun.

Hawkins looks more casual in jeans and a threadbare Prospect High Miners T-shirt, an ugly windbreaker thrown on top. Sunday, off-duty, at least until this. But his weapon is there at his hip, beside the star on his belt. "Samuel here?" Hawkins takes a single step forward. I don't move from the doorway.

"He left for Wyoming this morning." Still sounds like a fact. "To see about work. Sheridan and then Gillette."

I remember breakfast. The eggs I made, the way I pushed Samuel's bread into the toaster a second time because he likes it black. He'd cleaned his plate. Helped with the dishes before he left. Smiled from the door. That's all. I think about it again, study each recalled minute and second, but there's nothing else. Breakfast. Dishes. Smile. *He's somewhere beyond Bozeman by now*, I tell myself.

"Wyoming," Hawkins says. Like he can taste the truth of it.

The deputy starts toward the barn. "Nothing out there but some hay and an old mule," I call. The deputy stops midstride, looks at me, Hawkins. Seems to consider going back to the truck, settles on standing awkwardly in the middle of the drive.

Hawkins turns back to me. "He ain't in there, is he?"

"Hay and an old mule," I repeat, clinging to this bit of certainty.

Hawkins squints a little the way he does when forcing himself not to look away. I want to slam the door, clap my hands over my ears, but I make myself wait for the words. "See, Jo, we've got, uh, reason to believe Samuel might've been involved in this business down in Elk Fork."

"He's gone to Wyoming." I hear the desperation in the repetition, the effort to build truth from speech.

Hawkins's features close; he's heard it, too. He maintains that resolved eye contact, and I try to silence the echoes of his last statement—*reason to believe, might've been involved*—so I can brace for whatever comes next. "There's a smoke shop kind of kitty-corner behind the courthouse," he tells me slowly. "Been having some trouble with vandalism in the alley, apparently. They installed a security camera just yesterday; Samuel wouldn't have known about it."

After my mother was killed, Hawkins drove to the hospital and then the rehabilitation center every Sunday afternoon. He'd bring me an orange soda, maybe an *Archie* comic or a copy of *Western Horseman*. Afterward, he'd walk around the grounds with Samuel, who always came back to my side with his jaw a little more relaxed, his smile a little easier to coax forth.

"Can I come in, Jo?"

"No."

Didn't expect that. I see it in the stunned blink, the twitch at one corner of his mouth. An apology rises in my throat, and I swallow it. I want to tell him it's not personal. I want to tell him *no* is the only word I can form right now, the only sentiment I recognize. *No*, this is not happening. *No*, you're wrong about Samuel. *No*, this sick dread squeezing my chest doesn't mean I believe you. *No*.

"I got a warrant." The words apologetic, but with an edge behind them.

I stay in the living room with the deputy while Hawkins searches. Down the hall to my bedroom and studio—hardly a moment there, a cursory, courteous glance—then to the bathroom, the hall closet, the kitchen. Then upstairs.

I pick up the tape gun and start assembling a second box, though the first is still empty. The deputy watches, looks away when I meet his eyes. He's my age, early twenties, but the patch on his uniform says Split Creek, not Prospect, and I don't know him. Bits of hay cling to his boots; he checked the barn after all.

I listen to Hawkins's footfalls above. He steps more heavily than Samuel, his strides longer. He stops at the doorway to my childhood bedroom, at the end of the upstairs hall. I hear the groan of the floorboard swell and fade as he leans into the room and back out. Hasn't changed since I last regularly occupied it at ten: lavender walls, lace curtains, plastic ponies standing at attention on the bookshelves.

Next Hawkins inspects the bathroom—I hear a second's pause—and then he is in Samuel's room. What does he find there? I rarely go upstairs, and when I do, Samuel's door is shut. His bed is there, of course, probably with the same bear paw quilt he had as a teenager, meant to look like an heirloom but purchased on clearance at Kmart. Clean clothes in the closet, laundry on the floor. Bookshelves filled with veterinary texts, survival manuals, law books, maybe a novel or two. I wonder if he ever replaced his Bible.

What else? There was a Nazi flag on the wall, back when I was in high school. It was an identity Samuel tried on and almost immediately discarded, his racist phase brief but committed. (He still disparagingly mentions "the Jews" now and then, and says things like "our kind" and "those people" more than I wish he did, but that's nothing like the old tirades.) He burned the flag in a barrel in the yard a couple months after I spotted it, but the swastika tattoo on his biceps wasn't so easily disposed of; he wears long sleeves year-round now.

So the flag is gone, but what has replaced it, I don't know. Until today I have been content not to know.

Hawkins comes downstairs. "Where do you keep your guns?"

"Haven't got any."

"Samuel does." It's not a question. Twice he caught Samuel poaching, back when there wasn't much money for food. Twice he let him go with a warning. Twice I opened the back door to find a bag of groceries on the stoop.

"He'll have taken the rifle with him," I say, and immediately regret it.

Hawkins nods. "The FBI is sending some people out," he says. "I'd guess they'll be here in a few hours. News folks will be, too." He looks at the empty boxes behind me, and a wince crosses his face. "You still have the number of that lawyer?"

"The one who lost our house?" Not fair, maybe. The lawyer warned us it was unlikely we'd be able to keep the house; he was right. When the eminent domain notice came, Samuel wanted to handle it sovereign-citizen-style, by filing dozens of lengthy documents, cluttering up the court with pages upon pages of pseudo-legalese. He went to a few of their meetings a couple years back and ultimately dismissed them as overly focused on tax protest to the exclusion of what he called "broader concerns"—by then I knew better than to ask what he meant—but he admired their ability to use the government's judicial system against itself. I talked him out of it—it was one thing to appreciate a tactic like that, another to actually try it—and convinced him to hire the lawyer. We did it my way, the ordinary way. And we lost.

"Call him," Hawkins says. "You'll need a statement and someone to read it for you. And you maybe ought to talk to him about . . . anything else you think you ought to talk to him about."

I don't know whether to be insulted or flattered that Hawkins seems to think Samuel has let me in on something, offered me hint or warning. Of course I'd have stopped him if I'd known. If there was anything to know. If it was him. Hawkins mentioned a security camera, but I've seen the grainy images they produce; they're never very clear. So my brother holds some fringe beliefs. He talks, that's all. Talks and talks until he loses interest in whatever he's been talking about and goes in search of something else. It doesn't mean anything. Hawkins should know that, shouldn't have accepted Samuel's guilt so readily. It's too early for certainty.

Hawkins starts toward the door. I want to challenge him somehow, prove I don't share his certitude, but I'm afraid to ask about the bombing itself, so instead I say, "You're so sure Samuel had a part in this, how come you bothered to knock?"

There's something like admonishment in the downturn of his mouth. "Jo, you know there ain't no way I'd bust through the door of this house with a gun in my hand. Not ever." He hesitates at the threshold, gestures toward the young deputy. "Carson's gonna stay till the FBI folks get here." Takes me a moment to realize it's so I don't destroy evidence.

I wonder whether there's any evidence to find, if I would recognize it if I saw it. What I'd do with it if I did.

So many things I should do. Call the lawyer, like Hawkins said. Call my boss at Fuel Stop. Make sure Hawkins closed the gate across the drive, check that its NO TRESPASSING placard is still legible after weathering so many winters. Maybe try to surreptitiously search the house, see if there is anything here, anything that might prove Samuel went where he said he's gone. Anything he left me to explain this.

Instead, I go to my studio. The deputy follows, glances around the room, then positions himself outside in the hall. Still just a step away, only the illusion of privacy. I do my best to ignore him, stare at the half-finished painting on my easel beside the window. I started it two days ago after a brief but substantial rainstorm, energized by the brightening green of the late April meadows, the clouds fading from gray to white as they scattered high into the warming sky. Mountains. Meadows. Trees and streams, slopes and sky. My materials, as surely as brush and acrylic.

I am not an artist. Not the way people mean. I've never been to art school, never had a teacher, never hung my canvases in a gallery. I have talent enough to know what talent I lack. But I am good at painting what people want to see, good at rendering this corner of the West the way visitors and residents alike often expect or wish it to be. My brushstrokes are sweeping, my hues vibrant. The elk and deer who populate my paintings are never mangy or scarred, the cabins always sturdy and lit warmly from within, the mountains unscathed by mines, and on the rare occasions winter descends upon my scenes, there's always a fire crackling in a corner of the canvas.

These are largely practical decisions. I don't paint as a hobby, or not only as a hobby. My canvases are meant to be sold, and the folks buying paintings in Prospect are mostly tourists on their way to or from more spectacular parts of the state; no tourist wants a painting that includes mine tailings or aging trailer parks. So there's some calculation in it, yes, but it's not purely mercenary. I enjoy casting the world in its best light. I take satisfaction in creating the most beautiful version of this landscape I have known all my life. Each idyllic portrait of this valley feels like a gift to the place that is my home. If I overlook the flaws of that which I love, I'm no different than anyone else.

"Don't you ever get tired of painting the Disneyland version of Montana?" Samuel asked once. I shrugged, knowing he'd take that as acquiescence, but really I don't. Didn't.

But I've been thinking about Samuel's question more in the weeks since the court's decision. I've painted the view from my studio window countless times. Always the idealized version: a willow instead of the wind-whipped juniper, a barn paneled in classic red wood instead of practical gray steel. Most of those canvases I sold, and I was glad to trade each for the few dollars it brought, but suddenly they seem precious, and I a fool to part with them. It seems impossible I might someday forget this land, the rise and fall of the hard line between earth and sky, the easy spread of grass and trees, but I feel a new urgency to record them, and, for the first time, to do it honestly. To paint the juniper, not the willow, the gray barn, not the red. To prove that they are real, and mine.

I paint, and try to forget the radio, the knock on the door, the deputy in the hall. I try to imagine Samuel in his truck, approaching Billings now, humming along to a country CD and tapping one hand against the wheel. I paint and try to lose myself in the colors, to appreciate the way cerulean eases to dove gray at the height of the canvas, the yellow-white dance of sunlight on the arcing green of the grass. I mix the paints precisely, apply them meticulously. Build another beautiful world. But it isn't right, because I've done it again: painted the version I create for others, the version I've always been content to pretend is real.

And have I done the same thinking of my brother? Have I painted him into his truck in my mind, into the story he told me this morning?

I carefully dip my brush in bone black and cross it over the canvas again and again.

The first time my cell phone rings, I answer, then hang up before the reporter finishes telling me his name. Answer again the second time. Another reporter. I answer—and hang up—the third, fourth, and fifth times, too, and only after the sixth ring in half an hour do I mute the thing, though I keep it in my palm, watching new calls light up the old flip phone's tiny screen. The numbers are never ones I recognize, never Samuel's. I let it ring until the battery gives out and don't plug it in to charge.

The gate across the drive isn't visible from the house, and I doubt anyone is out there yet—it's a two-hour drive from Elk Fork even if you take the curves too fast—but I use the back door anyway. The sun is bright overhead, the day younger than seems possible.

The barn and house are separated by eighty yards and a small stream that runs strong this time of year; the water rushes just below the wooden planks of the footbridge when I cross it. The creek looks clear, but the mines have laden it with lead, zinc, and arsenic, and we have to fence part of it off so the mule can't drink the poisoned water. Lockjaw, grazing in the pasture, sees me coming and brays loudly before sauntering into a stall. There's a radio in the barn aisle—Samuel says the music soothes the mule—and I let my hand hover over the dial for a second before I switch it off: . . . *were attending services at Light of the World Church at the time of the explosion* . . . All I hear. More than I want to hear.

I saddle and bridle Lockjaw, promise the deputy who has shadowed me to the barn that I'll stay in sight, then mount and begin riding toward the rear of the property. I've always loved Lockjaw's easy, relaxed stride, the way her long ears dip to the sides with each deliberate step. I let the reins drape and try to settle into the rhythm of the mule's gait, but the shock of the day's events collides with the simmering worry of the last couple months, and I know I'll never again enjoy riding the property the way I once did. The day is like any other for Lockjaw, though, and she heads for the barbed wire and then turns left, hooves raising dust in the narrow, worn track beside the perimeter fence line.

Our great-great-grandfather Eli purchased this land in 1920, after thirty years working in Eden Mine. He built the house in the center of the forty acres, the barn to the southeast; to this day they are two of the last structures visible from the highway before reaching the Canadian border twelve miles north. The mountains rise from the eastern edge of the property, and the oldest depths of Eden burrow into the hardrock slopes behind the house. The mine expanded to the south in the years since, Eden's tunnels and adits reaching farther and farther before being overtaken by the newer Gethsemane Mine. The town followed, the newest homes and businesses always built just south of the ones erected prior.

Being left behind suited Eli; once he retired, he wanted as little to do with the mines as possible. Family legend says he left a lamp burning in his bedroom each night, having sworn off darkness. He intended this land to be a cattle ranch, but after the first year half the cattle died of blackleg and the rest sold for less than he'd paid. He could've made up the loss by selling some land, but he'd never owned anything before, and he made his son swear never to sell a single acre. Samuel told me our father made him swear the same thing.

In thirty-seven days, the state of Montana will force Samuel to break that promise.

Rather than ride the fence line all the way to the road, I cut across the pasture behind the house. Samuel hasn't yet mowed this year, and the grass reaches almost to Lockjaw's knees; she snatches a few mouthfuls without breaking stride. I close my eyes, concentrate on the tentative heat of the spring sun, the ease of the journey over this land.

"Josephine Faber?"

I open my eyes. A man in his late forties stands in front of the bridge over the creek. Average height, dark hair gone gray at the temples, eyes narrowed to a squint in the sun.

"Samuel's not here."

"Are you—"

"Yes. I am." The man's suit looks like the one Samuel owns: plain black, a few loose threads protruding from the holes in the plastic buttons, a decent if imperfect fit. His shirt is white, his tie an inoffensive red-and-gray stripe. He also wears black cowboy boots, and they aren't near scuffed enough to make me think they've touched dirt before today. "You're FBI?"

"Senior Resident Agent Will Devin." He holds up an ID, but he's too far away for me to read it. I wonder if he's done that on purpose, hoping I'll dismount. The plastic window in the wallet catches the sun, and a small square of reflected light skitters between us.

Lockjaw reaches for another mouthful of grass, and this time I stop her. "There are more of you at the house?"

Devin shakes his head. "Not yet. We've flown up some specialists from the Joint Terrorism Task Force in Salt Lake." I flinch at the word *terrorism*, repeat it in my head until I'm numb to the syllables so the next time I hear them their sting won't show on my face. "They're still down in Elk Fork. I'm based at the resident agency there."

I glance at his boots. "So you're, what, the down-home, folksy, local-boy agent I'm supposed to trust because you wear a pair of Justins?" *Shouldn't have said that.* But I don't know what I should have said instead. I don't know how to behave in this situation. I do know what Samuel thinks of the FBI, and maybe that's why I've defaulted to confrontation, which is so unlike me but so like my brother.

"Something like that." Devin nudges a stone with the toe of one boot. "They're Lucchese, actually."

I don't care how much he paid for his boots. I should never have mentioned them, should never have tried to emulate Samuel.

I urge Lockjaw forward, and Devin steps aside. I ride behind the barn and have already halted Lockjaw beneath the mounting bar by the time Devin comes around the corner. I see him take it in: the zigzagging ramp Samuel built, the metal bar overhead, and my wheelchair waiting on the platform at the top of the ramp. He keeps his expression neutral, but I don't think he knew.

He takes a step toward Lockjaw, and I say, "I don't need help." I unwind the lead rope from the saddle horn and loop it over the bar above, letting the knotted reins drop to Lockjaw's withers. Then I reach down and remove each of my feet from the stirrups before grabbing the bar overhead with both hands and pulling my body from the saddle. I move my hands sideways along the bar, like a child at a playground, and Lockjaw stands immobile even as my right leg drags across the saddle. When I've positioned myself properly, I settle into my wheelchair, one hand still holding Lockjaw's lead. I release the brakes on my chair, back Lockjaw away from the mounting bar, and only then turn to face Devin. "A complete spinal cord injury," I explain. "No feeling or movement below my waist."

He says nothing as I wind my way down the ramp. Lockjaw obediently follows my path on the ground. In the barn, I unbridle her and tie her in the alleyway. Devin stands a couple yards away—between me and the exit, which can be no accident— but he stays silent as I finish untacking Lockjaw, and makes no more moves to help, even when I reach to pull the saddle from Lockjaw's back and the bridle in my lap falls to the ground in a tangle of leather and metal.

He's good. Not that most people gawk and point when they first meet me, but they tend to studiously avoid looking at my chair, and often fix their eyes on a point a couple inches above my head. He does neither, and I find myself wishing he would.

I don't want to be Jo Faber right now—don't want to be a suspect's sister—and I'm desperate for almost any alternative, even Woman in Wheelchair. At least I've had practice playing that role.

I settle the tack on its racks in the barn aisle and hang my helmet on a hook near the stall, beside the dressage whip I carry to replace the leg cues I can no longer give. Then I run a brush over Lockjaw's coat, pick the packed dirt and stones out of each hoof in turn. I do these things slowly, trying to draw each second long. *Samuel is almost to Wyoming. He's about to cross the state line and can see the Bighorns.* Finally I untie the rope halter and slide it off Lockjaw's head. I cluck my tongue against the roof of my mouth, and the mule walks past me through the open door of the nearest stall. I shut the door behind her, check the latch. No more excuses for delay. I look at Devin.

"Can we talk in your house?"

"I'd rather not." Another thing I shouldn't say. I expect Devin to insist—he no doubt has the right to—but he hesitates for a fraction of a second and then nods. I'm instantly suspicious, almost wish he had demanded we go inside. I don't like the way this feels like a chess match, and one that sets novice against master. Everything I do seems to mean something to him—even if it doesn't to me—and I can feel him adjusting his responses, calculating and correcting.

A breeze carries through the barn aisle, and Devin's tie flutters away from his chest before settling again. "I'll be up-front. I'm here to arrest your brother."

"He's gone to Wyoming." Every time I say it, it becomes less real. More like a story. More like a lie.

"If he has, he went after he detonated an explosive device at the district courthouse in Elk Fork." Devin says it with no particular inflection. I suppose that's deliberate. Wait to see how

I react, whether I choose to be ally or enemy. I try to keep my features still, and after a moment he continues. "I'm going to be spending a lot of time learning everything there is to know about Samuel Faber. What he's done, where he's been, what he wants, how he thinks. But at this point, I'm close to a blank slate as far as he's concerned." He looks at me. "Tell me the one thing you think I ought to know about Samuel."

"Excuse me?"

"The one thing I ought to know about your brother. Before I find out what everyone else thinks about him, what do you most want me to know?"

I study Devin's face. He looks back steadily, with an expression that is less hostile than I expect. Doesn't mean anything. He can probably call it up at will, probably practices arranging his features into a perfect facsimile of empathy and understanding. He's here to arrest Samuel; he said so himself. I am a source of information, nothing more. A means to an end.

In my place, my brother would say nothing. Not a word.

"He's—" I stop. Devin tilts his head, waits.

One thing. One thing about Samuel. So much seems important. I could tell Devin that after our mother died, Samuel sold everything we could spare: our mother's jewelry (he saved her wedding ring for me), the two horses and their tack, the station wagon. I could tell him Samuel treated every transaction matter-of-factly, until the day he sold our father's watch. I could tell him Samuel put on that watch the day after our father died—he was only eight years old, and in pictures it hangs low over his hand—and had worn it every day since, and I could tell him that the day he sold it, he came home from the pawnshop and punched a hole through the kitchen wall.

Or I could tell Devin that Samuel had planned to be a veterinarian, had been the best shortstop in Prospect history and was offered a scholarship to the state university, had decided instead to go into the Army with his best friend Kev, had told me but not our mother when our lives took the turn they did. I could tell him that instead of college or the military, Samuel went to work first at the movie theater, then the fried chicken place, the home improvement warehouse, the sprawling junkyard off the old highway, and finally the sawmill in Split Creek.

I could tell him about the time Lockjaw—we'd called her Muley then—ran through a fence and two weeks later went stiff and rigid with tetanus. I could tell him that our mother had been in the barnyard with the rifle, that Samuel begged her not to shoot, and that though the vet said there was no real hope, Samuel spent the next ten days at the mule's side, sitting silently with her in the darkened barn aisle as she spasmed, administering the medications the vet left behind, hand-feeding her soft bran mash when she was finally able to eat, until at last she recovered.

I could tell harsher tales, too, about what happened the night our mother died, or how Samuel came to get a swastika tattoo, or what he said the day the notice about the house arrived. I could tell him how Samuel's faith in government had started to slowly erode even before it shattered into distrust, and how it had transformed into something much darker in the years since. I could tell him that I was sure the worst was behind us, that my brother had tried on half a dozen ideologies over the years but abandoned them all, that at last his soul seemed to have settled until that damned letter arrived. I could tell Devin that as much as I want to deny it, as much as I've been trying all day to deny it, whenever I think of that bomb in Elk Fork—whenever I can't stop myself thinking of it—I think of Samuel, too.

I weigh each of these things, and more. I think of why Samuel sold the watch, why he took the jobs he did, why he stayed with

Lockjaw, even why he got the tattoo. And finally I decide. I meet Devin's eyes. "Samuel," I say, "would do anything for me."

———

I wonder if you know where I am, Jo. If you've thought about it you do, but I wonder if you've let yourself think about it yet.

I really did mean to go to Wyoming. That wasn't a lie. After Elk Fork, I meant to go to Wyoming. Heard my name on the radio before I got to Billings. Don't know where I went wrong. I was careful, really careful. I was careful, Jo, and those people weren't supposed to be there. There wasn't supposed to be a church; I had no idea there was a church. That little girl wasn't supposed to be there.

Do you remember how we only had room for three books when we came here together? I brought Black Beauty *because it was your favorite,* The Call of the Wild *because it was mine, and* East of Eden *because it was the longest book in the house neither of us had read, and because of the name. (Remember how I kept trying to skip the parts I thought were too old for you, but you always caught me at it?)*

I don't have any books this time. It wasn't supposed to be like this. I made preparations just in case—in case of this, I guess—but I didn't think about books. All I have to read is this map of Montana. I'm writing in its margins now, words all along the Canadian border.

Did you believe it right away, Jo? That it was me, that I did it? You probably tried not to. You would do that for me. Maybe you're still trying. Maybe you're doing your best to ignore whatever they've told you, explain away whatever evidence I didn't mean to leave. But deep down, I bet you believed it right away.

Don't worry about it. You were right.

———

I wake in the dark to a sharp cracking sound. At first I think it's a gunshot. Always think I hear gunshots. Then the deepest haze of sleep clears, and I decide it might be thunder; the clouds over the Cabinet Mountains to the west had darkened suspiciously the evening before. But there is no rumble, no lightning bursting through the night. It cracks again, sharp and sudden, and at last I place the sound. The left shutter of the window in my old bedroom upstairs. The latch is broken, and anything more than a slight breeze sends it banging against the house. Samuel has been promising to fix it for weeks, but there's always something more pressing.

"Samuel," I call. Still feel a small thrill of terror when I raise my voice in the night, like a child who has finally gotten up the nerve to call for her parents after a nightmare. "Samuel!"

And then I remember. All of it.

Before bed, I steeled myself and turned the radio on. The bomb had destroyed the south facade of the courthouse, though early reports estimated most of the structural integrity of the building remained intact. No one had been inside. One man was injured by flying debris while walking his dog nearby. (The dog, the reporter assured listeners, was unharmed.) The rest of the injured—eleven in all—had been attending services at Light of the World Church across the street. The church met in a storefront, and when the bomb exploded, the windows facing the sidewalk shattered inward. I listened to the description and imagined the glass splintered into the air like a suspended sculpture of glittering shards, and I wondered whether it had been beautiful for a moment. If it had been beautiful before it was terrible.

Most of the injured were treated and released. Three remain in the hospital, two in serious condition, one critical. That last, the *one*, is the pastor's daughter. She is nine. Her name is Emily.

The shutter slams against the house again. I turn on the bed-side lamp, but the relief I usually feel when light eradicates dark doesn't materialize. I glance at the clock: 2:41.

I could go upstairs on my own. I've never tried it, never had to, Samuel always there to carry me. But I think it's possible; I'm strong. It would mean transferring to my wheelchair, then to the floor at the base of the stairs. It would mean using my hands to cross my right ankle over my left and raising myself backward one stair at a time. Eighteen stairs. Half my body dead weight. No wheelchair at the top. And I'd have to get back down after. Still, I think I could do it.

I consider it a moment more. Even grab the side of the mat-tress, ready to push myself into a sitting position. But I don't want to find out I'm wrong, don't want to learn I'm not strong enough after all. So I stay in bed and lie awake and listen to the shutter crack against the house until at last, near dawn, the wind dies down.

———

It was night then, too. Samuel the first to spot the headlights, understand what they meant. I remember the urgency in his voice when he said, "Mom," the expression on her face when she looked out the window and recognized Ben Archer's truck. Samuel went to the front door, locked it, headed for the back. Mom pulled me down the hall, tucked me into a corner of the closet in her bedroom. The smell of potpourri, the brush of wool on my neck. "Stay here, Josie," Mom told me. "It'll be all right, just stay here." A smile that even at ten I had known was forced. No time to object, to cry. The door closed. Dark.

———

I still haven't called the lawyer. Hawkins is right; I should. But I don't need a lawyer to tell me Samuel is in serious trouble. Besides, a half dozen FBI agents already traipsed through the house yesterday evening, carting away boxes and bags filled with what had been Samuel's possessions and were now classified as "evidence." I sat outside while they worked, stared hard at each person who crossed the whitewashed planks of the porch. I told myself I wanted the agents to meet my eyes, told myself they were cowards for refusing. Told myself I wasn't relieved to be ignored.

They left a receipt when they were done, but I should go through the house and inventory it myself. If I do, will I be able to identify what's missing? I imagine Samuel's room, new empty spaces on the bookshelves and dresser and desk interrupting the dust like chalk outlines. For each familiar object I'd find—the sweater I gave him last Christmas he wore only often enough to show dutiful appreciation, the horseshoe he nailed above his doorway for luck—there would be another absent item I'd fail to conjure in my memory, and yet another I'd never known was there at all.

The radio is still here. Samuel and I haven't owned a television since the day during my sophomore year when I came home to find it in the tall grass behind the house, a heavy rock resting in the center of the shattered screen. *Propaganda of the Zionist Occupied Government*, Samuel said. I've never been able to determine why my brother tolerates the radio but not the television—I think he simply likes music too much to give it up—but he does, and it stayed.

Few stations come in clearly in Prospect, and most have gone back to playing country or Christian pop, but I find one of the talk stations on the AM dial. No one has died in the night. *He hasn't killed anyone*, I think. Try not to add *yet*. I expect them to call Samuel a "person of interest" or something like that, but no, he's a "suspect," not to be approached, armed and dangerous, et cetera. (They give his name as Samuel Henry Faber; the only time I've heard his middle name spoken aloud before is once when our mother was angry with him for staying out all night with Kev.) Lincoln Street in Elk Fork will remain closed at least through the end of the day. There will be a prayer vigil for the pastor's daughter—*Emily, her name is Emily, she has a name and it is Emily*—on Tuesday evening.

Off.

There will have to be a statement; Hawkins is right about that, too. It's surprisingly simple to write. I didn't realize how often I'd heard similar statements on the news, how easily I'd internalized their components: First, express sorrow but don't apologize, because apology is close to admission. (Doesn't matter that nothing is proven yet, that I have nothing to do with it in any case, that I had no idea, that I'm devastated, too . . . *devastated* is a good word; I use it twice.) Second, cross out the sentence that casts your accused loved one in a positive light. (So Samuel raised me since I was ten. So he gave up plenty to do it. No one cares.) Third, say you feel for the victims. No, say you'll pray for them. (I won't. I haven't prayed since I was a kid, and even then I suspected I was talking to myself.) Fourth, think but under no circumstances write that it could not have been your loved one, because he is your loved one, because he has strange ideas but they are just ideas, because he is your brother and how could your brother have done this? End with a futile plea for privacy.

I hear footsteps on the porch as I finish writing. One knock, not loud, then Hawkins's voice. "It's me, Jo." He sounds like he isn't sure I'll answer.

"Just me," he says, when I open the door. I move aside to

let him in, see the glint of metal and glass beyond the row of aspens beside the road. "Quite a crowd out there," Hawkins tells me. "Reporters, mostly. I gave 'em all a stern talking-to about trespassing." He'd have tapped his star at the beginning, tipped his hat at the end. "FBI's got a car by the gate, too." It isn't a surprise—Devin told me the night before—but it's hard to get used to the idea. "There'll be more of them, you know. You won't see 'em, but they'll be watching the house."

I close the door. Hawkins is in uniform today, unflattering khaki head to toe. He's lost weight the last year or so, and it's aged him. "That's a warning for Samuel," I say. "Not me."

Hawkins looks like he means to say something but keeps it to himself. He goes to the couch and perches stiffly on the arm, rests a manila envelope on one knee. I follow him into the living room, park my chair near the hearth. "You here as a sheriff or a friend?"

Hawkins sighs, runs a hand over his face. He had a mustache for years but shaved it last fall when he realized it was graying faster than the hair on his head. He used to smooth it down when he was thinking and hasn't shed the gesture as easily as the mustache. "I don't know, Jo. Both, I guess. I wanted to make sure you were okay."

All he's ever wanted to do.

"I'm fine." Hawkins narrows his eyes but seems willing to accept the lie. "What about you?" I nod to where one hand is pressed against the small of his back.

"It's nothing," he says, taking his hand away. A couple years ago a drunk in a pickup slammed into Hawkins's truck while he was working a traffic stop. The accident left him with back trouble, but he rarely mentions it in front of me.

"Here." I hand him the statement. Hawkins takes a pair of reading glasses from his shirt pocket, skims the words.

"You didn't call a lawyer."

"Read it for me. Sheriffs do that kind of thing."

He folds the paper and puts it in his pocket.

"One more thing." I rock my chair forward a few inches, back. Stop. It's a nervous habit, and Hawkins knows it. "I don't want to talk to that FBI agent anymore. Devin."

Hawkins crosses his arms. "I get that it ain't a pleasant thing, Jo, but under the circumstances—"

"I'll talk to you. You can talk to him."

He sighs again, a short huff with more than a hint of a scoff in it. "This might surprise you, but the FBI don't exactly hold the office of the Sheriff of Prospect County, Montana, in terribly high esteem. No one's got the first idea where your brother is"—he pauses, ever so briefly—"so at the moment, you're about the best lead they've got. They're gonna want their own man on this."

"Tell them I don't recognize their authority. Tell them I consider myself a sovereign citizen of these United States and I acknowledge no higher office of law enforcement than the local sheriff." The words come easily. There are more I can say if these don't work; I can rattle off the right terminology to claim allegiance to any of the half dozen or so extremist ideologies Samuel has cycled through over the years. Despite how much I hated hearing the words from his lips, saying them now makes me feel closer to him.

Hawkins closes his eyes for a long moment, opens them slowly, like a man fighting off a headache. "You ain't ever held to any of that bullshit, Jo, and you know it."

"They don't." I thought carefully about this last night. Devin is dangerous. Smart. More skillful at reading me than I am at reading him. Hawkins knows me better, of course, which might be dangerous in its own way, but I have no secrets from him.

Samuel has no secrets from him. Almost none. "Those FBI folks are gonna read whatever file they've put together on Samuel, and once they have, they won't have a bit of trouble believing his sister subscribes to all the same crazy nonsense."

"I ain't lying to the FBI, Jo. Not even for you."

"Then just tell them the best chance they've got of getting anything useful out of me is by letting me talk to you, not them. Because that's plain truth." If Hawkins calls me on that, it's over. This is borrowed bravado, my best impression of what I think Samuel would do in my place.

"I don't like this," Hawkins says at last.

"You think I do?" I hear my voice crack on the last word. I grip the handrims of my chair hard, stare at the rug on the floor in front of me. It'd be easier to move around the room without the rug, but there's still the ghost of a stain on the hardwood. "I wish with all I've got that Samuel didn't do what you tell me he did. I'm still hoping you're wrong. But I don't want this getting worse than it already is. I've spent years listening to Samuel's diatribes; I probably know more about Ruby Ridge and Waco than half those FBI folks. And I don't want that for Samuel, Hawkins. Whatever he did or didn't do, I don't want it to end like that. But if I'm going to talk to anyone about this, I need it to be someone who knows more about Samuel than what you say he did yesterday."

I'm surprised by my own speechmaking, and I think Hawkins is, too—both of us are used to Samuel being the one prone to oratory—but I see the words working on him, and at last he sighs. "I'll tell them," he allows. "But I can't promise they'll listen."

I nod.

Hawkins stands, presses his hands against his lower back. He walks toward the door, stops just before he gets there. "You ought to see this," he says quietly, and lays the manila envelope on the table beside the door before he leaves.

I ignore it at first. Go into the bathroom, put up my hair in a braided bun for work. Clean the kitchen counters. Wash the dishes, which is usually Samuel's job.

I can't do this forever. Refuse knowledge. Embrace ignorance. But each piece of truth that settles in my soul brings searing understanding with it. *He is probably not in Wyoming. The glass shattered inward. Her name is Emily.* It doesn't, I hope, make me a monster for waiting until each piece of information starts to become a familiar sort of pain before seeking out the next.

So I fold laundry. Put away the brushes I left scattered in my studio yesterday. And finally, after sitting a few feet away and staring at it for several long minutes, I open the envelope.

A single photograph inside, printed on cheap copy paper in grainy gray scale. There's a time-and-date stamp in the corner indicating the still is from 10:00 Sunday; the image isn't as blurry as I imagined it would be. I don't recognize the truck. Samuel's is an extended-cab Ford, the front bumper tied on with baling twine; this one is smaller and older. For a moment I feel elated—*It isn't his truck*—and then my eye goes to the figure in the bed, bending over a small suitcase. He wears a baseball cap and sunglasses, and I've never seen that sweatshirt before, but the hard jawline, oh, that I do know, and the strong build, and the slight hollow in his left cheek where he's missing two teeth.

Despite what I told Hawkins, when I rose this morning I thought I'd accepted it: Samuel set off the bomb. But I must have doubted, must have been more loyal to my brother than even I knew, because when I look at the photograph, I feel the breath go out of my lungs and stay gone. For several seconds I do not move, do not breathe, do not think. And then I inhale, and the air comes rushing back to me, and with it a certainty so heavy I don't know how I'll bear it another moment, let alone minutes, hours, days, weeks. A lifetime.

Samuel. Yes, it is Samuel. It's Samuel.

It's him.

———

I steer my car down the long driveway, slowly enough the grind of gravel beneath my tires sounds like a series of distinct cracks and crunches. As I approach the highway, the glints of metal and glass I've seen through the trees reveal themselves to be a dozen vehicles butted up against one another on the grassy verge. Most are ordinary cars, but several are news vans with microwave antennas resting coiled atop their roofs like sleeping serpents. I've already been spotted, and people crowd together on the far side of the gate, some wielding cameras and microphones.

I set my jaw. Wouldn't be so bad if I could just step out of my car, open the gate, and be back in the car in a matter of seconds. I'm quick with the transfers into and out of my wheelchair, but it will never be as fast as simply standing, and I hate the thought of being a spectacle for the cameras. Just as I put my car in park, I see a khaki uniform wading through the tide of people. Carson, the deputy from Split Creek. He meets my eyes briefly, hauls open the gate, waves the reporters back. I nod to him as I drive past, then turn onto the highway and set my eyes toward town.

I love my car. Samuel surprised me with it for my high school graduation, the hand controls already installed. A practical gift—his long shifts at the sawmill make it tough for him to ferry me around—but I've always loved driving, sometimes go all the way to Elk Fork or Kalispell or into Idaho, just to enjoy the mountains and the sky and the speed. I'm sure all

Samuel sees is a waste of gas, but he never tells me not to go. I think about turning around now and heading north, or east, or west, driving till dark or later. Driving toward wherever Samuel might be. *And where is that?* It's just one more question in a sea of others: *What did he think a bomb would accomplish? Did he consider what it might do to others? To me?*

I continue south toward town, pass a handful of other properties like ours, wide fields and aging farmhouses. Horses graze in one pasture, a handful of cattle in another. Deer gather at the edges of the fields. On the side of one barn, the words WE SUPPORT NORTH LODE MINING CO. are just visible, two and a half decades of Montana winters having faded the letters till they almost match the equally weathered wood. Six properties on the east side of the highway between my home and the town limits. Six other properties the government could have decided to build a road through.

The sun is directly overhead now, and the valley will stay light late into the afternoon. The mountains on the east side of the valley are the high ones, the rich ones. The reason Prospect exists. They contain silver, or did once, and their surfaces are covered in tall, spindly pine and dark, rusty rock that turns the color of old blood when it rains. They keep the town in shadow until almost noon, and in winter their peaks vanish into the low blanket of cloud for weeks on end. They have names of their own, those mountains, but I almost always hear them referred to by the names of the mines that bore into their hearts: Eden. Gethsemane. The last ore was extracted more than twenty years ago; after the Gethsemane collapse in 1994 the company made a few gestures toward reopening the mines, but the mountains were mostly depleted, and now all they're good for is bearing the burden of a road no one here wants.

There are mountains on the west side of the valley, too, but this close to town they're just foothills, overlapping mounds of earth clothed in prairie grass that is a fleeting green today but will soon fade to a dull, dry brown. Steeper than they look—I climbed them often as a kid—but dwarfed by the higher peaks behind them, by the Cabinet and Purcell Mountains beyond. North, in Canada, are the most striking mountains of all, jagged rows of them, their color like gray mixed with cobalt, all tipped with white.

The speed limit drops to twenty-five at the town limits, and I slow as I approach the WELCOME TO PROSPECT sign; it's pocked with bullet dents and boasts a population of 649, which I consider exceedingly optimistic. I pass the old Gas-N-Go with its bright, remodeled facade that seems out of place among the brick and timber of the rest of the town. Next comes the school—only the elementary building still occupied, the high school students bused to Split Creek now—and then the post office, City Hall, the first of three bars, a pair of churches, four empty storefronts, Prospect Drug, and a coffee shop that doubles as the offices of the formerly-weekly-now-biweekly *Miner*. At the heart of town are the Gethsemane Mine Memorial and the patch of grass beside it that passes as a city park, the cemetery and funeral home beyond. When I was a kid, there was also a general store, a doctor's office, and a small but grand single-screen movie theater called the Orpheus, but the town has withered since the mines closed. Even with many storefronts vacant or boarded up, the center of town feels cramped, narrow two-story brick buildings pressed together, private homes stacked almost atop one another up the slopes to the west, defunct mining buildings and smelters and other rusting structures clustered at the base of the mountains to the east. Things ease to the south, with the relatively newer buildings claiming patches of lawn around their perimeters: the library, the dollar store, the second gas station.

I shouldn't like Prospect. Even in its youth it wouldn't have been an attractive town, and its crowded, jumbled layout speaks of necessity and thrift rather than planning or care. A few years after the mines closed, the city council hired a consultant who suggested making the town a tourist destination for gardeners and flower enthusiasts, but the project was called off halfway through—the soil was so contaminated by lead and other mining offal that officials had to plead with people not to plant petunias in their own yards—and the only remnants of that hopeful time are a single aluminum sculpture of a daisy next to City Hall and a *Silver Gardens City* mural on the side of Prospect Drug that fades a little more each year. Then there was chatter about an Indian casino going up outside town—I practiced dealing cards at the kitchen table—but the casino never materialized, the chatter fell away, and with it the remnants of faith that something would come along eventually. Jobs left. People left. Prospect stayed, diminished. The new bypass road, once built, might finish it off entirely.

And yet it is my home. I've experienced enough heartbreak here I could feel justified hating the place, but I don't. In some ways it might be easier for me to love Prospect than it is for Samuel, because I don't remember what it was like before the mines closed. On the other hand, perhaps that's what makes him so fiercely loyal to the place; every change is one more loss, one more thing relegated to memory. In any case, Samuel and I share a devotion to this valley. It cradles the bones of those we've lost, and stands in their stead; they lived here as we do, walked where we walk, saw what we see. It's the kind of love for a place only an orphan might understand. However damaged it might be, however poisoned, however marred, it's not just our home; it's what remains of our family. If I believe Samuel did what he did—and I must, I do—then I also recognize this is at least part of why. This place is ours. It is not for others to take.

I drive past the SEE YOU SOON! sign at the town's southern limits, then pull a hard U-turn. The car that's been tailing me since it pulled onto the highway outside my gates blows past, and the one behind it has to wait for oncoming traffic before following me.

I've worked at Fuel Stop part-time since my last year of high school. Gregory One Bear, the owner, had the misfortune to open the gas station six months before the Gethsemane disaster and two years before the mines closed for good. I doubt Prospect ever really needed two gas stations, but it certainly doesn't now. One Bear tries to carve out a place for Fuel Stop in the town's economy: in addition to the usual convenience store staples of Fritos, M&M's, and Bud Light, half the store is devoted to souvenirs aimed at the occasional tourists from Idaho or Canada who pass through Prospect on their way to Glacier or Yellowstone. Most days the tourists fail to materialize.

One Bear is behind the register when I go inside. "Jo—" he starts, but I interrupt.

"Might be a couple guys coming in behind me." I head quickly for the back room. It's generally a dismal place—gray folding table, windowless walls, OSHA posters, a couple lockers that don't latch—but today it feels like a refuge. I shove the bag on the back of my wheelchair into one of the lockers, check that my name tag is pinned straight on my red polo.

A copy of the *Elk Fork Chronicle* lies scattered across the table, the main section facedown, a used-car-lot ad covering the back page. I tell myself not to look, flip the paper over anyway. I skim the lead story. It's mostly about the explosion and the resulting damage, nothing I haven't already learned from the radio. Only a single paragraph about Samuel, and just one line that mentions me: . . . *a resident of Prospect in northwest Montana, where he lives with his sister.* There's one photo, Samuel's mouth lifted into that rare ghost of a smile I so often try—and fail—to draw out of him. He is twenty-nine but looks a decade older. Short brown hair, a shade darker than my own, and our mother's gray eyes. Skin that is tanned and taut and stretched too tightly over the bones beneath. The photo has been cropped closely around Samuel's face, but there's a small slash of yellow in the corner. My sleeve. My arm around his shoulders. We went to Glacier late last summer, drove the Going-to-the-Sun Road the final weekend it was open. We stopped at the Trail of the Cedars, asked a tourist to take the picture.

I leave the paper, go out onto the floor. I spot the reporters in the parking lot, one staring at his phone, the other smoking a cigarette. One Bear must have exercised his "right to refuse service to anyone." He's still behind the counter, pen in hand, occasionally marking a sheaf of papers beside the register. He doesn't look at me, and I'm glad.

The souvenirs and gifts are crowded onto shelves in the back of the store: mugs and shot glasses printed with *Montana*; teddy bears dressed as cowboys; coin banks shaped like elk; beaded moccasins bearing *Made in China* tags; T-shirts screen-printed with romanticized images of grizzlies and wolves; huckleberry-flavored everything. The store even offers a small selection of my paintings; they line one wall above a display of stuffed mountain goats.

"Paint some lightning bolts on the horses' legs," One Bear advised me once. "Some feathers in their manes. A circle around one eye. Hell, paint a star on some horse's butt and tell the customers it's so it runs with all the speed of a shooting star."

"I don't suppose that last one's authentic?"

He laughed. "White people love all that *Dances with Wolves* shit."

I figured he'd given me permission, so I painted lightning bolts and feathers and circles (no stars). The Fuel Stop paintings don't feel any more disingenuous than my others, with their clear skies and well-groomed wildlife. I usually sell two or three a month, enough to pay for paint and help with groceries.

I grab a filthy feather duster and start cleaning the coin banks. They aren't particularly dusty. I glance outside. One of the reporters is gone. The other meets my eyes and I look away. I finish the coin banks and move on to the shot glasses. I dust and listen to the fourth track of the country compilation that plays over the tinny-sounding speakers on a loop all day every day and do my best not to think. Yesterday's events still lie beyond a veil of surrealism, the hardest edges of knowledge blunted by shock. There's a reckoning ahead, though, and not far off. I can feel the weight of it settling near my heart and smoldering there, ready to burn.

"I didn't expect to see you today, Jo."

One Bear stands at the end of the aisle, arms crossed.

"I'm on the schedule." He glances away and doesn't say anything more. I went to school with his son. The afternoon before my first winter formal, Samuel sat me down and told me it was important I hang out only with my own kind of people, did I understand? I said yes. I thought he meant people who lived outside town and occasionally ate squirrel; only later did I realize he was warning me not to dance with Reggie One Bear.

Most of the people in Prospect pretend not to remember Samuel's tattoo. Pretend not to notice he never wears short sleeves. One Bear, I think, remembers. One Bear notices. At the very least he must have realized that Samuel never comes into this store, never hands One Bear any of his money. But he's also never held it against me, never lumped me in with my brother.

The door chime sounds, and both of us look up. Not a reporter—not one I recognize, anyway—but not a local, either. The man starts perusing the jerky offerings. One Bear watches him a few seconds more, then glances at the reporter still loitering in the parking lot. "Um." He picks up a *Montana*-branded lighter, lights it. Snaps the lid shut on the flame. "I could use another set of eyes on the books." He gestures toward the papers he's been marking. "Help me out?" I hesitate, and he adds, "Just for today."

I want to tell him not to make promises he can't keep, but instead I say sure and follow him into the back room. The books notably do not need another set of eyes. If I were in my boss's position, I'd make a couple mistakes on purpose, just to bolster the charade, but it apparently hasn't occurred to him to do so. I spend the rest of my shift at the gray table in the gray room, trying not to look at the newspaper with my brother's face on it and wondering how long it will be before One Bear removes my paintings from the gift shop and what excuse he will give me when he does.

———

That evening, there's a knock at the door just as I'm finishing dinner. To call it "dinner" is generous; I can muster neither the energy nor the enthusiasm for cooking, so I've poured cereal into a bowl, only to remember there's no milk. I eat it dry. Samuel told me that after our mother's death, the women of Prospect supplied him with food for weeks. No one has brought me anything now; apparently there is no casserole that says "Sorry your brother's a terrorist." The word—*terrorist*—still stings, but it no longer shocks the way it did that first day. The knock repeats, and I peer through the lower peephole Samuel drilled in the door. Devin, the FBI man. Same suit, different tie. I open the door and go out onto the porch.

Devin shows no surprise at my failure to invite him in. "I hear you don't want to talk to me." He glances around, presumably for a chair, and, finding none, leans against the porch railing. "Apparently you don't . . . 'recognize my authority,' I think it was?"

It sounds foolish when he says it aloud, and I feel heat in my face. It never sounds foolish when Samuel says things like that—misguided, certainly; radical, perhaps—but never foolish. I'm surprised Hawkins used that line after all. I wish he hadn't; I don't want to pretend to believe it now. "You can hardly blame me for not wanting to talk to you."

Devin makes no indication of either agreement or disagreement. "I want your help finding your brother," he says. "If you're more willing to give me that help with Sheriff Hawkins as intermediary, I'm not necessarily opposed to the idea. He knows the area; he knows you. I don't discount that." My gut tightens; I didn't propose Hawkins as go-between in order to aid Devin. "I am not, however, going to disappear, and you need to accept that." I say nothing, and Devin continues speaking, though only after a pause long enough to make me uncomfortable. "I spent most of the night reading the file we pulled together on Samuel."

It's a gentle evening. Still a pale gold glow above the ragged mountain horizon to the west, and though the forms of the aspens beside the creek have faded into the dusk, I hear their leaves fluttering against one another in the breeze like rustling paper. Something else I'll miss.

"Samuel's what we call a lone wolf," Devin says. "He's not acting as part of any organized group, not inspired by any one person or entity. He's tried out plenty of movements, but never seemed to find one he liked enough to stick with, though he appears to have adopted a handful of beliefs from several."

"You're profiling him." It should bother me—it does, because it reduces him to what he did yesterday—but I'm curious, too. I want to know if Devin will be able to explain the things about my brother I have never understood: Why has he tried so hard to believe in philosophies I could see through even as a teenager? Why has he so often sought meaning in anger and hate?

Devin continues as though I haven't spoken. "He has no social media presence. He occasionally posted on a handful of extremist message boards, but by the skewed standards of those communities, the opinions he expressed were downright moderate. He enjoys pointing out the flaws in others' ideologies. An intelligent man." It's a transparent attempt at flattery; I ignore it. "Most of the information about him comes from records kept after the death of your mother"—Devin lets his eyes fall from mine then, just for the briefest moment—"and from recent state court documents." He glances toward the front door. "I'm sorry about your house."

"I doubt that," I say. "You work for the folks razing it." Not strictly true. The state of Montana is razing it, not the feds. But, as Samuel would say, *Both stomp on their citizenry.*

"Eminent domain is enshrined in the federal and state constitutions," Devin says. He presses his lips together then, almost a grimace, and I wonder if the words were automatic, if he regrets them. If I've seen Devin make a mistake.

"Yes," I say, "I did learn that during my crash course in legal ways your government can screw you over."

Devin looks at me closely, as though reconsidering whether

I share Samuel's views. There's something sharp in his gaze, and I want to look away but don't. "After this, talk to Hawkins," he says finally. "You'll still hear from me—and I expect you to talk to me when you do—but if I can go through him, I will."

I can't bring myself to thank him. It should feel like a victory. But I never really expected Devin to agree to my proposal, and now that he has, I'm already wondering why. Is it an olive branch? A kindness? A trick?

"I actually came tonight to tell you something else."

I cross my arms, hope I look skeptical rather than apprehensive. I can't shake the hunch that Devin can read my thoughts, or at least guess their tenor.

"I don't think your brother meant to hurt anyone." Devin says it plainly. "I think he detonated that bomb on a Sunday because he knew the courthouse would be empty. I think he placed it at the south facade in part because it was shielded from Main Street and he wouldn't be seen, but also because the stores across Lincoln Street were closed Sunday mornings. I think he had no idea a church had moved in the week before."

Yes, I want to say. *Yes, you see it, too.* Amid all the other evidence—the damning photographs and the eyewitness reports and whatever was hauled out of the house in FBI boxes—are these small truths. And here is proof I haven't imagined them. It isn't an excuse. It doesn't make the bomb okay. But it does mean something that he intended to destroy stone, not flesh. Maybe it doesn't matter to the law, but it matters to me. And I am not the only one who knows.

I don't let Devin know how relieved I am, how grateful, though I have to push away a surprisingly strong impulse to confess my own ignorance and hurt, to offer up Samuel's history to this man who seems to think he might make sense of it. I remind myself that Samuel would not trust Devin, would not want me to trust Devin. I channel my brother's wariness, his silence. Secrecy is safer; he taught me that. I clear my throat, pitch my voice carefully. What I mean to say is something like, *Thank you for telling me, and good night.* What I say instead is, "Emily."

Devin looks at me. Waits. I am suddenly angry with him again. He has to know what I mean; he doesn't need to make me say it. "How is she?"

Devin pushes away from the porch railing, straightens. He adjusts the knot of his tie, smooths a palm down the front of his coat. I'm afraid he's going to refuse to answer, tell me it's none of my business. And it isn't, really, but at the same time I feel I must know. I need to know, need Emily to be okay, need my brother to not be guilty of anything more. "She hasn't regained consciousness," Devin tells me. "They say it could go either way."

———

I'm having nightmares, Jo. Only right, I suppose. I even expected it, was willing to bear it as a consequence of what had to be done, but I thought the nightmares would be about the explosion, the aftermath. Instead, I dream about you.

I dream about that night, but not about Mom, and not even about the hallway, but about afterward, going into Mom's room and opening the closet door and finding you there. My dream starts when I see you huddled in the corner. Your eyes are squeezed shut, and tear tracks streak your face. There's not much blood. I don't even see it at first, and for a second I feel this tiny spark of relief through the rage and grief. But then I notice the light coming through the little hole in the back wall, and I remember hearing you scream, and I thought I was scared before but now I'm scared, now I know what it is to be scared. None of this should have happened, none of it, but especially not this. I know I must look frightening, so I wipe my palms across my face and they come away red, and I kneel down and try to be calm and pray in my head, just one word over and over: please. Please please please. I say your name. You open your eyes. I wake up.

I don't have to guess at the meaning of these dreams. I know what you looked like, Jo. The girl from the church is a mystery.

———

Tuesday I listen to the radio: they've found the truck I saw in the photograph; it had been stolen from a parking lot in Elk Fork, abandoned across town. I wash the dishes. Go to work: the back room again, more meaningless paperwork. Return home and stare at the moving boxes in the living room. Leave them empty. Thirty-five days left.

Hawkins read my statement for the reporters the afternoon before, and it made the evening news. So, he warned me, had the photo I'd seen part of in the *Chronicle*, but this time in its uncropped state, me beside my brother. Afterward the number of vehicles parked outside the gate fell by half.

I cook an early dinner. Nothing fancy, just a fried egg sand-wich. I eat it and remember they're Samuel's favorite, not mine. Afterward I go to the barn to feed Lockjaw, and I would like to linger there. My mule treats me no differently, looks at me with the same patient expression she always wears. She knows noth-ing about eminent domain, extremist politics, explosives. Samuel is the one who feeds her carrots from the flat of his hand; I am the one who tosses her hay and rides her into the hills.

I leave for Elk Fork in late afternoon. The deputy opens the gate for me again, and this time no cars follow when I turn onto the highway. Just south of town I pass the turnoff for Split Creek, where Samuel has spent the last decade working at the sawmill. (He comes home every day carrying with him

the piercing scent of freshly slaughtered timber; it is simultaneously comforting and violent and will always remind me of my
brother.) Then the old road that connects the highway east of
the mountains to this one, the road that crumbled in a mudslide
two years ago after a brutal wildfire season and a wet winter,
that will not be repaired, will instead be replaced by the new
road soon to pass through what is now my living room, because
it has been determined by people who do not live here that it
is more practical, more useful, more *beneficial* to pave the old,
overgrown access lanes that cross the low saddle at the northern
edge of Eden Mine, just beyond my home.

I continue south. The highway is mostly empty, the curves
familiar. I wish they weren't, wish I had to work harder to focus
on the drive. Samuel, too, might be driving now. He could have
gone anywhere once he realized his name had been attached to
the bombing. Probably not Wyoming, but anywhere else. Perhaps to the Bakken oil fields, where he could try to lose himself
in the waning boomtowns, or farther into the Dakotas, where
there's plenty of space to disappear into. Canada, even; there are
ways to get there that don't involve official border crossings. Or
maybe he hasn't gone so far. I hit play on my car's CD player,
spend the next couple hours doing my best to concentrate on the
music and nothing else.

Elk Fork sits beside the interstate in the center of a round
valley ringed by low, barefaced mountains; every winter it fills
with woodstove smoke, every summer with wildfire smoke. Perhaps because I so often see them veiled, the mountains here seem
less distinct than those in Prospect, impressionistic rather than
solid. I reach the city just as the sun is beginning to sink toward
the western slopes, exit near the center of town and find Lincoln
Street still closed to traffic. I pull to the curb just beyond the
blocked intersection, hope I look like just another rubbernecker.

I peer past the oaks lining the sidewalk and see reams of caution tape, orange plastic barriers, a hastily erected chain-link panel fence into which someone has tucked a tiny American flag. It trembles in the wind.

Samuel used to talk a lot about America, about the Constitution. I agreed with what he said then: that the most important thing a government could do was leave its citizens alone, that people in suits on the other side of the country couldn't be expected to know what it was like to live in a tiny mountain mining town and shouldn't pretend to, that regular folks were always meant to hold the real power. Those ideas didn't sound much different from the ones I still hear around town, or on the radio—from the ones I still hold myself—and I can't quite pinpoint when they became something more sinister.

I can see very little of the courthouse itself from this angle, and the fading light doesn't help. I've been here so recently for the hearing that my mind sees what my eyes cannot. Samuel placed the bomb outside the south facade; the radio hasn't said where, exactly, but I imagine it tucked beside the stone staircase leading to the heavy double doors. On the other side of the thick walls: parquet flooring that clacks beneath women's heels, long benches crowded with people in department store suits, brass-framed signs posted at hallway crossings. The courtroom in which we lost the house.

They found where he built the bomb. Hawkins told me. A storage unit in Split Creek. I'm relieved to know he didn't build it in our home, or the barn, but the more details I learn, the harder it is to picture. The transition from thought to action. The many chances to change his mind, ignored. The time it must have taken, and the effort to keep it secret.

I think again of the shattering glass. The sound, the dust, the debris. The blood.

As I pull back into traffic, I force myself to glance across Lincoln Street, but the storefronts are indistinguishable from one another, a line of shattered windows boarded up with plywood. No way to know which had been the church.

The prayer service is being held in an elementary school a few blocks away. The lot is already full when I arrive, but I find a handicapped spot near the school's front entrance. I sit behind the wheel for ten minutes, watching people walk inside. Most are dressed casually, but a few wear more formal clothes, some in colors dark enough to suit a funeral. When the trickle through the doors has slowed to almost nothing, I pull my chair from the backseat, reassemble it, and transfer into it. I rearrange my skirt, touch my hair to make sure it's still tightly braided.

Inside, I roll slowly toward the auditorium. I pass a trophy case filled with prizes lauding the Sacajawea Hawks, a sagging butcher paper banner promoting a schoolwide read-a-thon, a poster advertising the upcoming spring field day. Outside one classroom a row of student papers are taped to the wall at elementary school student height. I stop beside them: identical worksheets outlining the process of photosynthesis. Bold arrows arc around each paper, pointing from the sun to the leaves of an apple tree and back toward the sky. Some of the papers show careful attention to detail, crayon colors precisely contained within black outlines. Others are sloppier, with bare white patches and printed lettering that gets bigger or smaller toward the end of each word. One child has colored the sun purple. I move on, careful not to look at the names on the papers.

The lingering scent of tater tots and canned green beans betrays the auditorium's double duty as cafeteria. There are more people than I expected—several hundred, surely far more than are affiliated with a church that meets in a small retail space—and all are standing, eyes on the screen above the stage, where the lyrics of a hymn are projected four lines at a time. I quietly make my way to the rear corner of the room, take a place behind the last row of chairs. I glance around one more time, checking that no one has turned in their seats, noticed me. Tell myself I'm not hiding, that this is the easiest place to park my chair.

On the stage, a young man with a guitar sings into a microphone while behind him a woman plays an upright piano. The hymn is contemporary, the melody wistful but not gloomy, the lyrics filled with words like *renewal* and *hope*. I don't know it. When the song ends, the musicians leave the stage, and another man steps to the microphone. He is younger than I would have guessed a pastor to be, older than me but probably no older than Samuel. He wears dark jeans and a pale blue dress shirt open at the collar, sleeves rolled to his elbows. His stride is long, his back straight, and he moves like someone used to being watched by others. I can't see his face clearly, but it seems he's looking at as many of the people seated before him as possible, moving from one set of eyes to another. It's dark where I sit, but I wish I had transferred from my wheelchair to one of the chairs in the neat rows before me. I stay very still.

"It is heartening to see you all here tonight," the man begins. "My name is Asa Truth, and I am the pastor of Light of the World Church. Many of you are strangers to me, and my congregation and I are deeply grateful for your support at what is a very trying time for our church community, as well as for Elk Fork as a whole." His voice is clear and would carry easily even without the microphone. There's something commanding in it, something calming, too, and I wonder whether that balance came naturally or if he's cultivated it. It's a voice that suggests assurance, solidity, certainty, and almost in spite of myself I find I want to listen to it. To believe what it says.

Of course I do.

It's like listening to Samuel.

I haven't been to church in years, not since I was twelve or thirteen. When I was a child, our mother took Samuel and me to one of the churches in Prospect, but I can't recall her ever speaking of God and we did not pray at home, not even over dinner, so church must have been a social occasion for our mother, a small-town survival strategy. I liked it well enough. In Sunday school we acted out skits based on Bible stories and made greeting cards with the words of John 3:16 on the inside. On Good Friday, we sang "Go to Dark Gethsemane," and I imagined Jesus on his final night, descending a thousand feet into the earth to pray. It must have been dark indeed, I thought, especially if he hadn't brought a headlamp, though I allowed that Jesus himself might have emitted a gentle glow, perhaps just enough to make out the rock walls of the mine.

After our mother's death, the pastor of our church visited me in the hospital. I remember his visit only dimly, perhaps because of the medications, perhaps because I'd paid so little attention to him during his sermons. In the hospital, the pastor was kind but seemed at a loss for words; he kept repeating, *We'll pray for you.*

Samuel took me to church after that. The older I got, the more it bored me, and the less I believed in it. Or the more I realized I never really had. Sometimes I wonder if what happened the night Mom died was responsible for my lack of interest in religion. The old *why me* question, as though all the bad things in the world had been no obstacle to faith as long as they were

happening to other people. It seems too simplistic. Maybe tragedy can only steal faith from those who truly had it in the first
place, and I don't think that was me.

It was different for Samuel, though. One Sunday—after
Mom, but not long after—I opened my eyes during the final
prayer and glanced at Samuel, half expecting him to sense my
lack of participation, give me a warning look. But he stood
straight, eyes shut so tightly there were wrinkles at the corners
that made him seem older than his eighteen or nineteen years.
His lips were moving silently, and I tried to make out the words
but couldn't. What I remember most are his hands, the way
he held them in front of him, palms up, as though waiting for
someone to place something in them, gift or burden.

The service continues with prayers, one led clumsily by Elk Fork's
mayor, the others more easily by the pastor. There are hymns,
too; I recognize only "Amazing Grace" and "This Is My Father's
World," which, we are told, is Emily's favorite. As the hour draws
to a close, the projector screen illuminates once again, this time
with a photograph of a balding middle-aged man.

"We pray for the healing of those injured in Sunday's explosion," the pastor says, "and particularly for those still hos-
pitalized. Garrett Folsom." A few moments' silence, in which
I hear a shuddering intake of breath several rows ahead. "Ruby
Harper." The projector switches to a photograph of a woman
with gray hair and a sly, closed-mouth smile. I study each face
as it appears. The radio said both have been upgraded to fair
condition. Fair seems promising. Fair is better than I was when
I was taken to the hospital. But there's also—

"Emily—" The pastor stops, his hand raised before him as
though in benediction or blessing. It falters, dips and trembles.

His shoulders rise and square as he takes in a long breath, holds it, lets it go. The hand rises again, higher than before, steadies. "Emily Truth," he says.

And she is on the screen. It's clearly a school photo, a head-and-shoulders shot with a carefully neutral mottled gray background. Emily wears a blue blouse and a delicate necklace with a tiny silver cross that rests in the hollow of her throat. Her hair is a glossy auburn, her eyes a vivid green, and her broad smile is missing a tooth at the far edge. I imagine the photograph framed on a living room mantel, glued to a scrapbook page, tucked into a plastic sleeve in the pastor's wallet. Her father's wallet. I try not to think about what the face in the photograph looks like now, in the hospital, whether it has been changed by the explosion, and how.

Whatever reasons Samuel had for what he did, they're not good enough. Whatever reasons he had did not justify hurting these people. This child. Still I hear part of my mind whisper, *He didn't mean it.* I try to banish the thought. It doesn't matter to anyone but me.

The screen goes dark, and the pastor resumes speaking, his voice clear and strong once again. I bow my head, close my eyes, and listen to the pastor pray for healing and strength and peace. It's not a passive prayer; his delivery suggests these things aren't inevitable but must be searched out, fought for, earnestly and genuinely desired. When he speaks of healing his voice takes on a sharper tone, each word ringing with a confidence I envy. I want the things he prays for, want them as deeply as it is possible to want something, want them so much the wanting is almost painful. I wish for Garrett Folsom and Ruby Harper to recover from their injuries, and most of all I wish for Emily Truth to be okay, to heal, to live. I wish for it with every thought and feeling and breath, and if fevered, fervent wishing can be a kind of prayer, then yes, I pray for it.

"You're his sister."

I jerk my head up, eyes open.

"I saw your picture on the news." The woman is in the back row, just a few feet from where I sit. She's turned, one hand on the back of her chair. "What are you doing here?" Her voice began as a near whisper, but it rises with each word. People close by crane their necks to look. I'm used to stares, of course—the wheelchair—but this is different. "Why did you come?"

I know now I shouldn't have. I thought it would be like the prayer service I heard they held in Prospect after the Gethsemane collapse, a place to share worry and show care. I thought people wouldn't notice me, and if they did, I thought they would see I was like them, I was sorry, I was sad. I thought they would see I was not my brother. Samuel would have known I was making a mistake. He would have told me not to come, would have told me I was being naive, breaking the rules we've fashioned for tragedies like this. He would have told me they would not let me separate myself from him. Would have told me I shouldn't try.

The woman won't be quiet. "This is a space for people who have been hurt." The man beside her lays a hand on her shoulder, but she shrugs it off. Tears dart down both cheeks. She is the age my mother would be.

"I'm—" I swallow, try to think of words I can say, right words, good words, but none come. The pastor has stopped speaking; I don't dare look toward the stage.

The man touches the woman's shoulder again, gingerly. "Margaret."

"We don't want you here," she says, each word a sentence unto itself. She isn't speaking loudly, but the room has gone silent.

I stare at her, jaw clenched. My hands are on the handrims

of my chair, but they seem no more willing to move than my paralyzed legs.

Then the pastor's voice enters into the silence. "Just as we pray for our loved ones and our community," he says, "let us pray also for the man who detonated the bomb, for, like us, he is a beloved creation of God." The pastor speaks more quietly than during the rest of the service, but his words command the attention of the room. Even the crying woman—Margaret—turns to face him. I feel the people around me resist his words. And why not? How can he say these things? How can a man whose child lies in the hospital at this very moment ask them to pray for my brother, who put her there? And do I hear something strained in that voice, something dutiful but no more? Or is that my own guilt bleeding into the words as they reach my ears? I bow my head, but not in prayer. Try to disappear into the darkness that isn't nearly dark enough. "And let us pray also for his family and friends, for their suffering may be different than ours, but it is no less real."

The pastor continues to speak—I'm sure he does, though I'm also sure he's looking at me, so I keep my eyes cast down—but I no longer hear what he says. I feel like a child again, that child in the hospital, a victim to be pitied, not knowing whether she's grateful for the prayers of others or resentful of them. Or, and this is a new thought: simply undeserving.

I test my hands again, and this time they obey. I cut across the room, not caring that several people turn to watch, and though the door gives me a few moments' struggle, still I do not look up, and finally I'm in the broad fluorescent light of the hall and I feel my pulse return to me, steady and reliable. I push the handrims as hard as I can until I'm moving quickly enough to let it all blur.

I'm in the parking lot before I hear footsteps behind me. I turn sharply, and the pastor slows immediately, stops when he's still a couple yards away. "Ms. Faber," he says, and despite the wheelchair, despite the picture in the paper and the accusing woman inside, there's a hint of a question in his voice, so after a moment I nod.

He is tall and narrow, the knobs of his wrists prominent, his cheekbones sharp angles beneath pale skin. His hair is a very light brown, probably darkened from a boyhood blond, and his eyes are green like Emily's, and bloodshot. I look for judgment in those eyes, but their opacity reminds me of Samuel's, and I instantly feel I've done something wrong, almost vulgar, in comparing the two men. The pastor puts one hand in front of him, and I recoil before I recognize it as a peaceful gesture; he sees me start and pulls back, and I remember the way his hand faltered when he prayed over his daughter's name on the stage. "It shouldn't have gone like that in there," he says, and his voice is different now, not clear and commanding like it was during the service, but soft and a bit broken, a huskiness wounding the vowels. "People are . . . It's a hard time."

All I can think of is Emily's photograph, and Emily's favorite hymn, and Emily's father standing here before me, looking at me and talking to me and all the while not knowing if his daughter is going to live.

Behind him, the school doors open, rectangles of harsh light cutting into the dying dusk, and people begin to file into the parking lot in ones and twos. The pastor steps closer. He moves as though he is fragile, or the world is, or both. He lifts his hand again, seems about to touch me, lets it drop gently back to his side.

I can't look at him. Can't speak.

He presses a small card into my hand. He takes a half step

back, but waits for me to fold my fingers over the card before he
lets it go and walks away.

I drive home five miles an hour under the speed limit, which
is much too fast when it's dark. The mountains blend into the
night, but their peaks and ridges reveal themselves by masking
the stars in the clear sky. I painted a scene that way once, all
midnight blues and blacks, moonlit silver edges, and a spray of
white stars. Hadn't turned out the way I hoped. I made the stars
too bright.

A few miles from the Split Creek turnoff, I spot a shifting
of dark on dark and shove hard on the hand brake. Loose gravel
rattles against the undercarriage. A whitetail buck stands immobile in the road, his eyes reflecting the glare of headlights. He's
close enough I can see the velvet coating each short curve and
tine of his new antlers, the flare of his nostrils with his breath.
He stares back for several long seconds, then flags his tail and
bounds out of the road and beyond the reach of my human eyes.

I drive the rest of the way home more slowly, thinking of
how many things in the world a person might not see until it's
too late.

———

I remember little of Ben Archer. He and my mother hadn't
dated long, a few weeks at most. At our second meeting, he
gave me a toy unicorn; though it was horse-shaped, it was not a
horse, and this small error, this misunderstanding of who I was
and what I liked, had seemed to me to indicate some deeper
flaw in his character. Perhaps if Archer hadn't been so inexo-
rably drawn to beer and whiskey, he would have simply been a

clumsily well-intentioned suitor my mother could have kindly turned away. But there was the beer, and the whiskey. And then there was Hawkins at our house, and serious conversations and papers signed, and a warning not to talk to Archer if I saw him, and then there was a long quiet time in which I almost forgot about him.

———

A new canvas.

My studio is on the eastern side of my bedroom. The room is large, as wide as the kitchen and dining area combined, though not so deep. Several tall windows in both the eastern and western walls let in light all day long. I hadn't wanted to move into this room after our mother's death—made Samuel carry me upstairs to my old bedroom for months afterward—and it wasn't until I set up the studio years later that it truly began to feel like mine.

When the room was my mother's, I sometimes came here in the evenings to curl up and read in one of her two whitewashed wicker chairs, or to play with my toy horses on the braided rug. My mother would have a book of her own, and we sometimes let an hour or even two go by without either of us speaking. Samuel never joined us, and at the time I had been glad, had guarded those precious hours alone with my mother, but now I wish I could remember him here.

Where the wicker chairs used to be stand a pair of easels. The desk has been traded for a storage chest filled with paints and palettes and brushes, the braided rug replaced by a spattered dropcloth. The room, which once wore a subtle scent of aging paper and mild potpourri, now smells mostly of paint.

I take the painting I ruined the day of the bombing off one of the easels. I consider trying to salvage something from the blackened canvas, decide I don't want to even if I can; nothing will stop me seeing the memory of that day on it. I fold the smaller of my two easels until it looks like a bundle of aluminum kindling, compact enough to close my hand around, and slip it into the bag slung across the back of my wheelchair. I add a box filled with pencils, erasers, and charcoal. Then I sort through the handful of prepped canvases and boards propped against the wall, finally select one twenty inches by twenty-four. I balance it on my thighs and go outside, down the long porch ramp, and over the patchy lawn to a spot twenty yards from the house, beneath one of the tall ponderosa pines that punctuate the property.

I have painted this house my great-great-grandfather built many times. It has appeared in winter scenes, buried under deeply drifted snow; in spring, with crocuses pushing through the soil in front of the porch; in summer, when the white exterior stands stark and bright against the fading fields; in autumn, when curling leaves gather along the foundation and the larch on the mountain slopes behind the house burns a brilliant yellow. Like most of my work, those paintings are light, impressionistic, never detailed enough to show the hard edges beneath the veneer of beauty. It's a picturesque farmhouse, and on my canvases its paint is never peeling, its gutters always straight, its shutters never broken.

The first Christmas after our mother died, there were gifts from neighbors and our mother's friends and near strangers in town, people who had worked with our father years ago or whose children attended school with me or Samuel. The second Christmas, there were almost no gifts (Hawkins gave me a book about mules and gave Samuel a bone-handled pocketknife), and no money to buy any.

I made a coupon book for Samuel, an envelope filled with construction paper vouchers for tasks I already did: make dinner, feed Lockjaw, play three games of gin rummy. It felt like a feeble gift even then, and too young for me—I was twelve—but Samuel thanked me sincerely. I suppose he was embarrassed by his gift for me, too: a shoebox containing five half-empty tubes of paint, two stained and splayed brushes, and a pad of drawing paper that held far fewer than the one hundred sheets promised on its cover.

I'd never expressed much interest in art before my injury. Sometimes I doodled in the margins of my school papers, but I didn't think of myself as having any noteworthy artistic talent or inclination. In the hospital, the nurses gave me a box of markers and a package of paper, and I started drawing there because it was one of the only ways I could find to feel close to the things that were important to me. I drew horses and mules, the house and barn, the meadows and mountains. Over and over I drew them. By the time I left rehab, I'd already gained some appreciation for the promise and limitations of the pen, for the joy of putting right on paper what was not right with the world, and the sorrow of knowing it was mere illusion.

The tube of black paint proved to be hardened and dried beyond recovery, and there was just a bit of white left, so most of my earliest paintings were comprised of colors blended to their truest, boldest intensity. No shadows, no darkness. My first attempts were terrible, but when I gave one to Samuel for Christmas the following year—a portrait of Lockjaw that, while painted with great affection, regrettably suggested the mule might continue to suffer from her eponymous affliction—he immediately hung it beside the kitchen table. Before long I learned to see its flaws and begged him to take it down, but he refused; it gazed back at us at dinnertime for years.

I position the canvas on my easel lengthwise, take a soft pencil from the box and begin to sketch. The canvas is already primed with a thin coating of neutral gray; my markings are faint but visible. I start with the mountains, their outline so familiar my hand moves almost of its own accord, shaping the low build of Eden on the left side of the canvas, working toward the sharper angles of Gethsemane on the distant right. I pencil in the wooden fence along the edge of Lockjaw's pasture, the creek, the handful of aspens and pines scattered across the fields, finally the barest shape of the house. I settle it to the right of center, closer to the bottom of the canvas than the top, but it is clearly the focal point. Ordinarily I don't bother with details at this stage—those come with the paint—but today I take extra care with the house.

I can't save it. The house. In just over a month it will be mine no more. Will *be* no more. It's almost refreshing to acknowledge this. To prove that I know how to do more than deny. That if I missed something these last weeks and months, it was because my brother hid it well and not because I refused to see what was. So maybe I am trying to prove something with this painting. Maybe I am trying to reject the kind of willful optimism I've crafted on canvas in the past. But I'm not used to thinking of my art in such lofty, purposeful terms, and mostly I think I simply want to paint the house exactly as it is, just once while I still can. Not better, not brighter, not more beautiful. To record it, forever, the way it stands before me today, so anyone who looks at the canvas in the future can bear witness to it just as I do now.

I hold the pencil lightly in my hand, angled beside the canvas, and for the first time in my life draw the long, low incline of the zigzagging wheelchair ramp alongside the porch; the motion is unfamiliar, these lines new and intrusive, and I feel awkward but persist. Then, before I can change my mind, I shift my pencil a few inches and sketch a wide patch of peeling paint. A dangling gutter. The broken shutter.

―――

I've covered most of Canada with my words, Jo, with these letters to you. It's a map of Montana, of course, so there's not much of Canada, just small strips of Saskatchewan, Alberta, and British Columbia, but I've already had to move on to the Dakotas. I find myself wanting to cover the far-flung places first, to avoid encroaching on Prospect.

I suppose you've had to offer words of your own. You are my only family; the propagandists would have demanded it. Did they leave you alone afterward? I hope so.

I know what I've done has caused you trouble. I know it's caused you pain. I'm sorry for that, so sorry. I regret plenty, but—I want to be absolutely clear about this—I don't regret what I did. If it had gone the way I'd planned, I'd regret nothing. It's not right, Jo. I know you're facing a house of things to pack or sell or throw away, and I know you're facing it alone because of me—that's not what I wanted, not what I meant to happen—but you shouldn't be facing it at all. The government has no right to take our home.

All these years I've played their game. I've paid their illegal, extortionate taxes, even knowing it was wrong, even knowing they have no constitutional right to levy taxes against my own property, because I didn't want to risk losing our home. I allowed myself be treated like a tenant on my own land. I sent them my money so rich men could get richer, so the undeserving could continue to suckle at the welfare teat. And what do we get for being docile, accommodating sheep? A notice evicting us from our own home, from the land our family has lived and worked and died on for generations. Do you think anyone had even a pang of conscience about that? Of course not. The government has been corrupted by avarice, by greed for money and power. It oppresses those it was meant to serve. We cannot—I cannot—acquiesce, not to this. If we don't stand up for our rights, they'll leave us with no rights at all.

I left no note, no manifesto. I didn't mean for them to know it was me, didn't want anyone to connect it to you. But this is some of what I would have written if I had. This is what it takes a bomb to make them hear.

I'll stop now. I've used up my slice of North Dakota and most of South Dakota, and I know you don't care for my "politics," as you call them. I don't want this to come across as an "I told you so." But admit this much, Jo—some part of you, however deep down, is at least a little glad I did what I did.

———

Thursday I finally tackle the empty box still waiting in the living room. I take a stack of paperbacks from the bookcase and push them into the corner of the box, then pull another stack off the shelf and shove them beside the first, and so on until the small box is full and I can tape it shut. Do it in less than a minute, don't stop to look at the titles or make sure the edges line up or that I've made efficient use of the space. Don't give myself any excuse not to fill the box and fill it fast. I scrawl *Books* across the top in thick red marker, then push it against the wall. There. I've started packing.

Friday I again work my shift in the back room and, when another employee calls in sick, volunteer for a second shift behind the register. One Bear thinks about it for a long minute before he nods. My paintings still hang on the wall above the stuffed mountain goats.

Saturday I take the easel and canvas back out beneath the pine, and I lay down a wash of Payne's gray across the mountains, a shade darker and bluer than the priming gray. Then I begin the painting in earnest, using the acrylics straight from the tube, even mixing a few with modeling paste, pushing and pulling with my painting knives until I've manipulated the thick pigments into textured ridges and swaths. The techniques are familiar; only the colors are different. My other paintings are saturated with color, mountains edged with violet, horses' coats reflecting bright yellows and reds. This painting will have subtler, stiller colors, like those glimpsed through a window on a rain-soaked day.

It's not right. I know it early on, but keep painting until I've got most of the canvas finished, until I can't pretend it might work itself out along the way. Maybe the knives, which work so well for most of my paintings, aren't precise enough for this kind of work. I replace the incomplete painting with a fresh canvas, begin again, trading my knives for brushes. This one takes longer. The brush feels clumsy in my hand, the whole process less certain, less intuitive than usual. Maybe that's good. Maybe slowing down will help me capture the details I so often gloss over.

Hours later I sit back and eye the nearly finished canvas. The subdued hues are disquieting. I meant them to be soothing, but they cast the house into gloom, and that's not how I see my home. But that's not the only problem. This painting is more accurate, certainly; I've accomplished that much. The image forming on the canvas is very like the one I see on any given day when I drive up to the house after work. There is more detail here than in any painting I've ever done, more realism. I haven't glossed over anything, blurred out, minimized or erased. It is faithful in a way my previous canvases were not. I take some pleasure in this proof that I have more range as an artist than I thought, but this isn't what I meant to paint. Isn't what I set out to do. Perhaps accuracy and truth aren't quite the same thing.

I'll have to try again, but not today. I'm losing the light.

Sunday strikes me hard from the moment I wake. Sunday is one week from the bombing, one week from the day Samuel left "for Wyoming." Sunday is the day he told me he'd be back.

I lie in bed too long, get up only when I hear Lockjaw's shattering bray from the barn. I hurry my morning routine, but almost an hour has passed by the time I make it outside. Lockjaw starts kicking her stall door as soon as she sees me, and I holler, "Quit!" The mule flattens her long ears but stops kicking. "It's not like you're in danger of starving," I mutter. I go to the feed room, scoop a quart of oats into a bucket, stack a couple flakes of hay on top. Then I look at the four bales stacked beside the bin and let my breath out in a rush. I've seen them every day this week, but I haven't realized until now. Four bales. Four. We never bring down more than two at a time.

I wonder if Samuel meant it when he told me he'd be back today. Maybe he really did intend to go to Wyoming, figuring a week would be long enough to be reasonably sure the FBI hadn't connected him to the bombing. Maybe he'd planned to drive up to the house this evening, come inside, drop a bag of burgers from the Gas-N-Go on the kitchen table. I wonder if he would have told me what he'd done. If he'd trust me with that knowledge, saddle me with it.

Whatever he told me, I'd have believed it. I believed everything. Not just Wyoming, but the lies he told me before. An extra shift at work. A trip to the store. *Sorry, Jo, big lumber order*

*so it's all hands on deck. Sorry, Jo, the first place didn't have what
we needed so I had to try another store. Sorry, Jo, there was a wreck
on the highway and it was all backed up.* And I'd always said, *It's
fine, Samuel. It's fine.* Which of those stories were true? Which
were lies? When was he at work? When was he in a storage unit
building a bomb?

I knew he was a liar, but until the bomb I didn't think he
lied to me. It shouldn't surprise me. Shouldn't hurt this way to
realize it. After all, I've seen him lie to others. Hell, I've lied
with him; he taught me how. He's good at it, better than me.
Does knowing that and believing him anyway make me a fool?
Does it make me something worse?

He said he would come back today.

I still believe he meant to.

And yet. Samuel knows what's easy for me, what's hard,
what's impossible. Retrieving hay bales from the loft is impossible. He brought down four.

I return to the house. I intended to pack more boxes today,
but the possessions I use least are upstairs. The break-it-out-
once-a-year kitchen appliances and utensils are in the upper
cupboards, out of reach. The bookshelves are bare save for the
top shelves. I have a grabber, but it's meant for things like cereal boxes, not electric mixers and dictionaries. I pack a single box with the good tablecloths and napkins from the linen
closet, sandwiching between them a pair of brass candlesticks
my mother put on the table at Thanksgiving and Christmas. She
never lit the tall ivory candles, reused them year after year.

I glance at my painting supplies, but can hardly stand to look
at them.

I go back to the barn, call to Lockjaw. I shouldn't ride alone.
Not without someone knowing where I'm going and when I
plan to be back. I've adapted well to riding without being able

to feel my seat or legs, but I'll never be as secure in the saddle as before my injury. If Lockjaw spooks or stumbles and I fall, I'll be in serious trouble, especially if I'm any distance from the house and barn. Once, years ago, Lockjaw was stung by a hornet and dumped me near the southern fence line. Samuel came home from work to find Lockjaw grazing in the front yard and me exhaustedly dragging myself a few inches at a time across the front field. If he hadn't been there, it would have taken me at least another hour to get back to my chair, and I hadn't even been hurt.

I consider all this. Then I saddle and bridle Lockjaw and lead her toward the mounting ramp.

There is a tree high atop the eastern ridgeline that I have always loved. It's a couple miles southeast of the house, roughly above where the Eden and Gethsemane mines would meet, had their tunnels ever united. The tree is just a Douglas fir like so many others on the mountain slopes, but its highest reaches stand above those of its neighbors, and as a child I ascribed almost mystical properties to the tree. I thought of it as a sentinel, a guardian watching over Prospect.

I talked Samuel into hiking there when I was eight or nine, and he agreed only after extracting promises that I wouldn't complain about the steep trails or the distance. I held up my end of the bargain, though it took much longer to get to the tree than I anticipated, and my legs started to burn and ache when we weren't yet halfway there. When we arrived at the tree, I was disappointed. It wasn't any larger or more majestic than its neighbors; it had simply had the fortune to plant its roots on a rocky outcropping that rose a couple yards above the surrounding ground. There were no eagles in its branches, no musical whispering of the wind through its needles.

"This was a good idea, Josie," Samuel said, his approval instantly banishing my disappointment. "That's one heck of a view." It was, too, a clear bird's-eye perspective on not only our own property—its sprawling acreage, the gray roofs of the house and barn—but also the entire town. From the tree, the foothills across the valley were dwarfed by the true mountains behind them, like the earliest ripple of a tide lapping at a beach, the peaks behind building higher and higher, the most distant ones capped with white like the highest breaking waves.

I sit atop Lockjaw now, one hand holding the reins and resting on the saddle horn, the other shielding my eyes from the sinking afternoon sun. I look at the mountains first, then the town, finally the house and land. There's an unfamiliar metallic reflection toward the front of the property. Still a couple vehicles parked outside the gate. I catch myself scanning the property for Samuel, hoping to see him walking to the barn or mowing the pasture. Sometime soon I'll stop forgetting what he has done, stop expecting things to be the way they once were. I can't decide whether it will be a relief when that happens or not.

I ride slowly down the mountain, giving Lockjaw a slack rein and letting the mule choose her path. I close my eyes, willing my mind to go as dark as my vision. Usually a ride to the high fir calms me, but my thoughts come quickly, in flashes and images, one after another, piling up so I feel hounded by them. The days till the eviction: thirty. The damaged courthouse. The photograph of Emily. Samuel driving back from Wyoming, Samuel still in Wyoming, Samuel never in Wyoming at all.

Hawkins is waiting in the barn when I get back, sitting on a storage bin in jeans and flannel, cleaning his fingernails with his pocketknife. He looks up when I lead Lockjaw into the barn. "You shouldn't ride alone."

"Don't have much choice, do I?"

He doesn't say anything else. Doesn't get up, either, though I know he has to make an effort to stay seated. Hawkins's instinct to help those he deems to be in need verges on Pavlovian, and being both female and disabled, I set off every *help that person* bell in old-fashioned Hawkins's head. Mostly he restrains himself unless I ask, and when he can't, he helps when I'm not looking. He mucked the stall while I was riding, for instance, but he doesn't point it out and I pretend not to notice.

He waits until I've untacked Lockjaw and am on the far side of the animal, grooming her coat with a soft brush. "What're you gonna do with that mule when . . ."

I wince, glad Hawkins can't see me from where he sits. "There's time yet to figure it out."

"Not a lot."

I wheel behind Lockjaw, toss the brush into the grooming tote with more force than I intend. "Jesus, Hawkins. I know I've got to take care of it, and I will."

I see his temples jump as he clenches his jaw, but his expression doesn't change. "Sorry," he says. "I know your brother usually handles that kind of thing, is all." He folds his pocketknife, tucks it back onto his belt. His hat has been sitting crown-down beside him—it's white, of course—and he puts it on now, stands. "I came to see if I could take you to dinner."

"I smell like mule."

He lets one side of his mouth twitch upward. "Puts you ahead of most folks at the Knock-Off."

The Knock-Off is just around the corner from City Hall, in the lower half of a two-story brick building on a side street so narrow it seems charitable not to call it an alley. When the mines were open, it was the most popular place in town, but these days most of Prospect's remaining residents prefer the newer sports bars in Split Creek, and the Knock-Off caters mostly to drunks and near drunks. This early on a Sunday, the place is almost empty; when Hawkins and I enter I see just one other customer and the bartender. We go to a table beneath high windows crowded with neon beer logos, and Hawkins kicks a vinyl-covered chair out of the way to make room for my wheelchair. The bartender saunters over with a couple menus; he drops them on the table, waits. Hawkins orders a fried chicken sandwich, I order a cheeseburger, and the bartender nods and scoops up the untouched menus.

I look at Hawkins, and Hawkins looks at the walls. A few pickaxes, black-and-white photographs from early days at the mines, an old-fashioned cap with a carbide lamp and reflector on the front. A photo memorial to each of the thirteen miners who died in the Gethsemane collapse. My father in the second row. He's smiling, sunlight bright on his skin, blue eyes squinted nearly shut. I can see Samuel in him. He doesn't look much like our father, really, but they have the same slim, sinewy build, and they stand the same way, rooted and sturdy, as though a person could push and push and push and still not move them.

"Nothing new to tell me about Samuel?" There isn't—Hawkins would have mentioned it before now—but I want to say his name.

Hawkins pulls his eyes to mine, shakes his head. I wave the bartender down, ask for a beer.

"You hate beer."

"Not drinking it for the taste."

Hawkins presses his lips together. "I don't like seeing you this way."

"I'm not allowed to be pissed off that my brother blew up a

building?" I don't care about the building. But it's easier to say than *Emily*.

"I just—" He passes his hand over his phantom mustache again. "I wish I could do something to make it better."

"You can't," I say, but I send the words across the table gently.

Our food arrives, and I'm glad for an excuse not to talk. I've forgotten to ask the kitchen to hold the pickle, but I leave the sour slices where they are; it isn't so good a burger that they ruin it. Hawkins shakes extra salt onto his fries and ferries them to his mouth by the handful. He doesn't drink—never does—and he's ordered a lemonade he leaves untouched. I don't think he really likes the stuff, figure he orders it because it seems like something an Old West lawman in a dime-store novel might do, a habit that would get another man mocked but that the sheriff can get away with because no one questions his righteousness or courage. Sometimes I think Hawkins looks in the mirror and sees Gary Cooper.

The lone customer at the bar pushes his stool back and ambles toward the door in a not-quite-straight line. He's tall, and thin in an unhealthy way; he doesn't make eye contact with either Hawkins or me as he passes.

Hawkins swipes at his mouth with a napkin. "I don't want to have to drag my ass out of bed tonight 'cause I've been called to your place, Branson." He cranes his neck. "You hear me?"

Branson doesn't turn but raises his hand in a brief wave that's half acknowledgment, half dismissal. Hank Branson was out sick the day of the mine collapse. He should've been in that stope, which means someone else was there in his place. I don't think he's held a job since, and I can't imagine he can afford to pay his extensive bar bill. I wonder who does.

Hawkins turns back once the door shuts behind Branson.

"The man gives me fits, Jo." I offer a tight smile. I've seen the Hawkins-Branson exchange before, and there's something performative in it. The two of them are like a couple actors in a long-running play, and Hawkins especially embodies his part well. I don't think he'd know what to do if Branson suddenly got sober. "He'll be back soon as he's sure I'm gone," Hawkins declares.

I nod to his empty plate. "Guess he won't have to wait long. Ready?"

He doesn't stand. Crosses his arms, sighs. "I got a question."

A question. Not a surprise, not really. Yes, Hawkins takes me out for a burger now and then, or has me over to his place for microwave dinners in front of the tube, but nothing gets to be that simple anymore.

I don't make it easier on Hawkins, though part of me wishes I could bring myself to; he's wound so tight, so obviously uncomfortable, that I almost expect him to huff and stamp a foot like an unhappy horse. Still I wait, silent.

Finally he meets my eyes. "Where did you and Samuel go that summer?"

Whatever question I thought he might have, this isn't it. For a moment it's so unexpected I can't imagine why he's asking—it seems as random as wanting to know who took me to prom, or what kind of soda I last sold at Fuel Stop—and then, in a single, awful, heavy moment, I understand exactly why he's asking. "I've told you that," I say, very softly.

"Tell me again."

I become aware of the buzzing hum of the fluorescent Coors sign over my head. "Did Devin tell you to ask that?"

Hawkins's voice hardens, just a hair. "Devin hasn't figured out he *should* tell me to ask that."

I spin my empty beer glass, widening the wet circle on the tabletop.

South Dakota. That's what we told everyone, when we came back. We'd been staying with Mom's friend in South Dakota, yes, we should have called, we could see that now, but couldn't everyone understand, we'd just lost our mother, we wanted to go somewhere we felt safe, now we were back and it was all fine, we'd only gone to South Dakota. I told the story so many times, to so many people, it started to seem nearly real.

I remember the day the social worker told me that when I left rehab, I couldn't go home with Samuel. He was only seventeen. (*Almost eighteen*, I protested.) We'd been traumatized by our mother's death. I had special needs. Not the most suitable environment.

I remember the way everyone worried that I never cried, not since the night my mother died. Not even when the therapists and social workers came to talk to me. Not even when they told me I'd never walk again. I remember that when they told me I couldn't go home with Samuel the tears finally came, and I couldn't stop them. (*Very nice foster parents*, they assured me. *Experience with physically disabled children. We can reevaluate when . . .*) I remember Samuel looking me in the eye and telling me everything would be okay, and I remember that then the tears stopped.

I remember him coming to visit me the day before I was scheduled to leave the rehab facility. We went outside together, as we had almost every day for a month, me pushing the handrims of my still-new wheelchair, Samuel beside me, waving to the receptionist in the lobby. I remember that instead of turning left toward the city park, he turned right toward the parking lot. I remember him telling me to hurry. I remember the rifle in the back window of the pickup.

And I remember the summer. Despite all that had happened in the preceding months—our mother's death, my injury—

those six weeks with Samuel are still a time I look back on with something like happiness. I felt peaceful. I felt safe.

Samuel made me practice the story before we came back. South Dakota, he said. Our mother's friend's name is Mary, you don't remember her last name. She lives in a yellow farmhouse in a small town, you don't remember where. Let me worry about that. He showed me a map, traced our imaginary route with a pink highlighter. We stopped at Devils Tower, he said. At Mount Rushmore. At the Corn Palace. And I told the story many times, to many people. To Hawkins most of all, because he asked again and again. South Dakota, I said. South Dakota. And finally he stopped asking. Finally he let it be truth. We'd gone to South Dakota.

We hadn't, of course.

Hadn't left the state.

Hadn't even left the county.

"Samuel wouldn't—" I bite the words off just in time. *Samuel wouldn't go back there*, I almost said.

He might.

"Where did you go, Jo?"

I still the glass in my hands. Lift my eyes to Hawkins's. "South Dakota."

I have prayed.

I have prayed with words. With any words that come to my lips, with eloquent words and words so jumbled they scarcely make sense. With words that say exactly what I mean and words that can't come close. I have prayed with my eyes shut and my hands clenched so tightly they ache for hours afterward. I have prayed at her bedside, and at mine. I have prayed as I walk down the street, as I swallow food I no longer seem able to taste, as I sit on the toilet. I have prayed at night in lieu of sleep.

When my own words fail me, I have prayed with the words of those who have come before me, with the words others have used to reach out to You: *Be merciful unto me, O God, be merciful unto me: for my soul trusteth in thee: yea, in the shadow of thy wings will I make my refuge, until these calamities be overpast.* And, *The Lord is my rock, and my fortress, and my deliverer; my God, my strength, in whom I will trust.* And, sometimes, more and more, simply: *Hear my cry, O God: attend unto my prayer.*

I am not brave enough to pray as Jesus did in Gethsemane. Every day, a dozen times a day, a hundred, I ask You to spare me—to spare *her*—but the second part of that prayer, the *Not what I will, but what thou wilt* . . . that I have tried to pray but cannot. They seemed rote words until I was asked to mean them myself.

Sometimes even the words of Your book are ash in my mouth, and then I have prayed without words, trusting You to know what is in my heart, trusting You to hear me even in silence. (Do I trust? Do I really? I try.)

I have prayed her name.

I have prayed Your names.

I have even prayed with my hands. One hand on her head, one on her heart—her pulse slight as a sparrow's; You see the sparrows, don't You?—and I pray with all that is in me that You might work through me as You once did when I was a young man.

I have prayed every way I know how.

I have prayed in new ways and old.

I have prayed without ceasing.

I drive to Elk Fork after work Monday. I need more canvases, paints, and a new bottle of glazing medium—never before have I used so many supplies without a completed painting to show for it—but more than that, I need to get out of Prospect. Out of the house that seems too empty without Samuel in it, and emptier with each box I pack. Out of the shadow of the mountains that haven't looked the same to me since my conversation with Hawkins.

This time I avoid Lincoln Street and the visible damage Samuel wrought, take an earlier exit off the interstate and make my way on surface streets to the outskirts of Elk Fork's small downtown. I park half a block from the art supply store; Martha Weatherby, the owner, sees me coming and holds the door. "Jo," she greets, "so good to see you again." I scrutinize her face and voice for any animosity, any hint she would rather I hadn't come, but find nothing.

"Running low on a few supplies." I force a cautious smile. I'm grateful for her kindness, but there is an odd artifice in this normalcy, a freshly foreign quality to these words we've exchanged so many times before.

"Let me know if I can give you a hand with anything."

The place is empty except for me and Martha, so I take my time as I make my way down the aisles, savor the scents of graphite and linseed oil as I roll past pencils and inks, papers and boards, watercolors and oils. The tubes of acrylics hang neatly on racks toward the back of the store. I choose a bottle of glazing medium and two tubes of paint from the lower racks and go to the register. "I also need three twenty-by-twenty-four canvases and a tube each of cobalt blue and alizarin crimson, please."

While Martha's gone, I study the flyers taped to the countertop. A sign-up sheet for a still-life watercolor class. An advertisement for a new gallery near the river district. A call for artists for a plein air painting festival.

"You should submit a portfolio for that," Martha says when she returns, tapping the plein air flyer with one of the paint tubes. "The deadline isn't until Friday."

"I don't think—"

"You sell yourself short, but you're quite talented, Jo. Besides, people would enjoy seeing you work with your painting knives. It's not a method most of the public is familiar with."

"I'm pretty sure they've all seen Bob Ross on TV."

Martha gives me a schoolmarm look. "Think about it. There's an auction at the end of the day, so look at it as an opportunity to make some money, if you must."

I might have let her talk me into applying a few weeks ago, though I wouldn't necessarily have expected to be chosen to participate. I can work quickly, have often tasked myself with completing a painting in a single sitting. It's challenging, but also freeing, because I don't give myself much time to think about the choices I make, and at its best, that kind of painting feels instinctive in a way it doesn't when I slow down. But the plein air festival is a competition to which the public is invited. It's for artists, real artists. I still feel like an imposter whenever I come into the store, still have to mentally justify spending money on professional-quality paints every time I purchase some. I know what I am: a talented amateur. I paint for tourists, not judges. That's why my paintings hang in a gas station and not a gallery. It's true I'm trying to do something more now, with this painting of the house, but it's also true I'm on my fourth canvas and no closer to a painting that feels right.

Still, the festival could have been fun, even if I were outclassed—and there is a very small voice in my head saying, *What if you weren't?*—but I can't do it now. Even if I were accepted into the competition, no one would want to watch the Elk Fork Bomber's sister paint a nice portrait of the city he wounded.

I can't explain that to Martha, though—can't say it aloud—so I just nod, try another smile. Martha purses her lips, then tears the flyer off the countertop and stuffs it into the bag with my purchases. "Think about it," she says again.

———

Another nightmare last night. I went outside afterward and lay on the ground so I could look at the stars. We used to do that some nights when we were here together, do you remember? We both had troubled dreams then, and sometimes we'd find ourselves awake in the night at the same time, and we would go out to watch the stars. You were fascinated with the idea of the earth moving, and you'd try not to blink, hoping you could keep your eyes open long enough to see the stars cross the sky.

You used to ask me about the constellations. I knew some of them because Dad had taught me: Orion, Scorpio, Ursa Major and Minor, Cassiopeia. I'd forgotten so many, though, and you wanted me to keep talking, keep telling you stories, so I made up new constellations. Last night I looked at all those stars and tried to remember which ones I had joined, which I had pointed to and said, See there? I tried to remember, but the stars were like scattered stones.

I do remember one of the stories. There was an eagle constellation, I told you. A long time ago there was a small village that lived peacefully but was surrounded by dangerous enemies. There were two friends there, a young man and a young woman, who had grown up together and were very close. One day word reached the villagers that their enemies were approaching, and there was no time to flee. The people prayed to their gods to save them, and just before the enemies reached the village, the gods turned all of the villagers into animals. The young man was turned into an eagle, and almost before he understood what was happening, he was soaring high above his enemies, out of reach of even their most powerful weapons. He watched them burn the village, but he didn't care. Just before he had become an eagle, he had seen his friend turn into a mouse and scamper into a field, darting between the enemies' feet. He began immediately to search for her. His eyes were very good for this now, but still it took him a long time to find her. He spotted her just before dusk, but as soon as he swooped toward her, she scurried into a hole. The eagle was alarmed to realize his talons were flexed, ready to seize the mouse, and he beat his great wings and took himself back high into the sky.

He had thought he was simply a young man in the shape of an eagle, but he understood now that he was *an eagle. His gods had saved him from his enemies, but in doing so they had made him into the enemy of his dearest friend. He circled the moon all night, then circled the sun when it rose, and all the time he prayed he would be turned back into the young man he had once been. But his prayers went unanswered. The eagle's wings grew tired, for he was afraid to approach the earth again in case he couldn't stop his eagle-self from destroying his mouse-friend, but he forced himself to stay aloft. He watched her from there, circling, riding the air currents as high into the sky as they would take him. He could not bear to leave her, but he did not dare go near. The eagle flew to exhaustion, but the gods were impressed by his loyalty to his friend, so rather than let him die, they made him part of the sky itself. Now he rests during the day, but at night he flies again, watching over his friend.*

As I write it out now, I see it was not a very cheerful story for me to tell my little sister. With gods like that, who needs the devil?

———

I tell myself I'm beginning to get used to the house without the sound of Samuel's footsteps, the clutter he left in any room he passed through, the butchered-timber scent he brought home from work. I'll have to get used to it. Whatever happens in the end, whether he stays gone, is arrested, or . . . something else, he will not be coming back here. When I first understood I was paralyzed, and it was permanent, Samuel told me it was okay to be sad, and okay to wish things were different, but it wasn't okay to pretend they *were* different. He would tell me the same thing now. I'm on my own. Accept it.

Four weeks until I have to be out of the house. I've already left the planning too long. We were supposedly going to receive "fair market value" for the house and property, but that barely accounts for the many modifications Samuel made over the years to make our home more accessible: the ramps, the wider doorways, the multi-height countertops in the kitchen. And I have no idea what the implications of Samuel's actions will be— still haven't called a lawyer—but the house is in his name; I have to assume whatever money he would have gotten for it will no longer be available to me. I have a little money in a savings account, maybe enough for a security deposit, but not much more.

I bought a copy of the *Miner* at Fuel Stop after my last shift. I spread it on the kitchen table now, leafing past the sports page and community calendar until I find the scant classifieds. Two apartments for rent in Prospect, both on second stories. No elevators in this town. Split Creek is a little bigger and might have a house or two for rent, but even those are likely to have a few steps to reach the front door. Ramps aren't cheap, even if a landlord let me build one.

Elk Fork will have more options. I've seen a couple newer complexes on my visits; they probably have some accessible apartments. The rugged western pride in independence that sometimes leads to a convenient amnesia regarding the existence of disabled people will be softened in a city, and in some ways my life would be easier there. But moving to Elk Fork would mean leaving Prospect. It would mean waking up and seeing the contours of unfamiliar mountains out my window. It would mean quitting my job. Selling Lockjaw. Giving up burgers with Hawkins at the Knock-Off. It would be exile.

I stare at the paper, willing more ads, better ads, to appear. Then I fold the newsprint around a ceramic bowl and tuck it into a moving box.

My newest painting is coming along. It's my fourth attempt at painting the house. This time I'm building the color slowly, layer upon layer. I've thinned the paints, and it's made for a more laborious process than I'm used to, more frustrating. It's not going badly, exactly. The painting looks like the scene in front of me. House, land, mountains, sky. Objectively speaking, it might even be one of my better efforts. But I could have said the same for the three canvases I've already painted over or trashed. I feel myself getting close to that point with this one, too, though I can't isolate exactly why the painting is so disappointing.

The sky is already finished. A thin, jagged strip along the top of the canvas, gray and overcast, enough light showing through the banks of clouds to keep the sky this side of foreboding. Now I'm at work on the mountains. I start not with what I can see, but with what I cannot, with what I know lies beneath the surface of the slopes. The darkest colors first, near-black grays for the deepest deposits of mudstone, then lighter grays for the limestone, finished with blood brown for the rock containing iron pyrite that roughly weathers to iron oxide. It matters to me that I paint the mountains with depth. That I not forget there is so much more to them than the flora on their slopes or the shapes of their peaks against the sky. But the layers of paint, carefully mixed and applied though they are, seem to barely hint at all these mountains hold, at how they've shaped the lives of those who enter their depths and live in their shadows.

I'm uneasy thinking so much about the mountains. The wilderness over the ridge is still vast, still empty. I know parts of it well, but that familiarity is starting to feel like a burden. We did not go to South Dakota.

On the mountains' lower slopes, I work up a pale green-tinged gold to match the new grasses, add some deeper green in the shaded patches, flick my brush to reflect the way the tallest stalks bend beneath their own weight. Mix in the slightest bit of red to suggest the fallen pine needles left over from fall, faded and crushed to a dusty mulch by a long season beneath the winter snows. It looks almost the way I want. Almost.

I push my chair back, squint at the painting, up at the mountains, back to my painting. Almost without thinking I lean to the side until my hand grazes the ground. I gather a small handful of soil, brush my fingers against each other above my palette, like a chef adding a pinch of seasoning to a dish. I blend the soil into my paint with a palette knife, dip my brush into it, feel the grit beneath the bristles. Touch brush to canvas.

Friday morning I drive to the tiny library in town, park beside Fanny Gordon's station wagon in the otherwise empty lot. The library is just a single room, with two shelves of books for adults and two for children, a handful of magazines, bound copies of the *Miner* and the *Elk Fork Chronicle*, a pair of computers. The collection skews toward true crime and romance, reflecting the tastes of Prospect's most voracious readers.

I've borrowed the few art books dozens of times. My favorite is on Caravaggio, though it smells of mildew and many of the pages are creased or torn. The first time I checked it out, I didn't think I would like the paintings; they seemed dark, the shadows too pronounced. But then the light caught my eye. The way each painting celebrated it, even if there seemed to be only the scarcest amount, only the yield of the smallest window or a single flame. *Chiaroscuro*, the book said. Shadow and light.

Fanny glances up from behind the checkout desk when I enter. "Jo, dear. How *are* you?"

I gauge her interest at half genuine concern, half quest for gossip. For a moment I imagine the reckless release of answering honestly—*I feel like I can't breathe. I check the radio a dozen times a day to make sure no one has died because of my brother's bomb. I lied to the sheriff and I think he knows it*—but anything I tell Fanny will be common knowledge this time tomorrow. "Oh," I tell her instead, keeping my voice neutral, "I'm as well as can be expected." I turn away before it occurs to her to ask exactly how people in my situation can be expected to be.

The table holding the public computers is too high—my

hands nearly at the level of my chin when I rest them on the keyboard—but I can see the screen clearly enough. I call up the website for the plein air festival in Elk Fork, plug in the flash drive I brought. The selection committee requires two sample images, and I choose one landscape and one equine painting.

I set to work filling out the brief application form. One question asks why I want to participate in the festival, and I compose a bland answer about sharing art with the community. The selection committee will like that reply, certainly more than the first ones that came to mind: *I want to know if I'm good enough. I need money and hope I can sell a painting at the festival auction for more than I can at a gas station. I'm tired of trying and failing to paint the house I'm losing. I want to not think about my brother and what he did for one day, just one day.* I click in the final empty field on the form, the one that asks my name. Let the cursor blink. *Josephine*, I type, and then: *Grady.* My mother's maiden name.

I click "submit" before I can change my mind.

———

The storm comes on suddenly. The morning was hotter than those preceding it, the sky a flawless blue from one mountain range to the other. My first hint that something has changed is the startling sound of the broken shutter upstairs slamming into the side of the house. It comes again, and I'm braced for it this time. Through the kitchen window, I see the tops of the ponderosa pines arch, straighten, arch more deeply with the next gust. A thin branch snaps off one of the trees and the wind flings it to the ground as sharply as a dart.

The clouds arrived without my noticing, but now they move so swiftly I can watch their eastward progress against the still ridge of the mountains. Lightning forks suddenly and I blink against its brightness; the thunder comes several seconds later, a rumble rather than a roar. The worst of the storm might miss us. Might go north.

Might not.

I pull on a sweatshirt and go outside. Lockjaw prances along the paddock fence line, nostrils flared. Another gust of wind—I duck my head and grab tight to the handrims of my chair to keep from being blown off the path—and a bigger limb breaks off another tree. It falls a few yards before being caught in the arms of its brother branches. Lockjaw brays, the sound pitched higher than usual, cutting through the din of the wind and the increasingly frequent thunder.

"Easy, Muley," I call, but Lockjaw doesn't so much as flick an ear in my direction. A storm like this sent her through the fence when she was younger.

I cross the bridge over the creek and the wind-buffeted water pushes its way above the wooden boards and licks at my tires. Another fifteen yards—easy, the wind at my back—and I'm in the barn. The rain starts suddenly, gray sheets coming in gusts, the sound like handfuls of gravel thrown hard at the aluminum roof. I go to Lockjaw's stall, pull the door open. "Hey, Muley!" I call again. "Hey, Lockjaw!"

This time Lockjaw turns at the sound of my voice, begins trotting toward the barn. Another boom of thunder and she spooks sideways, tossing her head in the rain, eyes rolling to the whites. "Come on, Lockjaw. It's all right, girl." She lopes into the stall and stops with a snort a few inches shy of me. I reach up and stroke her shoulder, feel trembling beneath my palm. Mules are generally steady creatures, and Lockjaw steadier than most, but storms are her weakness. "There's a good girl," I soothe. "You're okay now." I pull shut the exterior door leading to the pasture.

Some horses and mules panic and hurt themselves if stalled during a storm, but Lockjaw always seems to feel safer inside. I don't blame her. The barn is fragrant with orchard grass, the air is still, and the battering rain has steadied to a regular drum on the roof. Even after the power goes out, all the lights snapping off at once, the barn feels secure. The storm continues to send hard gusts against the building, the beams creaking beneath the weight of the wind, and the thunder comes every minute or so, but the wild look fades from Lockjaw's eye.

I wonder if Samuel is close enough to see this storm, to feel the brunt of it. He hates thunder almost as much as Lockjaw. I asked him why once, and all he said was, *Dad used to tell me it sounded like a rockburst.*

Another crack, not thunder but something else, louder and more immediate, and then a thud I feel in my chest. I go to the doorway of the barn, squinting against the rain, and see one of the pines on its side across the creek. I appreciate the tree's height only now that it's fallen; eighty feet is easier to understand stretched across soil than reaching toward sky. It stood on the far bank; now its top lies just a few yards from the barn doors, clusters of pine needles swaying almost at my feet. I'd liked the tree—it shaded my bedroom window as a child, and a family of gray squirrels often nested in its branches—but they'd have cut it when they tore down the house, so I don't spare much grief for it. Probably won't even bother to have it removed.

Except, I see now, it's fallen squarely across the bridge. The wooden planks are entirely hidden beneath the thick trunk and the broad reaches of needle-clothed branches. I roll down the path as far as I can, but the tree blocks my way when I'm still well short of the bridge. The creek is at its highest this time of year, but the water is still no more than eighteen inches deep.

It'd be nothing if I could walk. But the banks are steep near the barn, the creek bottom soft and silty.

I could saddle Lockjaw, ride across. But the storm will leave her on edge for the rest of the day; it would be a risk to ride her. And I slipped once trying to use my mounting bar after a rainstorm, the wet metal too slick to get a strong grip on. Even if I did ride back to the house, my chair would still be on this side of the creek. It feels like one of those logic puzzles I hated so much in school.

My cell phone is in the bag on the back of my chair. I return to the barn and open my contacts list. *Samuel. Hawkins. Fuel Stop.* That's all.

I dial Hawkins. Three rings, then his terse voice mail prompt. I hang up. He'll be busy after a storm like this. I try again, same result. Hawkins hasn't spoken to me since he drove me home in silence from the Knock-Off Sunday, since I told him *South Dakota* yet again. He'll answer if he sees my name on his phone, though. Surely after the storm. I wait half an hour, dial a third time. Nothing.

I try Fuel Stop—One Bear isn't exactly a friend, but he'd probably help me—but I get a busy signal. The landlines must be out.

The thunder has stopped, the wind eased, the rain still falling but not so fiercely. I'm wet from going outside to look at the tree, though, and the storm has left the air cool. I rub my hands hard up and down my upper arms.

I could call 911. This isn't what I'd call an emergency, but I might feel differently in a few hours. I wondered if the agent outside the gate would come investigate the fallen tree, but he hasn't, and despite my predicament, I'm glad. Still, I could call and ask to be put through to the FBI; Devin would probably love an excuse to come rescue me.

There must be someone else. Something of a marvel that I can live in such a small town for such a long time and not really know anyone. Oh, I know names, faces. I know jobs and families and histories and every kind of gossip. I say hello in stores and nod across parking lots, but that's it. That's the way it's been since Mom died. Samuel and I kept to ourselves. It seemed safer that way. I've never really needed anyone but him.

I hold my breath, call his cell. *The number you have dialed . . .* Of course not.

I reach into my bag again. My fingers find the card just where I left it the night the pastor gave it to me. Haven't even looked at it until now. *Asa Truth*, it says. Below that: *Pastor, Light of the World Church.* He's crossed out the printed phone number, beside it written *My cell*, and a number. I hold the card between thumb and forefinger, tap its edge against my thigh. Take a deep breath. Dial.

One ring, two, three.

"Hello?" The voice cautious, a little steely. He's probably received as many calls from reporters and strangers as I have, if not more. And he's waiting for news just as I am. Hoping for it, fearing it.

"Hi," I say. The word comes out raspy, and I clear my throat. "Um, this is Jo. Josephine," I add, and finally, "Faber."

A moment's silence.

"You gave me your card?" The rain starts to let up, as though softening its strikes against the barn roof to match the fragile weight of my words. "I was . . ." I don't know how to finish the sentence. Don't know what I was thinking. "Never mind. This was a mistake. I—"

"No," the pastor says quickly. "No, I'm glad you called."

"I shouldn't have." I wish the card had been in the house, safely on the far side of the creek. I've opened a door I should have kept closed. "I just . . . I didn't know who else to call."

"What's wrong?" He's gentled his voice, sanded down the startled, harsh edges of his earlier words.

I grip the phone tightly, think about hanging up. Already I can guess the pastor is the sort to call me back. "We had a storm just now," I say. "A big one. I don't know if you caught any of it down in Elk Fork."

"There was some rain."

"I came outside to bring our molly into the barn. Our mule. She hates thunder." I squeeze my eyes shut, shake my head. "One of our pines came down in the storm. There's a creek runs the length of the property between the house and the barn, and the tree's over the bridge."

"You're on the barn side?"

"It's not a big creek, but with my wheelchair . . ."

"I'll come right away."

"You don't—"

"Do you have a chain saw?"

"I . . . I don't know if there's gas in it."

"I'll stop and get some."

I hear him moving on the other end of the line, metal clinking against something hard, the rough brush of cloth against cloth. This isn't what I expected. Yes, I'd hoped he could help, but I feel as though part of me is still arguing against calling him at all, and now things are moving so fast; *he's* moving so fast. "I tried to reach a friend," I say, "but he didn't answer. This isn't—I shouldn't have called."

"I'm leaving now," the pastor says. "Tell me where to go."

He arrives in just over an hour and a half, which means he drove much too fast, especially accounting for a stop at a gas station. He pulls up alone in a dark green SUV; I watch warily as he steps out of the vehicle and unfolds his tall frame. Despite the pastor's willingness to come, something like shame or fear circles and nags at the relief I feel.

I wheel from the darkness of the barn onto the path that's now dappled with sunlight. "Hello," I call, lifting one hand in a cautious wave.

He looks toward me for only a moment. "I see your problem," he says, nodding to the fallen tree.

I stop a couple yards from the edge of the creek, behind what were once the tree's highest reaches. The pastor matches my distance on the far side. He wears jeans, a chamois shirt, and lightly scuffed work boots, safety goggles in one hand and a red gas can in the other. The clothes don't suit him; they're outdoorsy, and he seems like a man who ought to be on a stage. "Thank you for coming." There's so much more to say, and no good way to say it—none that I can think of—so I point behind him. "The chain saw is in that shed. It's not locked."

He nods, and I return to the doorway of the barn to watch him work. He paces the edge of the creek, crouching once to peer at the bridge beneath the tree. It takes him three tries to start the chain saw, but he's methodical once he has it going, chooses his cuts with care. He doesn't appear as at ease with this kind of work as Samuel, who moves with an economy and efficiency few can match, but he's careful and deliberate, and makes good headway in a relatively short time.

There's nothing I can do to help, and I try not to mind. There's a lot I can do—far more than I expected immediately after my injury, when even many simple tasks seemed overwhelming—but there remain a few things I cannot, and this is one of them.

When the pastor has most of the branches off the tree, he looks at the creek and then, without any visible hesitation, steps into the water, boots and all, and continues cutting the branches he couldn't reach from the far bank. He stumbles once, goes down on one knee in the water, and I gasp, but the chain-brake kicks in. He keeps the saw out of the water, restarts the chain, and continues with his work, never sparing so much as a glance in my direction.

More than an hour has passed by the time the pastor pushes the last round of trunk away from the bridge. The fallen tree still sprawls on either side of the creek, but now there's a gap in the middle, and the path and bridge are thickly dusted with fresh sawdust but otherwise clear. The sun has sunk below the western ridgeline, the first evening star already brightly visible in the darkening sky over the peaks. The power has come back on, and the barn lights glow behind me as I roll down the path and across the bridge. The sawdust's scent pierces the rain-cleansed air, and I try not to think of Samuel. "Thank you," I say.

The pastor pulls a handkerchief from his pocket, mops the sweat from his face. "Felt good to work." He glances at the piles of branches and rounds of trunk on the bank, at the rest of the tree's body. "You'll have plenty of firewood for winter."

Samuel always seasons pine at least a year, though he says six months will do in a pinch. Doesn't matter now. "Gotta be out of here before then," I say, and immediately wish I hadn't. Nod. Smile. Agree. Shouldn't have been hard.

"I forgot," the pastor says. "I saw in the paper. I didn't mean to—"

"It's fine." I glance at the pastor's soaking boots, his muddy jeans, his sweat-stained shirt. I wish I could not notice them. I wish I had been able to reach Hawkins. I wish my mother hadn't taught me to be polite. "Um . . . I understand if you just want to get going, but it's a long way to drive in wet clothes." I pause, to see if the pastor will preemptively decline the offer I haven't yet voiced. "I could dry them if you want." Another pause. "Maybe get you something to eat."

He studies me for a moment, then nods.

In the laundry room, I find a pair of Samuel's jeans I recently mended and the old Army sweatshirt Kev gave him. A T-shirt would be better, but of course Samuel never wears short sleeves. I hold the clothes out to the pastor. "They're Samuel's," I say cautiously. "I don't have anything else."

"They're fine." I listen for any hint he doesn't mean it, but either he really does think they're fine or he's a good liar.

I make sure my catheter supplies are hidden in a drawer in the bathroom, pull a clean towel from the cupboard. "Take a shower if you want," I say. "Water takes a minute to get hot."

In the kitchen cupboards I find some dried pasta and jarred tomato sauce, and in the fridge a bagged salad mix that's only a little wilted. I dump the sauce in a pan, sprinkle in some dried oregano and thyme, add the pasta to the larger pot. Soon I hear the water in the bathroom shut off, and a minute later the pastor emerges, his light hair damp-dark, the wet jeans wadded in one hand. I put them in the dryer, turn back to the pastor. "You're taller than Samuel."

"So I gathered." The sleeves of the sweatshirt end a couple inches above his wrists, the jeans more than a couple inches above his ankles.

If only you'd put those on before tackling that tree, you could've walked through the creek without getting a stitch wet. As soon as I think the words I realize I can't say them. This isn't the time for a joke; there will probably never be a time for a joke between this man and me.

I carefully lift the pot of pasta off the stove and balance it on a wooden board I've set across my lap. I wheel to the sink and pour the pot's contents into a colander, again carefully. I was less cautious as a teenager, once spilled boiling water on my leg. Didn't even notice until I undressed for bed and saw the burn. Still have an ugly scar on my thigh. The pastor doesn't offer to help. I would have expected him to. I wonder if he's being sensitive, doesn't want to make assumptions about my disability, or if he's angry, felt a duty to cut up the tree when I asked but nothing more. I wonder if the part of him that is a pastor is at war with the part of him that is a father.

I serve the food and take my place at the table. My fork is halfway to my mouth when I notice he's praying. Nothing ostentatious—hands in his lap, head bowed and eyes shut, lips moving quickly and silently—but I feel I've been caught cheating at something, and I keep my fork midair until he looks up.

We eat for several minutes in near silence, the only sounds the clink of silverware, chewing, and the clattering rumble of the dryer. The pastor studies the kitchen, his eyes gliding over the store-brand cereal boxes, the dirty dishes in the sink, the framed painting of a bowl of fruit I hung to cover the hole Samuel punched in the wall. The ordinariness of it all must frustrate him. "A little late for this," I say, after more silence, "but I'm embarrassed to admit I'm not sure what I should call you. Reverend, or . . ."

"Asa," he says. "Asa's fine."

"An unusual name."

"My father was a pastor, too," he says, his eyes still roving about the room. "A preacher. Tent revivals, hellfire and brimstone, faith healing, that sort of thing. He named me after an Old Testament king who lived a life faithful to God until he developed a foot ailment late in his life. Rather than trust God to heal him, he turned to physicians." He glances toward me. "He died."

His tone is matter-of-fact, and I'm not sure what to say.

"It could have been worse," Asa continues conversationally. "My grandfather—also a preacher—named my father Judas. As a daily reminder that, quote, 'We are all complicit in the death of Christ.' He's also the one that changed the family name to Truth from something blandly Germanic."

"Sounds kind of intense."

"You know what *Emily* means?"

The sound of her name almost makes me choke. Asa hasn't announced it as he did at the prayer service, has instead spoken it with such familiarity, such ease, that it brings her presence into the room in a sharper, more immediate way. I find my voice, offer a weak, "No."

"Neither do I. Her mother and I chose the name because we thought it was pretty. That's all."

I put down my fork. "I hope I didn't take you away from her today."

"You didn't." Asa looks down at his plate. "Her grandparents are with her. Catherine's parents. My wife died when Em was a toddler. Car accident." He touches his left hand with his right, spins an invisible wedding ring around his finger. I don't think he realizes he's done it. "Em's close with her grandparents," he continues. "They're good people. But since the accident I've always suspected they resent me a little. For not being there when it happened." He swallows. "For being alive when their daughter is not." He turns to look out the window, though it's dark now and I doubt he can see anything but his own reflection. "I've always tried to convince myself I was imagining it. But now when we meet at the hospital, they hardly look at me, and when they do . . ." He winces. "They blame me for what happened to Em, I think. It was my church."

A confessional quality to his words. And now a silence, a sense that he's waiting. I don't know what to do, what he expects me to do. Absolve him? Assure him? He's the pastor. "It wasn't your fault."

Asa jerks his head up, locks his eyes to mine. His features have hardened, and when he speaks it is with a growl. "Damn right it wasn't."

I've been half expecting anger ever since Asa answered my call—I thought I was prepared for it—but his fury so eclipses his vulnerability, is so absolute, so righteous, I know I don't hide the flinch. Asa stares hard at me, temples bulging as he works his jaw, lips pressed taut as though he doesn't trust himself with further speech. There's something wrenching in the realization that anger this hot is so close to the surface. That my brother is the reason it's there.

It's the moment for an apology. I can feel it on my lips, automatic but genuine. But I know that if I apologize now—if I start apologizing for Samuel now—I'll never be able to stop.

When I speak I do so very quietly, with as conciliatory a tone as I can muster, knowing it won't soften what I say. "It wasn't my fault, either."

He stands suddenly, his chair skidding hard against the linoleum, his hands in fists. I don't move. I try to believe my own words. Try to tell myself I am not my brother; I don't deserve this anger. Asa flexes his hands, balls them into fists again. The temptation of violence plain to see. Then he shakes his head minutely and hugs himself so tightly his knuckles blanch white. I brace myself for harsh words, or worse, but when I look Asa in the eyes, I see the heavy sheen of welling tears.

"I—it's just—" A single, choking gasp. "I can't," he says, and then he is gone.

———

I hiked back to the truck today. Wasn't the first time I've done it, but it ought to be the last. They could find it. They could be watching it. I went for the radio. I scanned the stations for almost an hour—too long—but there was nothing about me, about what I did. Just music and idle talk. I hope that means they're leaving you alone now, Jo. Still, I wish I'd found something. I wanted to know about the little girl. I wanted to know if she was still in the hospital. If she'd gone home. Or if she . . .

I don't want to have killed someone, Jo.

Not again.

———

Sunday I consider going to church. I suppose I'm only thinking about it because of Asa. I wonder if he's preaching to his own congregation, what he's saying if he is. His father was into hellfire and brimstone; his grandfather didn't sound like he was one for gentle theology, either. I wouldn't have imagined Asa preaching like that until I saw his anger Friday.

I visit the cemetery instead. I don't go often; it's too public, the patch of lawn right there off First, in the shadow of Gethsemane. When the cemetery was established, it would have been on the outskirts of town, but now it's in the center. Most of the oldest stones aren't stone at all, but wood, and now they're either gone or too rotted to read. I wonder if they ever accidentally dig up an old grave that has no marker, have to silently apologize and fill the hole, try again somewhere else. So much beneath the surface of the land in this valley.

I glance at the mining memorial as I pass. The iron figure on the pedestal points toward the sky, the headlamp on his hard hat burning twenty-four hours a day. It seems a little cruel. My father and the others died in darkness. No sky. No light.

Kev's headstone stands bright and white near the southern fence. It would be one of thousands at Arlington, but stands out starkly here. Something glints in the grass at its base: a can of Dr Pepper. Hawkins leaves one every week.

My mother's grave is beside the paved footpath; I can park my chair right beside it. The flat stone is simple, dark and polished, BELOVED MOTHER engraved below her name. The grass has been trimmed shorter around the stone, the green blades only just beginning to curl over the edges of the marker; Samuel must have been here not long before the bombing.

I've always thought our mother should never have been buried here. Our father wasn't. Still inside the mountain. It would have been better, to my thinking, for her to have been cremated so Samuel and I could scatter her ashes on the mountain later. I never said as much. It was a late funeral, more than two weeks after her death, but I wasn't there. Still in the hospital, and then in rehab for another month afterward. I don't know if my brother made the decisions or not, but there's no changing them now. And if he made the decisions, if this is what he wanted—a place to visit our mother, to see her name—then I'm glad he did it.

I should have brought flowers. My mother loved daffodils. Not that she would know. I wish I believed she would. I wish I could feel her presence here. I wish I could ask her what to do. I am twenty-two, but it doesn't feel as grown-up as I thought it would when I was a child. I didn't know what Samuel was going to do in Elk Fork—I had no idea—but perhaps I should have. And I don't know what to do now. Don't know if I should try to ignore what Hawkins suggested at the Knock-Off, or try to confirm it. Don't know what to do if I *do* confirm it. And though I am old enough to know this might not be true, I can't help but believe that my mother would have known. That she would have been able to tell me what to do. That if only she were still here somehow everything would be all right. And I wish I'd brought her flowers.

I reach into my bag and take out what I did bring. The Bible is small, with a stiff leather cover, a sharp crease across the front. My mother's gold wedding band hangs from the ribbon sewn into the binding; I touch the cool metal and then reluctantly let it go. I open the cover and look at the Polaroid tucked into the first pages: my father holding me as an infant, a smile I wish I remembered. Memories of vanished people. Then I hold the book spine-down in my hand, let it fall open to where I know it will.

The summer I was fourteen, Samuel spent weeks poring over this Bible at the kitchen table. He'd quit going to church the year before, and though I hadn't attended regularly in almost two, I'd been glad to see him with his Bible again. His lips had moved silently, eyes tracking rapidly across the text, fingers flipping hurriedly through the pages. One evening, he called me to his side and led me through a bewildering series of begats that, according to him, provided undisputable proof that Jesus was not a Jew. A year after that, I found the Bible in the garbage can, tossed on top of a moldy heel of bread and a winding orange peel.

It always falls open to the page with the Twenty-Third Psalm. I felt relieved the first time it happened. He'd rejected the Bible, yes, trashed it like it meant nothing to him, but he'd turned to this page so often the memory of the movement had imprinted itself on the book's spine. Even then I understood my brother was deeply troubled, was searching for meaning in dangerous places, and I'd been relieved to think he might have found a little peace in these familiar words of comfort, if only for a time.

Then I noticed the smoothed paper, the smeared ink. Samuel had run his fingers over the words dozens if not hundreds of times, I guessed, over these first few verses of the psalm. But not the Twenty-Third. The Twenty-Second, on the facing page. I knew it only for that first line Jesus had echoed on the cross—*My God, my God, why have you forsaken me?*—and was gutted, reading it through that day, to find verse upon verse of lamentation. My eyes fixed upon two particularly smudged lines: *my heart is like wax / it is melted within my breast.*

I read it again now, alone beside our mother's grave, the Bible open on my lap, and wonder if my brother ever read all the way through the psalm. If he read far enough to reach the turn in the song, far enough to reach the relief, the praise, the gratitude. If he read far enough to find comfort.

———

The latest painting of the house isn't working. My fourth failure. Adding the soil to the paint was an improvement, though I'm sure an art critic might have something to say about it, probably nothing nice: *sentimental* or *overly literal* or *childlike*—or worse, *childish.* That isn't what's bothering me; this painting is for me, and I don't have to care what anyone else thinks of it. But it feels like I haven't trusted my acrylics to do the job, yet haven't entirely committed to something bolder.

Maybe I should try pencils or ink or even pastels. I didn't like oils the few times I used them, but I've created a handful of decent watercolors over the years. Can't quite get the idea of the soil out of my head, though. There's something about incorporating the earth into this painting of a place, of *this* place.

I set my canvas aside, prop a Masonite board on my easel, tape a piece of canvas paper to it. Tap my brush against my palm. Finally I lean over and scoop a small amount of soil into a shallow dish, dampen it with a few drops from my water jar. I mix the mud with an old palette knife, dip one of my more battered brushes into the mix. Swipe it in an arc across the paper. The pigment—the mud—spreads unevenly, varying from quite dark to pale and watery. The sediment collects in the heavy tooth of the canvas paper, and when it dries a few minutes later, most of it brushes off with a single pass of my thumb.

I spend the afternoon experimenting. Use half a pad of canvas paper before switching to watercolor paper and use another half pad of that. At one point I gather mud from the creek bank, find it to be darker and redder than the soil from the yard. I collect an empty jar and a handful of coffee filters from the house. I scrape and mix and filter and pour. Try my knives, my brushes, even my fingers. Finally it occurs to me to mix the soil with water, filter it, then evaporate it. I pour some of the filtered mud into a cheap palette with half a dozen circular wells, leave it on the porch in the sun.

Might be another silly idea, and maybe more childish than the last. Who paints with mud? And for someone most comfortable with bright colors, moving toward a monochrome palette seems an odd and perhaps foolish choice. But I can't stop thinking about the land, the literal land. The polluted creek bed sediment that collected on the porch where Asa left his boots after cutting up the fallen tree. The sawdust-laced mud Samuel tracks through the house after work, the dusty lines and curves my tires make on the kitchen linoleum after I spend time in the barn. So much of it issues from the mountain, carried down to the valley in water and on wind. So much of it is tied to the place that made this town, the place that took so much from it, took my father and so many others. This earth. What it gives, what it takes.

Arrogant, perhaps, to think I can make use of that, create with it. But I will let the mud dry, and then I will try.

———

Asa comes back late Sunday afternoon. I'm packing up the winter things in the front closet and hear his tires on the drive, open the front door as he's climbing the stairs to the porch. "Here," he says, before I can greet him, "I didn't mean to leave with these the other night." He holds Samuel's jeans and sweatshirt toward me.

"You didn't need to bring these back." I put the washed and folded clothes on my lap and back away from the doorframe, and he hesitates only a moment before stepping into the living room.

"I shouldn't have left the way I did Friday." It's not quite an apology, and I'm glad.

"Don't worry about it." I go to the laundry room, put Samuel's clothes on a shelf. I stare at them for a few seconds, wonder how long I'd have to stay in the laundry room before Asa would leave. I realize his clothes are still in the dryer. I take them out, hurriedly fold them, try to smooth the wrinkles. Probably why he came back.

In the living room, Asa is perched sideways on the piano bench. I put the clothes beside him, but he doesn't touch them. He nods to the old upright. "You play?"

I shake my head. "It was my mother's."

Asa turns, plays a few bars, and I recognize the beginning of "This Is My Father's World."

"It hasn't been tuned recently," I say, though it's obvious. I never learned to play, and regret missing the opportunity to sit hip to hip with my mother at that bench, to learn something so beautiful from her. Samuel plays a little. Mostly late at night, when he thinks I'm asleep, the notes coming softly, precisely. He plays simple tunes, beginner's tunes, but with a gentle cadence that turns them wistful.

"I was wondering . . ." Asa touches a single key, lets the note hang in the air. "I was wondering if you could tell me about him. Your brother. I want to . . . I'd like to understand what happened. Why it happened."

It's not exactly a surprise—Asa came back for a reason, and the clothes weren't it—but I slump a bit in my chair. "I really can't tell you that."

He lets his fingers graze a few keys without sounding them. I anticipate the music, miss it when it doesn't come. "I stood up before my congregation this morning and told them that God has a plan. That everything that happens is part of something larger, that it's all working for the good, even if we can't see how. That even in difficult times—the most difficult times—there is comfort to be found in trusting that what happens in this world is God's will." He waits until I meet his eyes. "I've never felt like I was lying to them before, Jo."

He wants me to say something. I wish I could give him words that would satisfy, comfort. But I don't know what those words are. Don't know if they exist.

"I want to believe what I told them. I want to believe there was a reason. You can't tell me what it is, okay. Then just tell me about Samuel. Catherine's parents don't even want to hear his name, can't read any of the newspaper articles that mention him. Maybe that's better. Maybe that's normal. But I sit in that hospital room beside Em and look at her lying there, hour after hour, day after day, and I can't help but want to know why she's there."

"Is it . . ." I choose my words carefully. "Is it okay if I ask how she is? Your daughter?" I close my eyes. Emily's smiling face from her school photo waiting there in the darkness. "I think about her a lot."

Asa steeples his hands, then folds them like a child in prayer. "Have they told you anything?"

I remember Devin's words: *They say it could go either way.* I shake my head.

"When the bomb exploded—" He blinks hard, like someone trying to clear a bad dream upon waking. "When the bomb exploded, the big plate-glass windows shattered inward. I was facing the congregation, and I saw them, all these pieces of glass glittering in the air. One of them cut her here." His voice catches on the last word, and he draws a hand along his throat, beneath one side of his jaw. "There was so much blood. So fast."

Already I wish I could stop listening. Wish I hadn't asked. Wish he'd turned aside my question with a brusque *Okay* or *No change.* It makes me a coward, I know. Asa doesn't get to choose not to face the full reality of what Samuel did; why should I? But every word whittles away at the brittle resolve I've been relying upon these last couple weeks, and I want nothing more than for Asa to go so I can return to packing and try to pretend things are different.

"The doctors call it a hypoxic coma," he says. "The result of hypovolemic shock, which essentially means massive blood loss. Her heart stopped. The paramedics got it going again, but she hasn't woken up. The MRI results have been . . . not good. They say she'll probably have, um, neurological disabilities. But sometimes children with bad MRIs have good outcomes; the neurologist told me that." He looks up at me. There's something pleading in his expression.

"I hope she does," I tell him. "Have a good outcome, I mean.

I really hope she does." An impossibly insufficient response. The fact that the words are truth—the rawest, fiercest kind of truth—makes them no more worthwhile.

"She's never even had a broken bone before." Asa looks around the living room as though seeing it for the first time, lets his eyes linger on the bare mantel and the packing boxes lined up beneath, the stack of flat boxes still waiting to be taped together. "Is it just because you're losing the house?" he asks. "I don't mean that it doesn't matter, but is that the reason he did it?"

"It tipped him over the edge, maybe." As honest as I can be. "But he . . . I don't think it's the only reason."

"I'm glad," Asa says. I wonder why. I can't believe that any reason or combination of reasons Samuel might have for what he did could matter to Asa when balanced against Emily's life.

I try to hold both of them in my mind at once, Emily and Samuel. I think I'm hoping that if I do, I can stop caring about Samuel. That if I can remember—always remember, really remember—what he's done, and who he did it to, then I won't love him anymore. Then I won't have to wonder if caring about Samuel means I don't care about Emily, or her father. But it doesn't work. They're both there, and so are the truths that go with them: Samuel set off the bomb that injured Emily. Emily will never be the same. I want her to recover, to be whole. What Samuel did was wrong, so wrong. I still love him. So much.

Asa notices the books still occupying the top shelves of the bookcases. "Is anyone helping you pack?"

"No."

Asa stands, starts moving books from the top shelves to the lower shelves I've already emptied. I think about asking him to stop, but maybe he needs a task to focus on. And besides, as Asa has so plainly drawn out, there is no one else. Hawkins, maybe, but after our last conversation I'm no longer sure of that.

"Samuel's my only family," I say quietly. "My father died in a mining accident when I was very young. I don't remember him." Strange to be telling someone this. Everyone in Prospect lost someone in the Gethsemane collapse, if not a family member then a friend. And everyone in Prospect knew what happened to my mother. I've almost never had to tell anyone about my parents. "My mother died when I was ten," I continue. "Samuel raised me after that."

Asa has moved almost all the books. "How old was he?"

"Seventeen."

He turns. The top shelves bare. "Young."

"It wasn't official until he was eighteen." What those six weeks in the mountains were about. Waiting for Samuel's birthday, when the state might legally let me live with him. I remember the worry. Even more than the grief for our mother, the grief for my working legs, I remember the worry. Samuel wasn't supposed to have taken me from the rehab facility; we weren't supposed to be in the mountains. *Don't think about the mountains. Don't think about hiding in the mountains.* What if people were mad at us, what if we were in trouble? What if we went back to Prospect and they sent me to foster care anyway, kept me away from Samuel forever? I echo his reassurances now, reassurances Samuel couldn't have been sure of at the time, but turned out to be true. "We wanted to stay together, and the social workers had better things to do than take a paralyzed kid away from a relative willing and able to care for her."

"So you were already . . ." Asa nods to my chair.

Most of the time, if people ask about my chair, I simply say, "An accident," which is almost entirely a lie. But even if I don't owe Asa the whole story, I owe him more than that. I can't give him the answers he most wants about Samuel, but I will give him what answers I can. "Wait here."

I go to the closet in my bedroom, push aside clothes until I find my mother's camel coat, which she once told me made her feel sophisticated. She wore it rarely, and only to what passed as special occasions in a small mining town: school plays, spaghetti dinners at the Elks Lodge, Christmas Eve services. I pull a pair of newspaper clippings from the coat's pocket. One is the obituary, which I return to the pocket, and the other is the article that ran two days after my mother's death. I cut them from the *Miner* and *Chronicle* archives at the library when I was a teenager, and felt only a little guilty for doing so.

I go back to Asa, hand him the article. He unfolds it carefully, turns it to catch the light. There is a slight tremor in his hand, and the paper flutters lightly.

I wonder whether it's really a kindness to share this with him. Whether knowing more about Samuel is truly what he wants. Whether this is for me rather than him.

I watch his face as he reads. He inhales sharply at one point, and I wonder which detail has struck him hardest. The article starts with our mother: Marian Faber, forty-one, widowed in the Gethsemane collapse. Shot nine times, deceased. Then my brother: not named, seventeen. Tried to defend his mother, shot once, treated and released from the hospital. Then me: also not named, ten. Hidden in a closet, struck by a stray bullet that passed through a wall, airlifted to Elk Fork in serious condition. Finally, the ex-boyfriend: Benjamin Archer, forty-six. History of substance abuse, restraining order, deceased. There's one lie in the article—one omission—but I don't mention it.

Asa folds the article, closes his eyes—keeps them closed too long for a blink, *Is he praying?*—then looks at me. "A couple weeks ago, I would've had something to say," he tells me. "Some phrase I would've thought was appropriately compassionate. But no one's said anything to me about Em that actually helped."

In its way, that admission is itself a sort of comfort. I reach for the clipping, but Asa holds it up in front of him. "Is *this* the reason?"

I put my hands on the handrims of my chair, push myself away. "No." I hear the defensiveness in the terseness of the syllable. I wish I'd tempered my tone, but I don't think I'm wrong. It wasn't because of the house. And it wasn't because of that night. Not just the house, not just that night. It isn't that I don't see the temptation. Either one is an excuse. Not a good excuse—I can't imagine what a "good excuse" for setting off a bomb might be—but it would be comfortable, in its way, to be able to say, *Yes, that's it, that's why.* But I don't think it's that simple. I don't think Samuel is that simple.

I would have seen something simple.

I take the clipping back, fold it into a neat square. "It's part of the reason, maybe," I amend. The best I can offer. "I told you before I can't tell you why, Asa. I can tell you about Samuel, but I can't tell you why. I don't know why."

He opens his mouth and I brace myself for another challenge, but then he presses his lips together and nods.

I feel I should give him more, especially since I can't—won't? *can't*—give him an apology. And I could line up the evidence for him, sketch the profile I'm sure Devin has crafted by now: early trauma, distrust of government for reasons X, Y, and Z, the influence of friends and acquaintances with extremist views. But none of it should have added up to the explosion at the courthouse. I still wake each morning stunned by the reality of what Samuel has done. If he walked through the door this minute, the first thing I'd demand to know would be, *Why?* Probably wouldn't matter what answer he gave me. It wouldn't satisfy. And if Asa wants to play the same game, if he, too, wants to try to rearrange the pieces until they make sense, so be it—I understand the impulse—but he'll either end up as bewildered as I am, or he'll settle on an answer that's a partial truth at best.

Asa sighs, leans forward on the couch so his knees rest on his elbows, hands folded before him, index fingers steepled. He can't be much more than thirty, but gestures like this make him seem older. "Do you—" Asa hesitates. "Do you have a picture of him? Samuel?"

"You must have seen the ones in the papers," I say. "Or on TV."

"I want to see the one you'd choose to show me."

I find the ten-by-ten canvas behind a stack of larger paintings in my room. I asked Samuel to sit for a portrait for years before he acquiesced a couple summers ago, and I painted it hurriedly, afraid he might grow impatient at any moment. No brushes, just knives. The result is almost impressionistic, with sharper streaks of color along Samuel's jawline, cheekbones, the bridge of his nose. His eyes carry the most detail. Gray, with shaded hints of azurite and cobalt. Pupils the starkest black. I told him he didn't have to look at me while I painted, but he did, and I managed to capture the fullness of his expression: the hawkish intelligence, yes, the defensive arrogance that goes along with it. But also the wariness he tries to hide, the weariness he never entirely manages to shake. The gentleness that has become harder and harder for me to find, but is always there if I look long and hard enough.

In the living room, I hand the canvas to Asa. He holds it carefully by the edges. I didn't sign it, but he asks, "You painted this?" and I tell him I did. He studies the painting for what seems like four or five minutes. I wait to hear his verdict. To learn whether seeing Samuel through my perspective makes any difference, whether Asa finds the same things in the painted eyes I do.

The longer Asa looks at the painting, the more uneasy I feel. I start to wonder whether it's possible I did the same thing with this portrait that I do with most of my paintings: softened hard edges, tempered features, cast the subject in the best possible light. Did I paint what was there? Did I see what others didn't because I was willing to look more generously, more patiently? Or did I paint not what was, but what I wished was?

I worry Asa will sense my turmoil, but he just looks at the canvas silently and, when he's finished, hands it back without comment. "I should get back to Elk Fork," he says, and stands. "When do you have to be out of the house?"

"End of the month."

"I could help you pack," he says, glancing toward the stairs. "I'd like to."

My first instinct is to decline. Asa seems like a good person, sure, maybe a little stiff the way preachers can be. He helped with the tree when it would have been easier in so many ways for him to refuse. But when he's in the room, I feel myself edging closer to panic or breakdown with each passing second. I'm not entirely surprised by his offer, because he's still looking for answers, still thinks he'll find them in this house, in me. But I can't fix what has gone wrong, and whatever Asa might think, anything I can tell him about Samuel isn't going to fix it, either. I don't particularly want to be there when Asa realizes that.

Yet I can't pretend I don't want answers, too. I don't think we'll find them here. I don't think we'll find them until someone finds Samuel, and I'm not ready to face the question of whether I might be the one who can find Samuel. But it's excruciatingly clear I don't know my brother as well as I thought. Maybe Asa will see something I can't. Maybe if I help Asa understand Samuel, I will understand him, too.

"I'd appreciate the help," I say. "If you really don't mind."

"It'll give me something to do," he says. "And it would be nice to think that something positive can come of all this." He seems to realize how feeble it sounds, adds, "However minor."

He's trying so hard to reshape the circumstances, force them into some kind of sense. He smiles, and even that is tentative, wavering. I think again of Samuel telling me it's not okay to pretend things are different than they are. But right now I really want to pretend that Asa and I can be friendly toward one another, that it isn't impossible to care for Emily and her father and also for my brother. So I do my best to match Asa's smile, unsteady though it is.

———

I've used up all the other states. North Dakota, South Dakota, Wyoming, Idaho. Covered all of them—at least the portions on this map—with my handwriting, which I've made smaller but not small enough. There's room on the other side, but the ink bleeds through, and the index is there, so anything written there would be words on top of words on top of words. Now I'm venturing into Montana. I started this letter at the eastern border, just below the blue vein of the Missouri, and I'm winding my words along its banks.

I hope you're okay. I worry about you. Not because I think you're helpless or can't take care of yourself. I know you can; you've proven it time and again. But because there are things you relied on me to do, and now I can't do them. Because the goddamned house has stairs and I never managed to build that elevator we used to joke about. Because you're my little sister and I want you to be okay.

Is Hawkins helping you? He likes you, so he must be, though maybe his being sheriff has made it difficult for you both. Because of what I did. He's probably not even shocked. He's never looked at me the same since that night with Mom. And everything since then, every decision I made he didn't agree with, it's like none of it surprised him. Like he almost expected it of me. You've never disappointed him, though.

I know the bomb made him think of Kev. I thought about him, too, when I made the decision to do it. The bomb I built probably isn't much different than the one that blew him apart. I worry it's where I got the idea. Do you think if Hawkins knew I'd thought about Kev, it would make him feel any better, or would it just make him feel worse?

Has he asked you where I am? I never told you this, but I think he might have seen me once when I went back to the house that summer. I tried to be careful, but the second time I went, there was a bag by the back door with food—granola bars, dried fruit, that kind of thing—and some lantern batteries and a blanket. I didn't touch it, didn't bring it back here. But he's never believed we went to South Dakota. If he's asked you, what have you told him? Have I made you disappoint him?

I hope you're okay, Jo, truly I do, but if I'm absolutely honest, I have to admit there's a tiny part of me that hopes you're not. I read over what I've just written, about Hawkins and Kev and the bomb, and I think you'd be horrified. Since I've been back up here, I sometimes get these split-second flashes of how others must see me. Split-seconds in which I wonder if I'm wrong, if what people think and say about me is true, if I've become someone I'd never have recognized as a younger man. They don't last long, but they're terrifying. Sometimes I'm not sure what happened. How I got here. I'm not sure of things I thought I was sure of.

What I am sure of: The Samuel Faber who cared for his little sister was a good man. You needed me, and I was there for you, on that first night and ever after. You are a good person—I have no doubts about that, Jo, split-second or otherwise—and I had something to do with making you into that good person.

As long as you need me, Jo, there is something in me that is worth-

while. Worthy. As long as you need me, there is a part of myself I don't have to doubt. So I hope you are okay, because I am your brother and I care for you. But I hope you will forgive me for also hoping you are not okay, because if you are—if you truly don't need me anymore—does that worthwhile part of me still exist?

Look at that. I've buried the eastern plains in words.

———

Monday I go to work and sell two made-in-China *Montana* mugs to a Canadian tourist on her way home from Yellowstone. There's just one other customer while I'm working, and I spend most of my shift restocking the candy shelves, ripping the display tops off new boxes, consolidating the leftover M&M's and Reese's from the old.

Afterward I go to the library, where I delete two emails from journalists and am surprised to find a third from the Elk Fork plein air festival inviting Josephine Grady to participate. I hesitate only a moment before replying with a brief acceptance, then print the message, wondering if Jo Faber would have received such a swift and enthusiastic response.

My last stop is the Gas-N-Go. I doubt Prospect will be able to sustain two gas stations much longer, and my money is on the one that sells groceries rather than moose-shaped slippers. I shouldn't hasten Fuel Stop's demise by shopping here—and usually I don't—but Split Creek is a twenty-minute drive each way, and I want to ride Lockjaw before dark.

Devin is on the porch when I get home. I roll the window down. "Have you found Samuel?" I call. "Did something happen?"

He shakes his head. He's sitting on the porch steps, hands clasped, elbows on his knees. No coat today, and no tie. I immediately wonder whether, like a presidential candidate dressing down at a swing state barbecue, this is supposed to make him more approachable, more relatable. Maybe he's just hot.

Devin stays seated while I reassemble my chair, transfer into it, sling one canvas bag over the back of the chair, and settle the other in my lap. He stands only when I head for the ramp. "Grocery shopping?" It seems a clumsy effort, and I think an FBI agent should be able to fish for information with more finesse.

I tap the *Hi, I'm: JO* name tag on my shirt. "Work," I say. Hold up the printout of the festival email. "Library." Nudge the bag in my lap. "Groceries." I go into the house, leave the door open behind me. "I thought you were supposed to know all this already."

"Maybe I did," he says, and if there were any lightness to the words, I could accept them as an invitation to abandon the adversarial positions we've taken up. But even if he were to grant me that opportunity, he'd expect too much in return. "I'm sure you'd have mentioned it to Sheriff Hawkins," Devin continues, not sounding sure at all, "but your brother hasn't tried to contact you, has he?"

Good of him to phrase it that way. *Your brother . . . contact you.* Not the other way around. "No," I say. "He's too careful for that."

Devin nods. That much he believes. I wonder if he has any opinions about Samuel. Not professional opinions, not a profile, but thoughts about what kind of person Samuel is, apart from the bombing. It would be natural to speculate, wouldn't it? Maybe not for someone like Devin. Maybe he's just a human bloodhound, interested in whatever will help him track down my brother and nothing more. I put away the perishable items, leave the rest on the counter. I go back to the living room, take up my usual place by the hearth, wait for Devin to settle onto the couch. Its springs are shot, but he does his best to sit up straight. "You've been spending some time with Asa Truth."

"He's been here a couple times." No sense pretending otherwise with that black car at the end of the drive.

"I'm not sure that's a great idea."

"Is that the official FBI position?"

He gives me the kind of look a parent might give a back-talking teenager.

"I went to the prayer service," I say. "He gave me his card. A tree fell during the storm last week and trapped me on the other side of the creek. I called Asa and he cut it up for me. Came back a couple days later to return some things he'd borrowed."

"You could have called me about the tree."

"Yes," I agree. "I could have."

Devin sighs. "Okay," he says. "Do what you want. I just don't think it's a very good idea. Not with his daughter still—"

"I get it," I say. "Advice accepted. Your duty is done."

He presses his lips together, and I think he might get angry, but the moment passes and he relaxes. I glance down at those immaculate boots of his. I'm starting to despise them. Samuel would. They seem like proof the folks who comprise the government don't really understand life in this remote, rural place, that they see it only as a land for playacting.

Devin lets the silence grow until it's uncomfortable, then asks, "Still no thoughts about where your brother might be?"

The question I've been anticipating. Dreading. "Canada?" I venture.

"We're certainly looking into that possibility," Devin says. "Did Samuel mention anything about Canada recently?"

I shake my head.

Devin takes a small notebook and a pen out of his shirt pocket, makes a brief note. The pen is a cheap ballpoint, the kind that come a dozen to a package, and I wonder if he tends to mislay them. "No other ideas?"

I wish I knew if Hawkins told him about our conversation at the Knock-Off. Ordinarily I think he'd keep quiet, try to protect me, but if he got it into his head that it was his duty . . . And what is *my* duty? To tell the FBI . . . what, exactly? A passing thought? A possibility? That my brother and I went somewhere together once, a long time ago? "No," I hear myself say. "No other ideas."

Devin looks at me for a long moment. "I worry you're not telling me everything you could." He says it gently, like he wouldn't blame me if I weren't. Even without a lifetime under Samuel's suspicious tutelage, I'd know not to believe that.

But there's a temptation to it: *Tell him.* I counter the thought immediately: *There's nothing to tell.* Nothing I know, anyway, nothing for sure. Hawkins asking one leading question at the Knock-Off doesn't mean anything.

There's Asa, though. There's Emily. There's what my brother did.

If I tell Devin, it will be his burden. I'll be right about the mountains or I'll be wrong, but I won't have to think about it anymore.

He is my brother, though, and Devin is FBI. My brother has a rifle, and the FBI has more.

I stay silent.

I expect Devin to leave when I don't say anything else, but he doesn't rise from the couch, watches me intently. "Your brother loves you very much," he finally says. Fact, not reassurance. There's something hard about the statement, despite the benign words. Something different from what I've heard in Devin's voice before. "I've had a chance to read all those files. He sacrificed a lot to care for you after your mother was killed."

"Yes, he did," I say carefully. Devin hardly seems to hear.

"In fact, I'm a little surprised he detonated that bomb. Not because he doesn't fit the profile in most ways; he does: smart, angry with his lot in life, quick to lay blame on others. But I'm surprised because of you. Well, you told me, didn't you? He'd do anything for you."

"And?" My voice faint even to my own ears.

Devin meets my eyes. "And I find myself wondering what he'd do if we charged his little sister with obstruction of justice."

It's a relief, in a way. Validation. I don't trust Devin, or the FBI, and that doesn't make me wrong or deluded or hostile; it makes me right.

I am suddenly less afraid of Devin, despite the threat, because I'm certain he wouldn't have made it if he had any idea how close I came to telling him where my brother might be. He can't read me as well as he thinks. His files and training and profiles only go so far; he doesn't know Samuel, and he doesn't know me.

He watches me a few seconds more, then claps his hands together, says, "Well, I'm sure it won't come to that," and leans back on the couch, a smile across his face as though it's all been a joke.

I roll my chair backward a few inches before I can stop myself. Fold my hands, set them in my lap. "Is there anything else?"

Devin holds the smile a moment longer before he lets it fade. "Just one more thing." He takes the notebook out again, flips through a few pages. I watch his eyes; they don't move back and forth as they would if he were reading. "I said I've been looking over the files. About your brother. About his past, *your* past. And—this isn't totally unusual, of course, different sources being compiled, that sort of thing—but something doesn't quite make sense to me."

I take a breath. Did Hawkins talk to him after all?

"I see a lot of reasons for your brother to have turned to extremism, Jo. A lot of reasons for him to hate the government. The restraining order that didn't protect your mother. The threat of social services splitting the two of you up. Even the mining accident that killed your father—the investigation found that the government inspection a month prior should have flagged the risk of collapse, didn't it?"

I nod, once.

"And now the house, of course."

He's not telling me anything I don't know. I've lived in this house with Samuel all my life. I've watched him try out every crackpot antigovernment conspiracy theory to come along, and I've spent more hours than Devin ever will trying to figure out why all of it appealed to my brother, who should have been too smart for that kind of thing. "So what doesn't make sense?" I ask. "Makes pretty damn good sense to me, you lay it all out like that." I try to shake the anger I'm feeling. He wants me angry, or frightened.

"Well, you experienced all those things, too. And yet here you are, a bit jaded, maybe, but as far as I can tell, a law-abiding citizen. So what sets Samuel apart?"

"Aren't men more likely to do these things?"

Devin tilts his head slightly but doesn't answer. I should leave it at that, and don't.

"He's older," I say. "Had more responsibility."

Devin shakes his head. "On the other hand, when your mother died you were still a child. What could be more traumatic than losing a parent in that manner, at that age? And being injured the way you were on top of it."

I don't know what game he's playing now, but I'm tired of it, and I sure as hell don't need to listen to someone recite a litany of my life's tragedies. "How many paraplegic terrorists have you apprehended, Agent Devin?"

He doesn't blink. "My point," he tells me coolly, "is that you arguably experienced even more trauma than your brother. You are, at the very least, on equal footing. But you are not a suspected terrorist, and your brother is, and I'm wondering why. Now, you're right: you don't fit the profile the way he does. But I've been doing this a long time, Jo; I know when I'm missing something. And there's something I'm missing now. Something missing in the pages of those files." He looks at me, and I work very hard to keep my expression neutral. Because he's not talking about where Samuel is anymore. I take a breath, hold it, let it out. Hope I'm doing so convincingly, because I can't seem to remember how long a person normally takes to breathe a single lungful of air. "I wonder what it is."

The words land lightly, but as statement rather than question.

Devin stands abruptly, tugs on the cuffs of his sleeves. "It was good to check in with you, Jo." He strides briskly to the door. "Keep talking with Sheriff Hawkins, and call if you think of anything."

I don't move for a long time after he has gone. When I finally do, I go to the window to see the final dying sliver of sun sink below the ridgeline. Too late to ride.

———

I dream about it that night. First time in ages, familiar as yesterday.

After the headlights, after the closet door shut, everything was dark. Deep dark, black dark. Closet dark, mine dark, night dark. All dark. Dark until it was red.

No sight, only sound. Those sounds, those echoes.

I wake suddenly, scramble for the lamp on the bedside table. Feel the panic recede only when light floods the bedroom, when silence settles.

I remember this time. Don't call for Samuel. Know he isn't there.

———

I have the next day off, so Lockjaw and I go into the mountains and ride the trails on the far side of Gethsemane Mine. The cabin is the other direction, closer to Eden, and I pretend I haven't thought about that. The slopes are steep, but Lockjaw knows the trails well and has inherited the surefootedness of her donkey sire, so I give her a loose rein and let her choose her path. The trails meander along the contours of the slopes through coniferous forest, and trees rise tall on either side of the narrow path. When I look out over the eastern valley, I see it a slice at a time, each view punctuated by tall trunks, a timbered zoetrope glimpse of the landscape.

I love the gradations of color in these forests. When autumn comes, the larch will stand out bright as flames amid the evergreens, but I like the less spectacular view before me best. So many variations of green, so many subtle turns to a single color. I name them in my mind: cobalt turquoise, phthalo green, viridian green, chromium oxide green, sap green, green gold.

I stay on the trails longer than I should, and had Samuel been at the house, he'd have given me hell about it when I got back. I've attached a gel seat saver to my saddle, but I still have to be cautious of pressure sores, and long hours on a mule's back aren't the wisest idea. Even so, when I get back to the barn I remove Lockjaw's bridle and loosen her cinch, but leave her saddled and tied in her stall with a bulging hay net. I'll ride again after lunch.

In the house, I make a peanut butter and jelly sandwich, then go to the table with pen and paper. I look at the blank sheet for a long time. Twice I set the tip of the pen to paper, twice take it away without making a mark. I sigh, reposition the pen in my hand. *Molly mule for sale*, I write.

There's a note on Lockjaw's stall door when I finish the second half of my ride. *Supper at my place tonight. Come when you're ready. —H.*

Hawkins lives in the center of town, in one of the houses claustrophobically built up onto the lower reaches of the western slopes, the second-story window of one nearly level with the bottom porch step of the house above it. Hawkins's place is halfway up, a narrow steep-roofed structure fronted by crabgrass and dandelions. Good view of the mountains, though. I park near the detached one-car garage, as close as I can get to the ramp at the rear of the house. It's a rickety thing, warped planks of plywood rising a bit too steeply toward the house, one corner or another always coming un-nailed, but I appreciate it nonetheless.

"I wasn't sure you'd come," Hawkins says when he opens the door.

"I should've called." And that's it. We say no more about our last meeting at the Knock-Off or the days that have passed since.

Supper is microwaved frozen dinners. I'm not sure Hawkins has cooked a single meal since his wife moved out seven years ago. He has Salisbury steak and I have turkey and stuffing; Hawkins doesn't care for turkey, so he bought it especially for me. We eat in his living room, on opposite ends of the couch, our meals balanced on trays on our laps. Afterward we watch a cop show on TV. It has a downer ending, where justice isn't served and all the characters are angry but resigned about it.

"I did half the crap they do on this show, I wouldn't be sher-iff long."

I shrug. "You might be okay. No one else wants the job."

An old joke. Hawkins uncontested in the last three elections. I expect him to reward me with a brief smile, but he doesn't. "Want a soda? I got Dr Pepper or Coke."

"Coke's good."

He takes the trays into the kitchen, and I mute the televi-sion. I glance around the living room. I haven't been here in a few months, but I know the house well. I spent a handful of Thanksgivings here, a couple Christmas Eves, dozens of mun-dane evenings like this one. It's messier than usual, with junk mail piled on the coffee table, old copies of the *Miner* strewn be-side the couch, and dust bunnies gathering in the corners; Lila's influence is waning as Hawkins's bachelorhood becomes more entrenched. But most things haven't changed: the faded shag carpet, the wood paneling on the walls, the exposed beams of the ceiling. The paintings on the wall, one of which is mine and the rest of which look like they've been liberated from a roadside motel. The objects on the mantel: the framed photograph of Kev in uniform, the Purple Heart, the folded flag.

When I was younger, part of me was glad Samuel hadn't been able to join up with Kev. It seemed like just one more way to lose someone. After Kev's death, I never thought much about it again other than to try to push aside a sort of guilty relief. Impossi-ble not to wonder anew now, though. Instead of the thoughts I used to have—*What if he'd gone? What if Kev had come back and he hadn't?*—I have new ones: *What if he'd gone. What if he'd come back. What if it had given him something better to believe in.*

I close my eyes, rub the bridge of my nose. There's been a headache settled there for days, low but building. "You got an aspirin?" I call.

"Medicine cabinet," Hawkins replies from the kitchen. "Might be a little past the expiration."

In the small bathroom I reach to open the mirrored door. I find aspirin, yes, and also a small cluster of amber prescription bottles. Three are for serious painkillers, the kind they sent me to rehab with from the hospital; the label is torn from the fourth, just the glue and a few ragged shreds of paper left behind, but they look like more of the same. The bottles with labels are all prescribed to Hawkins: one from a doctor in Split Creek, one from a clinic in Idaho, the third from Spokane. Two are empty; the others are close.

He's not hiding them. The first thing I think. Wouldn't be hard to hide them from me; putting the bottles on the top shelf would do it. Not my business. But the sight of them makes me uneasy—there's something almost disappointing in it: *Opioids?*—and I close the cabinet without taking an aspirin.

Hawkins is waiting on the couch when I return to the living room; I pull up alongside but stay in my chair. He hands me a cold can, the top already popped. "I saw you had a tree down."

I wonder if I should say anything about the pills. "That storm last week."

"Sorry I didn't answer when you called. I tried you back and left a couple messages."

"I got it taken care of."

"I saw."

He probably saw before today. He'd have driven out when I didn't call him back, but ordinarily he would've let me know. If I hadn't lied to him about South Dakota again. I consider changing the subject now—I think Hawkins would let me—but I say, "Asa Truth cut it up for me. The pastor from that church?"

He didn't know—I can tell from the way he takes an extra-long pull on his can—but all he says is, "Good of him to do that."

"Yeah." I look away. Find the flag on the mantel, look away from that, too. "I think he wants there to be a reason for what happened."

"He finds one, you let me know."

Hawkins and Samuel must run into each other in town once in a while, and I assume they at least exchange pleasantries, though they're both the sort of men to reduce those pleasantries to terse nods. I can't remember the last time Samuel mentioned Hawkins. When I do he mostly listens silently. Wasn't always like that. My brother spent plenty of time here as a kid, with Kev, and he came for a while after that night at the house, bunking in his friend's room. Practically family. *Practically*, Samuel would have said, *but not*.

"How come you and Samuel fell out?"

Hawkins takes another swig of his soda. "I don't know I'd say we did." I think he's going to leave it at that—it would be typical of him; he often still treats me like a kid who might forget about an awkward question if it's just ignored long enough—but I look at him, and he sighs, sets the can down. "Wasn't any one thing, Jo. I don't mind saying I did get tired of hearing him talk about how the—what was it he was always saying, the 'Zionist Organized Government'?"

"Occupied," I correct wearily.

"Right. How the 'Zionist Occupied Government' staged 9/11 so we'd back the wars. That it was all about money. You know he once told me Kev wasn't a patriot? My boy not even in the ground a year. Said it in front of Lila, too."

I close my eyes, wish I'd taken the aspirin after all.

"Kev wasn't a patriot, but a pawn, Samuel said. Duped. I still remember the exact words he used. 'Conned into trading his life for a few pennies in a Jew's pocket.'"

That was a bad year. Kev gone. Money at its tightest.

Samuel wholeheartedly embracing the ugliest of the ideologies he'd adopt. "I never said anything to him about that tattoo," I say. "That swastika. I should have. I wanted to." I pull at a loose thread on the side of my jeans. What I'd always wanted to say was, *What would Mom think?* But it would have made me cry, and I never did.

"You were still a kid. What, thirteen, fourteen?"

Fifteen. But I never said anything about the tattoo later, either. Samuel came to regret it quickly enough, or seemed to, and once he started covering it with long sleeves I hadn't seen any point in bringing it up. I even convinced myself he kept it as a kind of penance, a reminder not to fall back into that kind of thinking.

"Well," I say quietly, "I can't blame you for not wanting to talk to him after that." I look again at Hawkins's thinner frame, at the junk in the living room. I feel a habitual impulse to justify them, to numerate the reasons they might not be connected to the pills in the bathroom. Should I resist the impulse, say something to Hawkins? Or am I overreacting because I failed with Samuel?

"You know I'm the one introduced him to the militia?"

I stare at Hawkins. I've always assumed it was someone Samuel worked with, maybe one of his old schoolmates.

"He was eighteen, nineteen," he says. "I could see he was having a hard time with what happened that night your momma died. I didn't take him to their meetings or nothing," he adds quickly. "Just bought him lunch with a couple guys I know. I thought it'd do Samuel good to spend some time with men who took kind of a no-nonsense approach to things. Who'd help him see himself as having done right." He drums his fingers against the can in his hand. "They were just old mining buddies. One of 'em was friends with your dad. I never thought . . ."

My first instinct is to ask what kind of sheriff introduces a troubled teenager to the local militiamen. But I know as well as Hawkins that the 'local militiamen' comprise a solid chunk of the town; they get together and play war games in the woods the way other men golf or watch football. I can almost see what he meant by it. And it's not as though Samuel wouldn't have found his way to them on his own; that side of Prospect's never been hidden. He never even joined; they were one of the first groups he sampled only to find fault with: *The Second Amendment's the only one they've ever heard of.* But when I look back at Samuel at eighteen or nineteen, when I try to understand now what he kept from me then, I see a young man who no longer knew what to believe. Who tried clinging to the things that had once made sense to him, like family and church, only to find them damaged or diminished. Who angrily rejected the patriotism that might have become his life, had things gone a bit differently. Who tried on one thing after another, looking for the one that would make him feel strong, whole. And that young man is not someone I would introduce to the militia.

Hawkins seems to know my thoughts. "It was a mistake, Jo. Don't you think I know it was a mistake?"

"You're not responsible for Samuel," I say. I try to mean it, and sort of do. "You always did what you could for him."

Hawkins laughs, and it's an utterly humorless sound. "I said that to him once, or something like it." He moves to rub a palm over his absent mustache, catches himself in the middle of the gesture; his hand falters and settles uneasily on the arm of the couch. "I didn't stop talking to him after he said what he said about Kev. I never did give up on him. Know that much. Whatever mistakes I made—and God knows I made plenty—I had the best of intentions."

The road to hell, I think, before I can stop myself.

"I talked to him a lot, Jo. Whenever he'd let me. I could see he never stopped hurting. I could see he was in trouble. But he got less and less interested in listening to me, and eventually I practically had to beg him to hear me out. One time I said, Samuel, please, you know I care about you. You know I've always been there for you." Hawkins meets my eyes. "And your brother looks right at me and says, Not always."

That night. The emergency call. The long minutes before Hawkins's arrival.

"You got there quick as you could." The words sound rote, and I know it's because I've said them to myself so many times. Because knowing something and believing it aren't the same.

"Not quick enough."

"It's not right for Samuel to blame you for that."

"He might as well; I blame myself plenty." Hawkins looks at me, something hollow in his gaze. I wonder if he plays his own version of the game I've played too many times myself. *What if.* What if Archer hadn't managed to kick the door in. If Samuel'd had time to open the gun safe. If Hawkins had been closer. "He never would talk to me much after that. I kept trying for a while, but . . . I'm sorry to say I let him go."

I want to tell Hawkins to snap out of it, reject this weight of responsibility. Samuel is responsible for himself. We all are. Whatever Hawkins should have done, or shouldn't have—whatever I should have done, or shouldn't have—we didn't force Samuel into anything. We didn't force him to build that bomb. To detonate it. I want to tell Hawkins he better not dare let his guilt pull him down, because if he does, what chance do I have?

Hawkins shakes his head now. "I should have done more to stop this."

"You couldn't imagine he'd do what he did." The reassurance is for me as much as him, and the words come out tentatively, like a lie I haven't fully committed to.

"I knew he was capable of it."

"That's not fair." He's thinking of that night at the house again. But anyone would've done what Samuel did that night. Anyone who loved his family. Who loved me.

Hawkins looks at me. Shrugs. He wants me to leave it.

You weren't there. What I want to say. *Don't judge my brother. What he did. What he's become. Because you weren't there.* But that would be an echo of Hawkins's last conversation with Samuel, and he's shown me how deep that echo would cut. I stop myself where Samuel didn't. I hold back the words he let loose.

"Come on," I say instead. "Samuel isn't such an outlier, and you know it. How do you think some of the other men in this town would've reacted if it'd been their house was gonna be razed for a highway?"

"Don't think they would've bombed a building."

"Oh, really?" He looks away. "You think there aren't some folks supporting him behind closed doors? There's no great love for the government in this valley. If that little girl hadn't gotten hurt, Samuel would probably be a folk hero."

Hawkins sits silent for a moment. Doesn't look at me when he finally speaks. "But she did," he says quietly. "Get hurt."

I close my eyes. It only makes the image of Emily's school photo crystallize into sharper detail.

"Do you know where he is, Jo?" His voice still soft. Gentle. The voice he used that night in the house, the voice he uses with victims, probably the voice he uses with people who have done something wrong and regret it enough they might confess.

"No."

"Do you *think* you know where he is?"

I say nothing.

He sighs. Lifts his hand as though to put it on mine, lets

it hover a couple inches off the couch, settles it back onto the cushion. "Don't make you a bad person if you tell me."

I look at my own hands, run the tip of one finger up and down my thigh. So strange, still, to feel only half that motion. "Does it make me a bad person if I don't?"

I wait a long time, but he doesn't answer.

———

The cabin seems smaller without you. Isn't that strange? You'd think it would seem bigger. Your cot isn't here, and neither is your wheelchair, your duffel bag with your clothes, your cath supplies, Black Beauty, *the hurricane lantern I brought so you wouldn't have to face the dark. And of course you aren't here, and I'm not kidding myself, Jo; I know that's the real reason the cabin seems smaller. I'm lonely.*

Boo-hoo, right? Poor terrorist Samuel (that must be what they're calling me; they impose the label on any citizen who stands up to their tyranny), all alone in the woods. But you were the reason we were here last time. It was all about staying together. It was about keeping you safe. We just had to wait long enough. Remember how we counted the days? You made little hash marks on the wall with my pocketknife like prisoners in old movies. I looked for them a few days ago but didn't find them.

So there are no stories this time, no games of gin rummy or go fish or war, no three-course camp meals. There's only me, the rifle, a sleeping bag, a flashlight, a water bottle, this map, a little food. I found the huckleberry patch right where it was years ago, but they're not ripe yet. Once I hiked over the ridge and shot a deer. Stupid. I shouldn't have gone so far, shouldn't have made so much noise, and in the end I had to leave most of it. I just wanted to get out of this cabin, because it's only me and the floor and the walls and a papered-over window, and it's so damned small. I'm waiting again, but for what? I could scratch the days in the wall, but what would I be counting toward?

I shouldn't complain. A prison cell would be smaller. A grave smaller still.

———

Wednesday I find Samuel's birthday present while I'm packing. He won't turn thirty until August, but I've already bought him a gift: a new multi-tool with a black leather case. After work I drive to Elk Fork and return it. Don't have the receipt, so they give me a gift card for the equivalent of a sale price ten dollars less than I paid. I hand it to an elderly man who is coming into the store as I leave.

Before leaving Elk Fork, I stop at two apartment complexes. Both tell me all the accessible units are occupied. Would I like to add my name to the waiting lists? No.

Back at the house, I haul my easel and supplies and the mud paints outside. The muds have evaporated into small cakes, like pan watercolors, and I've experimented with them enough to know they paint like watercolors, too. At first I was afraid the monochromatic palette would be limiting, but I'm enticed by the necessary emphasis of value when working in just one or two colors, by the power it gives light over shadow. I've decided to do a new painting of the house, intended to start it today. I sit and look at my easel for a long time, at the blank sheet of stretched paper taped to the board. I sit until dark, and for a little while after.

———

Asa comes to help me pack on Friday morning. I don't ask about Emily. I know I should, but I think he'd tell me if something was wrong, and every time I mean to ask, the moment passes before I can say her name. For his part, Asa seems content to make small talk as he removes things from cabinets or tapes boxes. Maybe it's as much a relief to him as it is to me to pretend he's just helping an acquaintance move. We finish the downstairs first, though there isn't much left. After we pack the last couple boxes in the kitchen, Asa labels them with neat, blocky letters and stacks them in the living room with the rest. "What else?"

I glance upward, just for a second. "You've done plenty."

Asa walks to the hallway, nods toward the second floor. "You need help packing upstairs."

"I can get Hawkins—the sheriff—to help me sometime."

"We can get it done now. Just tell me what to do."

Maybe he wants to see Samuel's room. Asa hasn't asked about him today, but he must still be searching for answers. I doubt he'll find them in Samuel's bedroom—especially not after the FBI carted most of its contents away—but I feel I owe him the chance to look. "You'll have to help me up the stairs." I let the words out slowly, give him time to object. "Carry me, I mean."

It's different than when Samuel carries me. My brother picks me up easily, as though only the parts of my body I can feel have weight. His hold is always confident, almost casual, his arm pressing against my upper back just firmly enough for reassurance. Asa is less certain, one moment cradling me like I'm made of china, the next squeezing as though he's in real danger of dropping me. It's not a particularly comfortable experience, and I hold my breath until we've reached the landing.

"Just set me on the floor there," I say, and when he has: "And bring me my chair, please." He carries it upstairs and sets it beside me, then goes back down to the living room for boxes and tape. I transfer to my chair while he's gone, and when he comes back he looks at me as though I've performed a magic trick.

The second floor is cramped, just a short hallway with a small bedroom on either end, a tiny closet of a bathroom opposite the stairs. "Been a while since I've been up here," I say. The nightmares don't come often anymore—or didn't until the bombing—but when they do, I have two choices: I can lie awake the rest of the night in the downstairs room, or I can call for Samuel and ask him to take me upstairs to my childhood bedroom, where I'll be asleep in minutes. Most of the time I choose to lie awake, but once or twice a year I come up here.

I haven't been in Samuel's room since we were children, though—he sometimes let me sit on the floor and draw pictures while he did his homework, if I promised to be quiet—and since I caught that glimpse of the Nazi flag in high school, he's kept the door shut whenever I'm upstairs. It's closed now. I nod to it, feeling a small surge of curiosity myself. "Let's start there."

The room is even sparser than I expected. The FBI took box after box out of the house, and Samuel isn't sentimental about material objects—our father's watch notwithstanding—but I'm still surprised by how remarkably little there is to pack. The first object I see is one of my paintings (an autumn-gold meadow, a stand of aspens, a bugling elk); it's the only thing on the wall. The closet door stands open, and most of Samuel's clothes are gone, presumably to be tested for residue of whatever he used to make his bomb. The bookshelves are almost empty; I'd expected them to take whatever extremist titles he might have had, but they've taken the homesteading references, too, the hunting books, even his collection of secondhand veterinary textbooks. Samuel's desk is nearly bare, nothing left but a sticky note reminder to call the farrier. The drawers of his filing cabinet are ajar; in them I find only my own report cards from middle and high school.

"I guess there's not much left to do here," I say. "I'll pack the papers and books. Maybe you could put what's left of the clothes in a bag? I'll drop them at the thrift store next time I go to Split Creek."

"You don't want to keep any?"

"Samuel won't need them again." Not if he goes to prison. Not if he . . . doesn't.

We work in silence. I glance at Asa a couple times, but his expression is neutral. I wonder if he finds anything significant in the off-brand parka; the swim trunks that, to my knowledge, Samuel has never worn; the Prospect High baseball cap, its brim discolored by a season's worth of decades-old sweat. Asa joins me at the bookcase when he's done with the closet—do the few books there tell him anything? A thesaurus with the cover bent in half, an encyclopedia of baseball statistics, *The Call of the Wild*.

I glance at that last one. I remember the story. Remember where I heard it the first time. I didn't tell Devin or Hawkins about the mountains, but I could tell Asa. He's a pastor; he must have heard confessions before. But I don't know Samuel's at the cabin. Why would he go to a place I know? It doesn't make sense. It would be stupid, and Samuel is a lot of things, but he isn't stupid. I try to find the words I would use to tell Asa, to explain that Samuel might be in the mountains but probably isn't, that we went there once but I don't know why he'd go back now, and then Asa is putting the book into a box and closing the flaps and I still haven't said anything, and I don't say anything.

I expected Samuel's room to be the challenging one for Asa—as much as he might claim to want to understand Samuel, it couldn't be easy to handle the belongings of the man who built and detonated the bomb that injured his daughter—but the moment I open the door to my old room, I realize it will be far more difficult. Still the room of a little girl.

Lavender bedspread, white lace curtains, a purple-and-blue

rag rug on the floor. Shelves filled with *Archie* comics and issues of *Western Horseman*, a nearly complete set of the *Black Stallion* books, a crowded row of plastic model horses. Above the bed hangs a dream catcher I made at day camp when I was eight, over the dresser a string of horse-show ribbons from the Prospect County Fair and the Silver Rodeo Fun Days. On the nightstand a three-part picture frame, my father on one side, Lockjaw on the other, me and Samuel and our mother in the middle.

Asa stands in the doorway behind me. "You don't have to do this," I say. "Hawkins will help me."

He looks at me, offers a tight smile. "No, we're on a roll."

I keep the *Western Horseman*s but not the *Archie*s, *The Black Stallion* but none of its sequels. The dream catcher goes into the trash, the ribbons into a baggie because I still think I might use them for a craft project someday. Asa takes the last blue ribbon off the wall, looks at it for a long time. I squint to read the gold lettering on the satin: *Prospect County Fair, Junior Western Equitation.*

"These are from before you were hurt?"

"Yes." I can see the roof of the barn out the window, but am sitting too low to see the pasture. The sky seems broader now that the tree is gone. "I didn't really ride for a couple years afterward, except double with Samuel."

"But you do now?"

"Samuel trained Lockjaw to accept a paralyzed rider. And I learned a few new ways of doing things."

"It's amazing you still ride."

It isn't. I hear that kind of thing a lot, though. Anything I do that other people don't expect me to be able to is *amazing* or *remarkable* or, worst of all, *inspiring.* "I missed it."

"Em is in that horsey stage right now," Asa says. "Keeps begging for riding lessons. I was—I decided to wait until she was a little older."

I take the ribbon from him, fold it and tuck it into the baggie with the rest. I wish I could say something comforting, or even offer to have Asa bring Emily to meet Lockjaw if—*when*—she recovers. But I won't be here, and Lockjaw won't be mine anymore. (Even now I have two unanswered voice-mail messages on my phone inquiring about "the mule for sale.") Instead, I force a confidence into my voice I don't feel and finally make myself ask, "And how's Emily doing?"

"Fine." Asa looks at me, quickly away. "The same, I mean."

"That's . . . good," I say, regretting the word too late, but Asa doesn't react.

He goes back to the bookcase, takes down one of the model horses and starts wrapping it in a sheet of packing paper. I'm trying to think of some way to change the subject when he does it for me. "You remember I told you my father was a preacher, too?"

"A revivalist, you said."

"Right." Asa pauses to concentrate on folding the edges of the paper around the horse's fragile ears. "Not so much a revivalist as a faith healer."

I choose a horse of my own, start wrapping it. "Like, he whacked people on the forehead and they threw down their crutches?" I immediately wish I'd phrased things more delicately, but Asa half smiles for a moment, there and gone.

"Last I saw him, he was just laying on hands, but maybe he got around to whacking people on the head eventually. He was a bit of a showman." He puts the horse in the bottom of an empty box, takes another from the shelf. "Actually, he was a con man."

I concentrate on wrapping, try to keep anything like surprise off my face.

"Maybe *con man* is too harsh a term." He pushes a hand through his hair. "He never went in for the most blatant fakery, the hired victims and chicken livers and whatnot. Most of the classic tricks of the trade aren't actually tricks, so to speak, but merely amount to listening to people, planting the suggestion first that they feel sicker and then better than they really do, choosing to 'heal' people of self-resolving conditions—the common cold, sore muscles—and claiming credit for it, or impressing an audience by choosing to bring on stage only those who are hard of hearing, not truly deaf, or mostly blind but not entirely—"

"Who use a wheelchair but can stand with effort, and not the completely paralyzed?"

Asa reddens, nods. "People see a hard-of-hearing person react to thunderous applause, or a legally blind person point to a spotlight—or, yes, the person in a wheelchair who stands—and they happily imagine miracles where none exist. My father was very good at convincing people of what they wanted to be convinced of. They did most of the work for him, really. They wanted it so badly, Jo." He glances up. "I'm not excusing it. Just trying to explain."

I don't say anything. I've done enough parsing of excusing-versus-explaining in the last couple weeks that I recognize someone trying to persuade himself.

"Some of those people really did seem to feel better after he laid hands on them. At least for a little bit, right afterward."

"A placebo effect."

"I suppose so." He doesn't sound certain.

I take a black Appaloosa off the shelf. The paint has rubbed off the tips of his ears and the edges of his nostrils, and one leg has warped so he stands only with the aid of a penny positioned beneath one hoof. He wears a chain of dried buttercups around his neck; it crumbles at my touch. "Maybe it's none of my business," I say, "but how did you turn out the way you did? You were raised by a man putting on these fake faith-healing tent shows or whatever, yet here you are an actual preacher with an actual congregation." I glance at him. "You *are* an actual preacher, right? You believe it all, I mean."

"I do." Clears his throat. "I try." Asa puts a wrapped horse in the box, but doesn't pick up another. "I didn't know it was fake when I was a kid. My father taught me my scripture, my hymns, my prayers. The tools of his trade. I didn't know he didn't believe in any of it. Not then. He told me later it was because a kid couldn't be trusted not to give away the game. Maybe that was all it was. I wonder sometimes." He looks at me. "He and I used to drive from town to town in this old RV, just the two of us. We'd park in fields or pastures or fairgrounds or empty lots on the outskirts of towns, wherever they'd let us set up the tent. I slept in that little bunk over the cab. There was a window by my pillow, and if it was warm enough I'd crack it open after I went to bed. My father would sit outside in a lawn chair, and some nights I'd hear him praying the psalms. And he *was* praying them, not just reading them. Always the King James Version. He'd preach using whatever translation was popular in a given town, but he always used the King James when he prayed the psalms at night. I still think they sound best that way.

"One day when I was twelve we were in the RV . . ." Asa sighs, picks up the picture frame on the nightstand—lingers over that center photo, the one with Samuel in it—puts it back down. "I don't really talk about this," he says. "Not even to my congregation. People tend not to understand."

"You don't have to—"

"No, I want to tell you. I just hope it won't change the way you think about me."

It surprises me to hear that Asa cares what I think of him, but I say, "Okay."

"When I was twelve, my father and I were driving after our last afternoon service, trying to get wherever we were going next before dark. I don't even remember where it was. Isn't that strange? You'd think you'd remember every detail of something so important, but I can't even remember the state. Somewhere with fireflies. It had just crossed into dusk, and they were glowing." He looks out the window into the fading light. "The boy came out of nowhere. He was just there in the road all of a sudden, on his bike. My father swerved but couldn't avoid him." Asa glances at me. "It was a hard hit. The sound . . ."

I put down the horse I've been wrapping. I know all about sounds you never forget.

"It was the middle of nowhere, Jo, I mean really the middle of nowhere. Fields and fields and not a single building in sight, not even a barn. The boy wasn't moving, but he was breathing—my father bent over him, and I remember that because I started crying then and couldn't see anything else. Finally my father decided to drive back to the last town we'd passed to get help. It was probably ten, fifteen miles back up the highway."

"He left you there?"

"He had to. I couldn't drive, and we couldn't leave that boy all alone in the road. It was so quiet after he left. I could hear the boy breathing, but they weren't normal breaths; they sounded like work. He was only a few years younger than me, probably nine or ten. Blond." Asa draws his hand down his chest. "He had this *X-Men* T-shirt on, and it was all faded and the screen printing was cracked, like he wore it all the time.

"I started praying. Familiar prayers, new prayers, whatever I could think of. I usually prayed silently, but that day in the road I prayed aloud, partly because I thought maybe it would be more powerful and partly because I couldn't stand listening to those raspy breaths. And I don't know how long my father had been gone, if it had been seconds or minutes or what, but even though I was praying louder and louder, I still knew when the boy's breaths stopped. Still heard their absence."

Asa closes his eyes, and I close mine, too, so I won't have to look at him. When I open my eyes again, his are still shut. He looks like he's praying, but more gently than up on that stage at the prayer service. That was a strong sort of prayer; this is tentative. Fragile.

"It was so quiet. So quiet. I picked up his wrist and there was still a pulse, but barely, much slower than my own. I didn't know what to do. Didn't want to admit there wasn't anything to do." He opens his eyes, looks right at me. "Mostly I didn't want to be alone with him when he died."

The sun has gone behind the mountains. Hard to see Asa's face. "What did you do?"

"I stood up. I started walking away—no, that's not right—I backed away, because I stumbled at the edge of the road and fell into the ditch." He lifts one hand, turns the palm toward me. "Scraped the heel of my hand. And I don't know why I did what I did next; I really don't. I don't remember deciding to do it. I went back to the boy and I put one hand on his head, here"—he touches his brow—"and I put the other on his chest, over his heart."

I pick the horse back up, roll one corner of the packing paper tightly between my fingers. I feel myself drawing back from Asa's story. Afraid of where it's going. Afraid it's going where I hope it will.

"I don't remember praying with words. It happened almost immediately, just moments after I laid my hands on the boy." He holds his hands at chest height, looks at them as though he doesn't quite recognize them as his own. "It wasn't comfortable. I felt something like heat move from my hands to the boy's body, but very suddenly, almost like a shock."

Asa pauses again. He seems reluctant to tell the rest of the story, and I can imagine why: it *will* make me think about him differently. "You healed him."

Asa looks at me for a long moment. Hard to read his expression in the dim light, but at last he nods. "He started breathing again. Opened his eyes. After a minute he sat up. Looked at his ruined bike, at me. Asked what happened." He shakes his head, lets out a sigh that's almost a laugh. "I was so stunned I didn't say a word. Just sat there staring at my own hands. The kid asked what happened again, then asked if I was okay, and I still didn't say anything. He finally gave up on me, I guess. Tried to get back on his bike, but it was well and truly wrecked, so he left it and started walking down the road. Not even a limp."

"You let him go?"

"I was so tired I couldn't even stand. Never felt that exhausted before or since. By the time my father got back with the paramedics and the police the boy was gone."

We sit in silence. I wish he hadn't told the story. Or maybe that he hadn't told it in such detail, with such certainty. He believes it. Hell, he's based his life on it.

"You don't believe me," Asa says. Not a question.

"I believe you told me what you understand to have happened," I say carefully. It's an inadequate, insulting answer, and I realize it immediately but can think of no way to mitigate it. Religious elements aside, I don't believe healing is so quick or clean. I know better. It takes time. It leaves scars.

Asa nods, the gesture calm and tinged with resignation. "I've never found the right words to explain it to anyone else. My father never believed me. Or maybe he did. He was . . . incredibly angry.

Told me it was all fake, that I was a fool for believing it, that a smarter kid would've worked it out on his own without his father having to spell it out. But nothing he said could touch the certainty of my experience. Nothing he said planted even the tiniest seed of doubt in my heart. Nothing ever has, until—" He stops abruptly, clears his throat. "I've wondered since then if someone who didn't believe it himself—in the possibility of it—would really have been so furious." He looks at me for just a moment, pulls his eyes away as soon as they meet mine. "My mother died when I was very young. Cancer. My father must have prayed for her."

"You think he tried to heal her?"

He shrugs, almost apologetically. "It could make a man lose his faith, don't you think?" And suddenly I'm thinking of Emily. "I've never done it again," Asa says. "Healing. Tried once or twice, but never in a situation as serious as that. Sometimes I wonder if I'd been there when Catherine had her accident . . ." He sighs, shakes his head.

And now? I want to ask. Has he tried? Will he? What will happen when it doesn't work? Because it can't work. It's not real. I've never envied the faithful, but right now I wish I could believe in it. For Asa's sake, I wish I could believe in it.

He's gazing out the window again, toward the last band of light fading over the western slopes. I wonder if he's still thinking of his wife. Or if his thoughts have already returned, as they must always return, to his daughter. "I didn't mean to—"

"It's all right." Asa turns toward me, arranges all his features but his eyes into a lighter expression. "You were wondering how I came to hold genuine faith. Now you know." He leans toward the bedside table, turns on the lamp. The silhouetted mountains outside disappear, obscured by my own harshly edged reflection. Asa takes the last horse from the shelf. "There's a name for this color. The yellow coat and white mane and tail."

I blink, swallow hard. "Palomino."

"Right." The model is of a Quarter Horse standing square; I always liked his sturdiness. He seems like he'd be a reliable sort, if he were real. Asa runs a fingertip down the model's nose, like it's fur and flesh rather than hard molded plastic. "'Em likes palominos." He pulls another sheet of packing paper from the box.

I meet my own eyes in the window reflection, look away. "Does your faith bring you comfort?" I ask, very quietly. Hear the hopefulness—the pleading—in the words.

Asa folds the paper carefully over the palomino's face. "I used to think so."

I can't read. Can't eat. Can't sleep. I sit beside her and watch her and wait. The only time I turn on the television is at 3:30, when *The Galaxy's Funniest Animals* comes on, and I watch it for her. Sometimes I bring the newspaper or buy a magazine in the gift shop, but I don't open them; they pile up on the bedside table. I keep my Bible in my hands, the one my father gave me when I was a boy, run my fingertips along the scuffed and softened leather at the edges of the cover. I spend hours paging through it, though I hardly need to. I know so much of it by heart.

My hands find the chapters I don't preach anymore, the stories I don't tell. The Book of Job: I know what I'm supposed to see in these verses, the theological lessons I'm supposed to absorb and impart, but when I consider them now, I see only cruelty and a heartless suggestion that one's children can simply be replaced. The story of the Flood, which seemed righteous enough when I wallpapered Em's nursery with pastel animals filing two by two into the ark, but seems unfathomably harsh now. The stories of Isaac, whom You saved, and of Jephtha's daughter, whom You didn't.

I don't linger on those stories, let neither my eyes nor my

mind rest on their words. (If I must overlook so many of Your words, so many of Your deeds, do I still believe? Should I?) Instead I seek out those that still bring comfort:

Leadeth me beside the still waters.

Be strong and of a good courage.

Which hope we have as an anchor of the soul.

I save the most comforting stories for the latest hours, the darkest moments. I read of the healing promise of God, the promise I know is there because I have seen it, I have felt it, You have shown it to me. The blind man, the woman with an issue of blood, the man sick of the palsy. I don't have to believe in these stories, don't have to burden my wounded, wavering faith with them, because I have one of my own. It is knowledge, not faith, and perhaps that makes it lesser, but I am grateful to You for it now.

Always, in the end, I turn to a story I never thought much about before the bombing, a story I want to avoid as much as I want to turn to its page and never leave. A healing left too late. (You are Lord; nothing is too late for You. I know this. I do.) I can't bear the backstory. Jairus falling at Your feet. The declaration of his daughter's death. The laughing crowd. Instead, I skip to the end. To the most important line. I read it over and over, a prayer unto itself. I whisper the words aloud, again and again until they dissolve into incantation, though You only had to say it once. *Talitha cumi.*

Little girl, I say to you, arise.

Saturday I wake and try to remember why I thought applying to the Elk Fork plein air festival was a good idea. Money, I remind myself. And more than that, the hope that it might be a few hours' respite from thinking about Samuel and his bomb. But this morning all I can think about is the fact that my picture has been on the news, it's hard to hide in a wheelchair, and I must have been a fool to believe there could be anything relaxing about this day. Easy enough for "Josephine Grady" to upload a couple landscapes to a website, but now Jo Faber has to paint for an audience.

I arrive at the Elk Fork park where the festival is to be held while it's still early morning, my easel, canvas, paint box, and other supplies in a bag slung across the back of my chair. I tell the volunteer at the artists' tent my name—my fake name—and wait to be called out as a fraud, but she simply hands over a map, a copy of the competition rules, and a name tag. I carefully pin the latter to my jacket. Maybe today will be a reprieve after all.

The park meanders along the banks of the Wounded Elk, and I choose a spot overlooking the river. There's another artist farther down the bank, but his easel points east, toward the high mountains at the edge of the city limits, so our paintings won't be too similar if they end up near each other at this evening's show. I assemble my easel, glance at my watch—I have only two hours to complete my painting—and start making a quick compositional sketch. To my left, two willows arch gracefully over an eddy, their branches trailing in the water. To my right, the river tumbles over a series of rocks; a kayaker steers his craft through the passage, and I lock the image in my memory. Straight across the water, a paved pathway hugs the bank, studded with new streetlights meant to look old-fashioned. Past the path, a row of brick buildings line First Avenue, one with a zigzagging fire escape cascading down its rear wall, another with a faded ad for a defunct brand of cola still ghosting its bricks.

And beyond them, just visible in a gap between two buildings, stands the blackened facade of the courthouse.

I stop sketching. Stare. Footsteps approach, pause behind me. People here to observe the artists. I trace over a couple lines of my sketch until they've gone. I look across the river again. Suddenly the courthouse seems to dominate the view. It's just a glimpse, really, a ragged-edged gray slash. No one will notice if I omit it. But I can hardly seem to see anything else. I could move, set up my easel somewhere else. Another glance at the watch. Fifteen minutes gone.

I sigh, settle a primed canvas onto the easel, fix it in place. Squeeze a rainbow of paints onto my palette. Choose a broad painting knife. I hold the knife over the palette, and hold it, and hold it. Takes me a moment to realize I'm stuck, because this has never happened before. I've never really had to decide what colors to blend and build; that's always been something I've simply known intuitively. I never expected that this most familiar sort of painting could feel so awkward, so alien.

Shouldn't be hard. How many times have I done this? Paint what people want to see. Make the colors more intense, amplify the beautiful, omit the ugly. Swirl brilliant blues together for the river, shape the willow branches from greens so vibrant they appear in life only for a fleeting day or two at the height of spring, play the sunlight off the brick buildings in an array of oranges and pinks. Paint something someone will happily write a handsome check for this evening so he can hang it over his fireplace.

A couple stops behind me. Still my palette knife loiters over colors that are already starting to thicken as they dry. So this will be how I humiliate myself: not by painting something inferior, but by painting nothing at all. I hear the couple walk away, their steps hesitant. To my right, the other artist has already blocked in the major shapes of the mountains and valley.

I drop the untouched palette beneath my easel, pull a couple paint jars from my bag. I only have the two, and they're small. They'll have to be enough. I choose my cheapest palette knife, use it to scoop up a hunk of the dark soil beside my chair. I tap most of the soil into the first jar, deposit the rest in the second. I shake out the tiny pebbles, the largest grains of sand, then pour some water into the jars from the container I brought—river water would be better, but I can't get to it—and mix the muds until each is the consistency I want.

More people behind me. I replace the blank canvas on my easel with a piece of stretched watercolor paper, wet a brush, hesitate only a moment more—too late to change my mind—and start to outline the wide curve of the river. The line goes down lightly, and I chase it with others for the trees, the path on the far bank, the buildings (just broad blocks at this point, no decision yet about the courthouse). I choose a wider brush, start laying down washes. This Elk Fork mud is grayer than the Eden mud, with no hint of the dried-blood red tinge I've come to expect. Grittier, too, since I haven't filtered it, with visible grains settling into the heavy tooth of the paper; I hope it will stay in place until

I can cover the painting with a sealant. For all its differences from my home mud, it feels comfortable, and the painting forms easily beneath my brush, the way I expected it to under my knife.

There's a small crowd around me now. I continue working, building the color as if I were working in watercolor, light to dark. Twice I reach down for more soil, add it to the first jar to thicken the slurry. Whispers behind me. I try not to listen, hear only *have you ever seen* and *monochrome* and, over and over again, *mud.* I paint the water, its dips and rises, the weeping trees, the buildings, each a slightly different shade of brick. I paint the tops of the barefaced mountains, where their rounded peaks peer over the buildings. I paint the clouds, their shapes threatening but the light gilding their edges reassuring. In the lower right-hand corner I paint my name, stop myself drawing the *F* for Faber just in time: *J. Grady.* And then, last of all, with only minutes left in the competition, when I'll have no time to change my mind or alter the painting, I paint the damaged sliver of the courthouse, its broken edge the darkest shadow in the piece.

I skip the afternoon artists' gathering at a downtown pub, skip the panel discussion at the Elk Fork Library, too. After sealing and framing the painting and dropping it off at the gallery, I spend most of the afternoon at a small, dark bar in one of the brick buildings that just missed appearing in my composition. I nurse a single beer for a couple hours, then order another to make up for the time I wasted on the first. When that's gone, I order a third, leave when I start to think I might drink it.

The gallery hosting the evening show is in the heart of downtown. It's a straight shot past the courthouse, but I go the long way, along the river path. The hospital is just a few blocks away, and Samuel walked this path every day when he took his infrequent breaks from my bedside after I was shot. Can't stop myself wondering if he walked it before the bombing, too.

What were his thoughts that morning? Whatever words I ascribe to them seem wrong, like a monologue written for someone other than my brother. I can imagine the actions I've been told about—parking the truck, carefully moving the suitcase housing his bomb—but I see those things from the outside, as an observer only. It's an impossible failure of putting myself in his shoes. I want it to be reassuring, this inability to imagine what was going through his head, proof that I could not have known, could not have prevented what he did. But instead it makes me feel that I didn't know him as well as I thought. That the closeness I've always felt to him was in some way a lie.

I time my arrival at the gallery well; it's reasonably full, but everyone is still milling around the hors d'oeuvres. I turn down a glass of wine and slowly tour the perimeter of the room. The gallery is a classy one, all polished wood floors and track lighting, the sort of place I usually feel intimidated to enter, and I can't help but feel a small thrill to see my own work on its cool gray walls. My painting is in the middle of the far wall, opposite the entrance; its monochromatic color scheme makes it easy to spot amid the pastels and watercolors. A couple stands in front of it, the man gesturing at the river with the hand that holds his empty wine glass.

"Josephine?"

A sudden memory of Devin blocking my path the day of the bombing, addressing me with the name no one who knows me uses. I put on a smile, turn to face the woman asking. She looks to be in her fifties, dressed with an effortless elegance I envy, just a little too much makeup on her face. I search her eyes for any indication I've been found out, that she's about to say Josephine *Faber*, but her expression remains pleasant. "I'm Frances Bailey, owner of Highcrest Gallery in Whitefish. Call me sometime;

I'd like to discuss your work." She hands me a business card and disappears into the crowd before I have a chance to respond.

"Is that yours?"

I look up to find Asa standing beside me. He gestures toward my painting. This is so far from the context in which I expect to see him that for a moment it's almost like I don't recognize him. I manage a nod.

"Watercolor?"

"No." I tuck the gallery owner's business card into my bag. "It's mud, actually."

"Mud?" The couple studying my painting moves on to the next, and Asa starts toward it. I follow reluctantly. He stops in front of my painting, clasps his hands behind his back and leans forward from the waist, as though he's at a museum and expects a guard to appear at any moment to ask him to *please step back, sir.* "Mud," he repeats. "How about that."

"I meant to use acrylics like I usually do," I explain, "but I've been experimenting with earth as a medium lately, and at the last minute I decided to try it today." It sounds so simple put like that, a casual decision. But it feels momentous, like something I can't go back from.

"It's incredible."

"It's not so different from watercolor. I can use washes and layers the same as I would with traditional paint." This should be an easy conversation. Something safe and impersonal, something I know enough about to fight off awkward silences with explanations and descriptions. But the longer I look at my painting—no, the longer I look at Asa looking at my painting—the more I realize it is, in some ways, an inversion of the chiaroscuro paintings I'm so fascinated by. Instead of a vast darkness illuminated by a single flame-point of light, I've painted a broadly lit scene in which everything points toward that darkly damaged edge of the courthouse, a black hole at the center of my painting. I came to the festival intending to paint a canvas very like those I've spent most of my life creating: bright, textured, warm. Sanitized. Instead I've done something very different—felt compelled to do something very different—and I'm still not sure why, or whether I am pleased to have done so.

Asa keeps his eyes on my painting, and I try to figure out what he's looking at. Is it something as simple as the brushwork, the undissolved grit visible in the washes, the shape of the trees and the water and the brick? Or is it that darkest of buildings, those few brushstrokes, those last layers of mud I did not want to paint but felt I must?

"There are a couple interesting pastels over here," I offer, rolling backward a few inches. Asa doesn't move. Has he seen the card beside the frame, the one that gives my name as something other than what he knows it to be? "I didn't know you would be here."

It isn't quite what I meant to say. *I didn't know you planned to attend the festival* would have been closer, or maybe, *I didn't realize you liked art.* But Asa steps back from my painting, finally, looks at me again. "I didn't, either." The words seem burdensome, somehow, his tone flattened beneath their weight. "I didn't mean to—I just happened upon the show and came in. I didn't plan it." He tugs on the hem of his T-shirt, distorting the clean water charity logo on the front, then lets it go, squares his shoulders. "I'm going to the hospital soon. Catherine's parents come to spend time with Em every evening, and when they arrive, the nurses tell me to go home. Get some rest, they say. I never do. Before Garrett and Ruby were discharged, I'd visit them. Now I sometimes take my laptop to a coffee shop and try to work on my sermon or answer email. Mostly I just wait to go back."

"I should have realized—"

"I'm always early," he says. "Every day. I'm supposed to switch off with Catherine's parents at eight, that's what we agreed, but every day I end up down here at least an hour before. I wish I could just go to the hospital now, but if I show up early Em's grandparents will leave and that's not fair to her or them, but somehow I still can't help myself coming early so I'll at least be nearby. I came in here because I saw the balloons and the sign and all the people, and because if I'm in here I'm not walking around outside. If I walk around I'll end up back at the church."

The boarded-up windows. The chain-link fence. The blackened courthouse.

And here I've painted it into my damn picture.

He's looking at it again, over my shoulder. "God created man from dust from the ground," he says. "Some would say that's where the artistic impulse comes from. He created us in His image, and we, in turn, are ourselves driven to create. How interesting that you have also chosen earth as your medium."

Asa doesn't voice it, but some people, I know, would say that children, not art, are the clearest expression of that creative drive. As for my paints, well, maybe Asa sees some divine significance in them, but as far as I'm concerned it's semantics. Yes, I sometimes paint with mud. But even parts of my store-bought acrylics come from the ground, from metals and minerals that have been mined: cadmium, chromium, cobalt and the rest. My newer paintings aren't greater, or truer, or more authentic acts of creation, just because I've started to use a rawer form of what the earth offers.

But I find Asa's words encouraging. Maybe it's just his tone. Maybe it's the fact that a preacher speaks a certain way, imbues his words with an authority even heathen ears like mine recognize. But maybe there's something in it. Not the God stuff. But maybe it's true I've found a medium that feels like mine. A medium that feels like I was made to use it.

A faint smile crosses Asa's face. "Look," he says softly. "You won."

I turn, see one of the judges pinning a yellow ribbon to the frame of my painting. "Third place," I correct.

"Still," he says. "Congratulations."

One of the pastels takes second, and a painting of sunlight on the river that I admired earlier wins first. Asa and I watch as the judge walks around the gallery and affixes the ribbons, applaud with the others when he is done. The auction will start soon.

"I should go." Asa looks gaunter than just a few days ago, more exhausted. "I'm glad I got to see your painting. You're very gifted."

"It was good to see you," I say, and think I might mean it. I should say more, something about Emily, but another artist taps my shoulder to congratulate me, and when I turn back Asa is gone. I glance at my watch: 7:04.

Still almost an hour for him to wander the streets.

———

I've started to think about what will come next. I've tried not to. But the hours are long up here, Jo, longer than I remember them being when I was younger. Writing these messages to you on this map has become the centerpiece of my day, and I make myself wait until almost sundown, both so I have something to look forward to and so I can't use up too much map before I lose the light. My handwriting is getting better all the time, because I linger over these moments, these words.

I stay close to the cabin. It's too risky to venture farther away; I was foolish to chance it before. So now I stay close, and I let the hours pass. Nothing to read; I told you that. I tried whittling, which confirmed you got all the artistic skill in the family. I watch the birds, all day sometimes—a red-winged blackbird came almost to my hand a couple days ago, but I haven't seen him again. I don't cook now that the deer meat's gone; I'm down to some trail mix, a bit of beef jerky, and some canned beans I can't hardly stand to look at anymore. Not much you can do with any of that to fancy it up. I'm on the last hole of my belt; when that's too loose, I'll try for squirrel. Thought I was done eating squirrel.

It looks like plenty written out that way, but really it hardly takes up any time at all. I don't mind looking at the trees and the mountains and listening to the birds and all that, but it lets in too much time for thinking, and if you think long enough about anything you'll start to doubt.

I'm not stupid, Jo. I knew it could go to shit. I didn't think it would, but I knew it could. So I thought about it just enough to bring a few things up here to the cabin a couple days before, but that's it. That and the hay in the feed room; I guess you'll have seen that by now. Not like me. Usually I've got every little thing planned out, every little worry accounted for, so I've been trying to understand why I dropped the ball on this one.

If you were reading this, you'd already have figured it out, wouldn't you, Jo? It's because I couldn't stand to think about not seeing you again. What I ought to do is leave. Get out of these mountains, maybe out of Montana. Lay low, stay off the grid. I know how to do that. But it would mean leaving you behind on your own, and I really do know you'd be okay—some things would be hard, but you'd be okay—but I can't seem to do it. I'd always wonder how you were. What you were doing. If you ever forgave me.

And even though I have to stay up here in this damned cabin, even though I can't come back to the house and ask you all those things, even though in just sixteen days—or is it fifteen? I might've lost track of one day—you'll have to abandon the house and go somewhere else, it still seems better than leaving.

Because if I stay here, Jo, I know you could find me. If you wanted to, you could find me.

"How come you never left Prospect?"

I shrug, meet Hawkins's eyes. "Where would I have gone?"

We're back at the Knock-Off, Tuesday night, two-dollar well drinks, the place packed for a change. Hawkins has shoved his ketchup-stained plate to the side of the table and leans over his crossed arms so we can hear each other. "I don't know. I was surprised you didn't go to college, at least. You graduated salutatorian."

"There were four people in my graduating class, and the Durnam twins were dumber than a box of rocks." I pick a sesame seed off the bun of my half-eaten burger. Hawkins's comments seem a little out of the blue, but I've thought about this a few times myself since learning we were going to lose the house. "I suppose I might have gone if Mom had still been around."

"You stayed because Samuel was here." Hawkins doesn't say it like a question, so I don't answer, but he's wrong. Samuel was the one who'd intended to leave. He stayed in Prospect with me instead of joining the military with Kev, accepting the baseball scholarship, becoming a veterinarian. He stayed to drive me to school, teach me to ride again, keep me safe. Whatever Samuel should have—could have—done with his life, the one he ended up with is because of me.

So Samuel might have left, freed of responsibility to me, but I've never wanted to live my life anywhere but Prospect. I love the way the mountains cleave the sky, and the valley cradles its people. I love knowing the heralds of each season and hearing comfort in the call of the creatures that make this corner of Montana home. I love that I don't have to explain myself to the people here, that my history and most of my hurts are known to them without my having to speak them aloud. Maybe I don't see the town for what it really is. Maybe I'm too willing to see the good in the place and not the bad, to overlook the poisoned land and broken bodies, the empty storefronts and struggling businesses. I don't think something is worthless because it's damaged. I don't think that because something's been hollowed out it can't still hold beauty.

I used to think these were admirable traits. That seeing the good in what others could not meant I was somehow better than them, kinder, more insightful. But now, more and more, I think I was just naive. Maybe if I loved this place less, Samuel wouldn't have felt the need to defend it with a bomb. Maybe if I loved him less, I would have realized he was the kind of man who would.

Too rarely did I work up the nerve to ask the questions he needed to hear, point out the fallacies in the Patriot- or Posse- or sovereign-endorsed talking points he brought home, object to his prejudices. I ignored the strains of conspiracy I heard in his speech, let them solidify into fact in his mind, told myself they were just ideas, just talk. Unimportant, insignificant. Too often I looked for the best in my brother when I should have suspected the worst.

I can't change how I saw Samuel, how I treated him, challenged him, or didn't. He's not here.

Hawkins is.

"You've got a lot of pills in your medicine cabinet," I say, staring at the remnants of my burger. I've kept my voice low, partly for discretion and partly because I'm only half convinced I should speak, and for a long minute Hawkins doesn't say anything and I think maybe he didn't hear me.

"You'll remember I got hit by a truck," he says finally.

"You're getting them from a lot of doctors." I remind myself I'm trying to do right. I'm trying not to make the same mistakes I made with Samuel; I'm trying not to ignore things I shouldn't ignore. I remind myself Hawkins could have put the pills on a higher shelf.

"That's how you got to do it these days," Hawkins says. "This crackdown because lowlifes sell their meds. Decent folks can't get what they need." He doesn't sound mad, exactly. He doesn't even sound cold, more sort of patient, like he's indulging me. Like I'm just little Josie who doesn't quite see the reality of the world the way the grown-ups do. I don't say anything. "I got pain, Jo." This time there's a hint of anger in his voice; it's oddly reassuring.

"I know you do." I risk a glance at him. Hard features. I remember the way he's made himself look me in the eye over the years even when he didn't want to, and I try to do the same now. "I just worry that maybe you shouldn't be using that kind of pill for your kind of pain."

He either doesn't know what I mean or—I think this more likely—he knows exactly what I mean. I could be wrong about all this. I don't think I am, but I could be. I hope I haven't made a mistake. I hope I haven't made things worse. But if I have, I've done it in a different way than I did with Samuel.

Before Hawkins can say anything else, a middle-aged man with a beer in each hand backs into our table, loses his balance, spills one of his beers across Hawkins's plate, sees the sheriff, and says, "Oh shit, man."

"Think you mean, 'Excuse me,'" Hawkins says. He holds eye contact with me a second longer before turning to the man.

"Shit, yeah. 'Scuse me."

Hawkins takes the unspilled beer out of the man's hand. "I think maybe you had enough, Jimmy." The other man nods a few too many times, starts backing away. "You ain't gonna drive, right?"

"Aw, no, man. No."

I watch the exchange in silence. I've seen it before. Not with this man, but with plenty of others; it's a reenactment of Hawkins's interaction with Branson last time we were here. The straight-arrow sheriff. The hapless but probably harmless drunk.

A stern but gentle sort of paternalism. I see Hawkins doing his best to be worthy of his white hat, his tin star. I see what the fantasy is to him, and I see his desperation to hold on to it.

"How 'bout you give me your keys and I bring 'em by your place in the morning?"

"I'm fine, man. I mean, Sheriff. For real."

Hawkins pulls himself straighter, holds out his hand. Jimmy sighs but hands the keys over, then shuffles out the door with one of his buddies.

Another night I might have asked Hawkins if he ever thought he was just encouraging them to head to Split Creek instead, transferring responsibility to the Smokies out on the highway. I might have reminded him that this isn't a western, that when people ride off the screen of Prospect, they just end up somewhere else.

But I've said enough for one day.

———

A prospective buyer is coming to look at Lockjaw Wednesday morning at eleven, and I'm up at six. Plenty of time to rake the barn aisle, clean the tack, groom the mule till she shines. But I do none of those things. Pick Lockjaw's hooves and give her a cursory brushing, that's all. I consider taking a short ride, in case it's the last, but I'll never enjoy it thinking that way. Instead I sit in a corner of Lockjaw's stall and watch her eat. She has pulled the flakes of hay from the feeder and scattered them across the floor of the stall, stands with one foreleg forward and one back, nuzzling aside the stems to find the tastier leaves.

When I was too young to know better, I liked to think that Lockjaw was the descendant of one of the mine mules from the early days of Eden. There had been a dozen in the beginning, hardy animals lowered down the shafts to pull ore cars in the tunnels. At many mines, the pit mules lived their entire lives underground, working until they died a thousand feet down, but at Eden they were each hoisted up the shaft once a year, turned out in a pasture for a month before being sent back down. It was intended to be a kindness, I suppose, but I wonder whether it's better to remind an animal of the sun or let him forget it forever.

When I was eight or nine, Samuel explained what it meant that mules were sterile, and I stopped imagining Lockjaw's strength and tenacity were the products of good pit mule genes; as I got older, I understood there was nothing to be envied in the life of a mine mule. Lockjaw will be valued in her new home. She's broke as can be, smart on the trail, knows how to pack game. Still, it's scary to sell an older equine—too many end up at auction, too broke down for anyone but the kill buyer—and not something I ever expected to do.

I hear a rattle on the long drive, go to the entrance of the barn to see a pickup towing an empty stock trailer. *Got to sell her*, I remind myself. My painting sold at the festival auction for the equivalent of six or seven of my ordinary paintings—more than the winning canvas—enough for a security deposit on an apartment or a rental house, but that doesn't help Lockjaw. Even if I could find a horse property to rent, I wouldn't be able take care of her on my own. What if she got cast in her stall, or hung up in the fence, or just plain decided not to be caught? And without Samuel's income, where would the money come from for the vet, the farrier, the joint supplements that keep the aging mule's arthritis at bay? *Got to sell her.*

The prospective buyer is a man from Columbia Falls looking for a companion for his Quarter Horse mare, something quiet enough his nieces and nephews can ride it when they visit. I ride Lockjaw first—the man seems impressed by her steadiness when I mount, her tolerance of my swinging legs—and then it's his turn. Lockjaw pins her ears briefly when he mounts, but she moves off when he clucks his tongue. Right away her gaits become stiff, her back hollow and neck inverted. The man bounces in the saddle, his elbows flapping at his sides. He told me he competed in reining, but I imagine he's never so much as seen a sixth-place ribbon at the local fair. I've already decided not to sell to him when he snatches Lockjaw in the mouth with the bit—an accident, I think, a loss of balance—and the mule throws her head between her knees and lets loose a buck that would make a rodeo bronc proud. Launches the man a good ten or twelve feet.

The empty trailer bounces back down the drive. I should be disappointed—*Got to sell her*—but I give Lockjaw a carrot and an extra pat before turning her out into the pasture.

It's one of those lush May afternoons I simultaneously long for and forget once they're gone, only to be surprised and relieved by their return the following year. The greenest days can be brief in the valley, but they're intense while they exist: the few deciduous trees are heavy with foliage, the high sun intensifying the color of the leaves, and the meadow is a shocking sort of green, an exaggerated hue that looks like something from one of my brightest canvases. In a matter of weeks the meadow will fade to gold, then to a shade that can most charitably be called yellow ocher, and soon after that the burn bans will start, and then the wildfires. But for now, for this short time, the landscape is a kaleidoscope of greens, and I can understand the decision to call the place Eden. The colors make me doubt my decision to paint this final piece using the earth. Might be better to allow myself the full palette of colors, to capture a favorite season one last time in this place. But the mud painting has started to take on the sepia tone of an old photograph, and that's better, isn't it? A painting about memory, after all. About the past more than the present, or at least of the past as a path to the present.

This newest—final—painting has progressed quickly since I found the perfect method of making the mud paint, of working with it on paper. I've already finished the mountains, the meadows, the sky. The barn is there, too, not quite done but well on its way. These elements all came easily, perhaps because I painted so many versions of them on my previously rejected canvases, perhaps because they don't carry as much emotional weight as the house itself. I've been avoiding the house.

But it's time to start on it in earnest. I've laid the lightest of washes down already, but on my paper the house stands as a blank shape in the landscape, a faintly grayish void surrounded by detail. With each layer it will get darker. With each layer there will be more shadow. I wish there were a way to paint the house that reflects the way it was built: beams first, then walls and floor and ceiling, roof, windows, house paint only at the very last. I wish I could paint it perfectly first, then add the years' decay bit by bit, so slowly the damage reveals itself only when one remembers what once was. I wish I could paint the house's history into the paper.

I sit for a long time, dry brush in hand. Think it might be one of those days when I bring all this outside—the easel, the board and paper, the cakes of mud, the brushes—only to take it back inside unused, unchanged. No. I don't have that luxury: just twelve days left.

I dip my brush into one of the jars, touch it to the mud cake. Start to paint the roof into place.

I'm getting ready for work the next morning when I hear a round thud from the living room; when I wheel into the room I see a single delicate feather clinging to the glass of the picture window. I find the bird in the bushes below the window, a sparrow, its body cradled in the narrow branches. I think it's dead, but when I pick it up one of its wings flutters desperately, and I feel the frantic beating of its heart against my palm.

I bounce it lightly in my hand to see if it's just stunned and will fly away, but it's hurt too badly. The kindest thing would be to wring its neck, but I don't have the stomach for it. Would Asa try to heal it? Maybe the idea would offend him. Maybe a sparrow wouldn't seem important enough to bother God with. But who is? Why did that boy on the bicycle in Asa's story deserve to be made whole? Why not Asa's mother, or his wife? Why not Emily?

The questions must have occurred to Asa, and I wonder if being a pastor means he has easy answers, or if instead they haunt him that much more. If he wants to believe in God or simply feels he has to. I don't understand belief, why it comes to some people and not others, why tragedy strengthens it in some and shatters it in others.

It doesn't seem like the choice people pretend it is. I wish it were that simple. Maybe I would choose to have faith, too, if I thought it was. Who wouldn't want to believe in miracles, in the possibility that all could be made right with just a touch, with only a few prayerful words? It's a tempting promise. But then there are the miracles not delivered. The questions. The doubt.

The sparrow gone still in my hand.

———

The end of my shift at Fuel Stop. Gregory One Bear suddenly in the doorway to the break room. "Have a minute to talk, Jo?"

"Of course." Never good when the boss asks that. I expected this conversation a couple weeks ago, maybe, when there were still reporters' cars parked in the lot, when my face was still in the papers. But the attention has dropped off dramatically—the last reporter quit staking out my driveway a few days ago; now he just stops by for an hour or two in the afternoons—and I'm surprised by, if grateful for, how quickly it has done so. (Does Asa feel the same way? Is it a relief to him, too, or does it feel more like abandonment?)

"Are you planning to leave Prospect when you . . . sell . . . your house?"

"I suppose I'll have to."

"It's just you haven't given notice."

"Sorry, I didn't think of that. If I end up leaving, of course I'll work out the notice. I can drive up if I need—"

"It's fine, Jo, it's not that. I'm not worried about that." One Bear glances at the register, speaks with his face turned away from mine. "It's just, well, you've seen the books these last few weeks. You know I'm not making much profit." He isn't making any profit. Enough to keep the lights on and the beer coolers cold; that's it. "How many sales did you make today?"

Three. A six-pack of Rainier. A T-shirt screen-printed with trout spelling out the word *Montana*. Ten dollars' worth of gas. "You're closing."

"Not right away," he says. "But when they build that road and there's no reason for the tourists to come through town anymore . . . You know I can't compete with that damn Gas-N-Go."

"What are you going to do?"

"I got a cousin has a private campground outside Glacier, says he can take me on soon as Going-to-the-Sun opens. He's looking to retire, so it'll be mine to run after this year."

I pull my keys from my bag, put them back. The jangling too loud. "Sounds like a good opportunity."

"You can stay till I close, if you want to. I figured you'd be leaving anyway."

I don't answer. Don't want to admit I still haven't made any plans.

"Well." One Bear scuffs one of his boots against the tile. "I'm happy to be a reference if you need one."

"Thanks." I try a smile, but it feels like the same forced expression I've found myself wearing time and again over the last few weeks. Something foreign, something practiced. One Bear knows me well enough to notice.

"It'll work out for you, Jo," he says. "You'll find something."

"I know."

"Probably for the best, really," he tells me. The sound of tires in the parking lot. We both look up, but it's only the elementary school bus making a U-turn at the end of its short route. "This town just don't got much to offer anymore."

There's a missed call from Hawkins when I get off work. I call him back from the parking lot.

"I ever tell you how much I hate senior prank season?" he asks by way of greeting.

"Every year." I'm relieved he sounds friendly, but wonder if it means he's already dismissed what I said about his pills. "What is it this time?"

"Car on the roof of the old high school."

"That's a recycled one. Class before me did that."

"So they did," Hawkins agrees. I hear someone shouting in the background, the heavy clank of metal on metal. "An old El Camino, I remember right."

Ordinarily I wouldn't mind small talk, but he's stalling. "You called me?"

"Devin wanted me to ask you something."

I'm silent.

"He wanted to know if Samuel hunted, so I said sometimes." I immediately think of the mountains. Samuel didn't hunt much when we were there. The noise. But he'd had the deer rifle, took a young buck once. "Then he wanted to know what he hunted, and I said far as I know just deer and maybe sometimes a turkey."

"Sounds like you answered for me." The words come out stiff.

Hawkins doesn't seem to notice. "Well, then he asks me if Samuel liked it—hunting—and I opened my mouth to answer and I realized I honestly don't know. Thought maybe he'd let it go, but he insisted I ask you."

"Did you tell him about the poaching?"

A pause. "That was a long time ago."

I don't say anything right away. Does Samuel like hunting? The question makes me uneasy, though maybe just because Devin is the one who asked it. Whatever crimes Samuel has committed, hunting isn't one of them—at least not since the poaching, and he hasn't done that in more than a decade, and then only for food. It certainly isn't a crime to enjoy hunting— Devin would have to lock up half the state if it were—though he should've noticed there aren't any trophy mounts on the walls of the house.

I think about a day not so long after our mother was killed, when I was still unwilling to be left alone. Samuel pulled me onto Lockjaw's back behind him, and we rode to the far side of the property, Samuel carrying our father's .22 rifle in his free hand. I spotted the rabbit a second before he did but didn't tell him. My arms were wrapped around his middle, and I could feel him exhale as he raised the .22, could feel his body still for the briefest of moments before he fired and the rabbit leaped and fell. I remember being sorry for the rabbit but glad for the meat.

"Samuel only killed what he had to."

———

Saturday I call the number on the business card Frances Bailey gave me at the plein air show. I half expect the owner of the Highcrest Gallery won't remember me, but she invites me over right away.

It's a longer drive to Whitefish than it was before the old road washed out, than it will be when the new road cuts close to an hour off the trip. I park on a side street just off the main drag downtown. It's not peak tourist time—ski season long gone, Going-to-the-Sun not yet open—but I still have to negotiate plenty of other people on the sidewalks. The Highcrest Gallery has recessed glass doors, and I glimpse pale gray walls through the windows. Inside, huge canvases dominated by splashes of red and orange paint punctuate the walls, the lighting arranged to illuminate their surfaces just so. The gallery is nearly empty, only me and a middle-aged couple wearing matching polar fleece.

Bailey emerges from a door in the rear wall and walks briskly toward me. "Josephine," she greets as she approaches. "So wonderful to see you. Come into the back where we can talk."

She shows me to a well-appointed office. She settles into the chair on the far side of her glass desk, has already moved the guest chair against the wall to make room for my wheelchair. The window boasts an enviable view of Big Mountain, but the art on the walls does its best to compete. The canvases here seem as carefully curated as those in the gallery, and as opaque: three narrow framed panels of arcing blues and violets; the shapes and colors seem somehow urgent, but I can't make sense of them. The flattery of the invitation is starting to wear off. This is real art, art you need a degree to understand. I don't make this kind of art.

You really come all this way just to quit? I hear Samuel's voice in my head so clearly I almost turn to see if he's there.

"Jo," I say.

"I'm sorry?"

"Jo," I tell her. "I go by Jo." I said that on the phone, didn't I?

Bailey smiles. "Of course." She pours two glasses of water from a pitcher beside her desk. There's something floating amid the ice cubes. Flowers? She places one of the glasses on my side of the desk, leaves the other untouched. "I'm so glad you were able to come by today. I've been thinking about your work since I saw it at the festival."

"I'm—that's good to hear." I have no idea what I'm doing. It must be hopelessly obvious.

"I'd like to talk to you about a show," she continues. "The main gallery is booked through next year, but I'd like to get you in sooner. I think we can finesse the schedule for the Slate Gallery— that's the smaller room on the east side of the building—and manage three weeks starting in the middle of next month."

"Next month?"

"You do have other pieces like the one I saw?"

"Well, I'm working on—I mean—that's a newer technique for me." I start to tell her about the mud paint, the soil and water from the mines around Prospect, the energizing idea of painting a place *with* a place. I practiced this part in the car on the way over, tried the sentences aloud, tweaked them until they sounded like the professional artists' statements I'd read in the catalog I picked up at the show.

"Do you have other paintings of Elk Fork?"

I look at Bailey. Her expression hasn't changed. Her voice hasn't changed. But something has.

"I don't . . . I don't live there."

"Of the courthouse?"

Silence. She looks at me, that same polite expression holding her features in place. Her hands are folded atop the desk; they don't fidget. I pick up my glass, put it down without drinking. Moisture has beaded on the outside, and I wipe my palm on my unfeeling thigh.

"Why do you want paintings of the courthouse?" I've waited too long to ask the question. I know why. She knows why. Now I'm making her say it, and in doing so it seems I've done something uncouth.

She tries to spin it, but even that precise elocution and carefully modulated tone can't make the meaning behind the words any less ugly. "Well, I was so struck by your festival painting," she says. "The courthouse. And you, well . . ."

"You know my name isn't Grady."

"I know you're his sister." She unfolds her hands, puts them in her lap, looks down. Something of the practiced smoothness falls from her voice. "I thought you knew."

"You want me to paint the courthouse because my brother bombed it." I say it more to myself than her.

"I do think there's great artistic interest in—" she begins, and I look at her and she stops. "I'm sorry," she says, more quietly. "I thought you knew. It's just . . . well, you *are* good, but you're very young, aren't you? Not formally trained. And . . ."

And my paintings hang in a gas station. I doubt she knows that, but now I also doubt she'd be surprised. I want to tell her that someone thought my mud painting from the plein air festival was good, bought it for more money than I've ever sold a painting for. But as soon as I think it, it stops being a point of pride. What if the person who bought it also knew I'm not Josephine Grady but Jo Faber? What if the person bought it because of who I am—who my brother is—and not because of what I know how to do with brush and canvas?

"I'd still like to the do the show," Bailey offers tentatively.

The worst thing is I'm tempted. I need money. How long did it take to paint that cityscape at the festival? I could churn out plenty more by the middle of next month, even with the move. They'd certainly sell for far more here than my acrylics do at Fuel Stop. I try to convince myself not to let pride stand in the way of practicality. I even try to convince myself that it's only fair, that Samuel screwed up my life enough that if I can cash in on his name, I deserve to.

But then I think of how it would make Asa feel, for me to make money off what my brother did to his daughter. And then, because I'm thinking of Asa, I remember what he said at the plein air show. About creation. About my gift. But why would I put Asa's opinion above this woman's? He doesn't own an art gallery. He probably doesn't know anything about art. He's a pastor. He knows about a single book, and a feeling he calls God. Maybe he doesn't even think my art is good. Maybe he was just being nice.

He made me believe it, though, didn't he? Or maybe that's not right. Maybe he let me see I already believe it. My paintings—my mud paintings—have worth. Earth is my medium. I am creating and my creation matters.

Maybe I'm wrong. Maybe Frances Bailey is right. Maybe this is my only chance to hang my paintings in a fancy gallery and sell them for real money. Maybe my mud paintings won't even sell to tourists, and no one else will ever understand why I paint them.

Maybe I can live with that.

———

I still check the radio every morning and evening. Just long enough to hear nothing has changed. Samuel hasn't been found. Emily hasn't . . .

A warning about a traffic accident on the interstate. A weather report promising showers. The relief of music. I turn the radio off. I think I should call Asa, but maybe I'm wrong. Hard to know if he'd want me to. It's crossed my mind that he's bargaining. That he's helped me with the tree and the packing not because he wants to, and not even entirely because he wants answers about Samuel, but because he is trying to prove to God that he is good. That he should be rewarded. That Emily should be spared.

A frozen meal for dinner. I wonder what Asa is eating. He probably does have an endless supply of casseroles from his congregation, but does he eat them? After my mother died, I wouldn't eat. The hospital would bring the tray and it would sit beside my bed, and then they'd take it away. They asked me to eat, then demanded I eat, but I didn't. One day they let Samuel stay through dinnertime. Brought us two trays. He didn't say a word, just sat beside my bed and ate whatever bland thing they'd brought. I stayed stubborn for about five minutes, then ate mine, too. I wonder if he's hungry now, wherever he is.

I want to tell Samuel about the gallery. I want to hear the sneer in his voice when he tells me the Bailey woman is just an entitled parasite, and I want to hear the pride when he tells me I was right to turn her down. I want to tell Asa, too, tell him his words helped give me the strength to say no to her, to trust in the value of my own art, but I don't know if he would understand, and if he did I don't know if he would care.

I toss the empty tray into the sink. I rehearse the lines I would say to Asa if I were to call. *Just checking in* and *Wanted to see how you were* and *Don't mean to keep you.* I rehearse the lines I wouldn't say, too. *When I was young, Samuel and I said we went to*

South Dakota but we didn't. There's a cabin in the mountains. I think
I know where he is. I don't know if a call would be too much or
not enough, and in the end I leave my phone in my bag.

———

I've left the rivers and plains behind on this map. Into the mountains.
I've started this letter around the Little Snowy Mountains, a spiral of
words unfolding toward the west, curving now around the Highwoods,
the Little Belts, the Castles, and the Crazies. The sentences are piled
atop one another, following contours, stacking toward the heights of the
ranges. It makes them hard to read, but it doesn't matter. You won't read
this, will you? Maybe I wouldn't write it if I thought you would.

A confession. Nothing serious, Jo, nothing like what you're think-
ing, nothing else like the bombing. I looked for your diary once, when
you were in middle school, maybe your first year of high school. I
wanted to read it, but not because I was worried about you. That's
why guardians usually read diaries, right? They're worried about
drugs, booze, boys. I knew I wouldn't find any of that. (Not because
of the wheelchair. Just because you weren't that sort of kid. Kind of a
goody two-shoes, really, Jo.)

No, I was worried about me. Every day since I took you out of that
rehab center and brought you here to the cabin, I've wondered if I did
the right thing. I know it was what you wanted. I know you couldn't
stand the thought of us being separated, of going somewhere else to live,
with someone else. And it made sense to me at the time. Why heap
more tragedy and loss on top of what happened to Mom? Why put
you through more changes when you already had to deal with being
orphaned and paralyzed? And those tears of yours, Jo. Kills me to think
about them even now. I'd have done anything to make them stop.

But I was so lost. And not just because I didn't know anything
about raising a kid, let alone a traumatized, paraplegic kid. I didn't

know what to do with myself after that night, Jo. I didn't know what to do about what I'd done. Hawkins was the only one I could talk to about it, and he never said anything other than "You did what you had to."

I wondered what you thought about me. That's why I wanted to read your diary. I was so afraid I wasn't the guardian you deserved. I wondered if you regretted running away with me that summer, if you wished you had an adoptive parent instead of just an older brother, if you knew what I did that night Mom died and if you were afraid of me because of it. If you blamed me for not doing more.

So I called in sick one day and went through your things while you were at school. I found a lot of sketchbooks—you must've drawn ten thousand horses by now, Jo; you had a good start even then—but the only diary I found was from when you were in grade school. You wrote in it twice. Once on your birthday to say you got it as a gift, and once a day later to say you fed Lockjaw carrot greens after dinner. And then three hundred and sixty-three blank pages.

So no diary, no journal. No way to know your thoughts. It was wrong of me to look. I still wonder what you thought of me, though. What you think of me now.

———

I haven't added Asa to my phone's contacts, but I recognize his number when it shows up on my screen. "It's Asa Truth," he says when I answer, as though I'd know more than one.

"Is everything okay?" I tuck the phone beneath my ear, wheel across the living room, spin my chair when I reach the wall of moving boxes on the far side. "Is Emily all right?"

"Yes," Asa says quickly. "Yes, she's . . . nothing has changed. Everything is the same."

I almost say, *That's good*, but I've learned not to force optimism.

"I wanted to see how you were doing. Make sure the moving plans were all in order and so on." The words come tentatively at first, then in a rush, and I know he has called for no such reason.

"Fine," I tell him. "You helped me get just about everything packed. Not a lot to do now but wait." I wish I hadn't said that. He's waiting, too.

Silence.

I rock my chair forward and back, then tighten my grip on the handrims, stop the chair short. Don't let go of the handrims because if I do I'll hang up. This is stupid. Worse than stupid. There is no friendship here, no friendship possible. Asa and I should not know each other. Should never have heard each other's names. I don't dislike him. He seems like a good man, and he has been good to me. But I cannot give him whatever it is he wants. Answers. Understanding. Healing. They are not mine to give.

I'm trying to figure out how to say that—if there is a way to say such a thing kindly—when I hear a deep breath on the other end of the line. "I was wondering—hoping—you would come visit Emily."

I want to tell him no. I want to say I'm too busy, sorry, the move and all. I want to tell him it will not do anything if I come, not for him and not for anybody. I want to tell him I couldn't even save the one person I love most; there's no way I can do anything meaningful for anyone else.

And I don't want to see her.

I don't want to see what Samuel has done.

I press the silent phone against my ear and stare at the rug on the living room floor. I'll leave it here when I go. Can't possibly bring myself to roll it up, reveal what lies beneath. "There's nothing I can do for her," I say quietly. "You know I'd undo what my brother did if I could. But I can't."

Asa is quiet for a long time, long enough I think maybe he

has hung up. Then he says, "It would be doing something for me if you came," and I know I will go.

Another prospective buyer for Lockjaw comes out the next morning, a boy accompanied by his father. The kid doesn't have a lot of experience—he's ten or so, and has been borrowing a pony from a neighbor—but the father does, and Lockjaw likes them both. The boy's balance isn't perfect, and neither is his timing, but he's careful and attentive, the kind of kid who wants to learn and will. The father strokes Lockjaw along the crest of her neck, just behind her ears, and she lets her lower lip droop. Feels a bit like a betrayal. I should be glad—ecstatic, really—to find people like this, but when the father holds the check out to me in the barn aisle, I can't make myself take it.

So I didn't sell the mule. I can at least get rid of the boxes and bags designated *Thrift* that are cluttering up the dining area. I cram them into my car to the roof, leave only enough room for my chair. Before loading the last box, I tear the tape off the top and rifle through it, retrieving one paper-wrapped package. I leave it on the porch, then take everything else to the thrift store in Split Creek.

Still time to kill before driving to Elk Fork. I work for an hour on the painting. I've been making slower progress over the last few sessions. I tell myself it's because I'm doing the detail work now, but really it's superstition; I want to believe I can't lose the house if I haven't finished the painting. By the end of the hour, the long patch of grass beneath the drainage spout is there, planted one stroke at a time, blade by blade; each shingle on the roof has been painted into place; and the delicate spindle of the railing lines the porch, each baluster carefully carved by my brush. I roll my chair back a few feet, squint. Almost done.

I haven't painted the shadows. Not the deepest ones. I know I need to. I know the painting won't be right until I do. It's not the only thing I've left unfinished: one window remains blank. One window still stands stark and empty.

———

The hospital in Elk Fork is one of the taller buildings in the city, but that isn't saying much. Five stories, maybe six. I'm headed to the third today. An older man gets onto the elevator with me, and before he disembarks at the second floor, he looks at my chair and says, "Get well soon." I don't bother to correct him, jab the "Door Close" button as soon as he's gone. A relief to get the oversized *Visitor* badge at the reception desk on the children's floor. I held off the nerves during the drive down, but they hit me now, and I would like to linger in the hall a few minutes more. But the receptionist called Emily's room when I arrived, and there's Asa now, leaning from a doorway halfway down the hall, one hand raised in a wave as though we've spotted each other across the grocery store.

The surroundings feel blessedly unfamiliar, the hot-air balloons painted on the walls bright and fresh, recent. I can't remember what was on the walls when I was here as a girl, but it wasn't hot-air balloons. Farm animals, maybe. I think I remember a cow with eyelashes and lipstick. "Thank you for coming," Asa says, as I stop near him. I nod. The truth is, despite agreeing to Asa's request on the phone, I wasn't certain I was going to come. Not yesterday, not this morning, not even in the parking lot. Only now, in the hall outside Emily's room, do I know that whatever reasons Asa has for wanting me here outweigh the reluctance I feel. His body is blocking the doorway, and I'm grateful for these final few seconds' reprieve before he goes into the room and I have to follow.

Emily doesn't look dead. A ridiculous thought, maybe, but my relief makes me realize I'd been worried about it. I could be wrong. I've never actually seen anyone dead, though I passed within inches of two bodies that night in the house. (*Close your eyes, Sweetie*, one of the paramedics told me. I didn't, but because I was strapped to the backboard all I saw was the blood on the ceiling and walls. Great arcs of it.) But no, there's the rise of Emily's chest beneath the blanket, the gentle fall a second later. Tubes snaking from beneath the edges of the blanket, but nothing in her throat, nothing obstructing her placid face. A girl with her hair in long braids on either side of her head, a stuffed dog propped at her side, a blanket tucked neatly beneath her armpits. She might be sleeping, nothing more, if not for the bandage around her neck. It stands out starkly, the same titanium white as the bleached sheets. I hear lyrics in my head, something from an old hymn. Crimson sin washed white as snow. I've never liked that imagery. Blood doesn't cleanse. It stains.

"She looks," I say, and then am not sure how to finish the sentence. "Like her picture."

Asa nods, goes to a chair on the far side of the bed. We'll have to talk across it, our words passing above Emily's still form.

The room is nothing like the sterile hospital rooms that appear on the television programs I watch at Hawkins's house: Every flat surface is inhabited by stuffed animals of all sizes and species; the walls are papered with dozens of greeting cards; a crowd of Mylar balloons just beginning to surrender the buoyancy of their helium is slowly sinking from its position above the television set mounted in the corner. My own hospital room had been well adorned with gifts, too, but not so lavishly as this.

Some of these must be from people who don't even know Emily, who saw what happened on the news. I take the plastic palomino horse from my bag, hand it across the bed to Asa. I've touched up the paint, given the horse a new glossy finish that highlights the yellow-gold color of his coat. "Not sure you'll find anywhere to put it."

He places the model on the table beside his chair, next to a book whose gilt edges betray its holy nature. "I'll donate most of this," he says, gesturing to the gifts. "But I want her to see them all if she wakes up."

The word—*if*—sounds sharply in my ears. I've been so alert for it in my own thoughts, so eager to eliminate it, I can't possibly miss it now. Asa puts his hand over his face, bows his head. "When," he says, and I barely hear him.

I try to muster the sort of purposeful cheerfulness my nurses used when I was a child. "You said things were the same," I remind him. "She's still doing fine."

"They are the same," Asa agrees, "but she is not fine." He takes his daughter's hand in both of his own, leans his elbows on his knees. "Every day things are the same, they're worse," he says. "Every day things don't change, they do."

Twin impulses pull at me: flee, comfort. I suppress the first, cling to the second. "You have faith things will get better," I tell Asa.

"Do I?"

"Yes," I insist. "You do. I know you do."

Asa meets my eyes for a moment, fleetingly, then suddenly stands and strides out of the room. I hesitate, glance at Emily— she is so still she seems almost like a doll, like one more beautiful gift crowded into this room—then follow Asa. I find him a couple yards down the hall, propped awkwardly against the wall, one leg bent at the knee, the other angled in front of him, as though he started to slump to the floor and stopped himself but can't summon the energy to straighten.

"I can't say things like that in there," he says, his voice only a shade louder than a whisper. "I can't say *if*. She could hear. They say people hear what goes on around them when they're in a coma. I can't say things like that in front of her."

"It's all right." I almost say I'm sure Emily didn't hear, but realize that won't sound like comfort. "Do you want to go to the cafeteria, get some coffee or something? Just for a few minutes," I add, when his eyes dart back to the doorway.

The cafeteria fulfills the hospital cliché: in the basement, lit by flickering fluorescents, stocked with burnt coffee and plastic-wrap-smothered sandwiches. We both get coffee— Asa almost dumps the contents of a salt packet into his before I stop him—and I buy a chocolate chip cookie with too few chocolate chips. I break it in half and put it on a napkin on the table between us.

"You stay the night here?" They didn't allow that when I was a child, but I think they do now.

Asa nods. "I haven't slept at home since the bombing." He stirs his coffee slowly, watches the tiny whirlpool chase the little balsawood stick around the cup. He looks like he could use something stronger than coffee; every time I see him, it's as though something else has been whittled away, hollowing him out from the inside, so much gone now he's starting to crumple. "Sometimes I leave for a few hours, but I never go home." He glances up. "It's one reason I was eager to help you at your place. I worried the whole time, every time, being so far away in case something happened, but at the same time sometimes I want to get on the freeway and drive as far away from here as I can. When you called me that first day, it was such a relief to have a reason to be gone. An excuse." He puts a hand to his face, speaks from behind its shield. "It's horrible to admit that. I'm a horrible father."

"It's not," I say. "You're not. You're absolutely not. It must be so— I can't even imagine how it must be to see Emily like that." If Samuel had known—if he could have seen what his bomb would do, what effects it would have—he would never have made it. I'm sure of it. Have to be sure of it.

But he does know. The thought arrives immediately, clear and true. I have been Emily. I have been the little girl in this hospital. For all I know, I have been the little girl in that very same room upstairs. And just as I have been the little girl in the hospital bed, Samuel has been the man in the chair at her bedside. He has spent time in this basement, forcing sustenance into a stomach churning with anxiety. The fear Samuel felt for me, and the hatred he felt for the man who had put me in that hospital bed, must both feel very familiar to Asa. And there is another parallel for Samuel, isn't there? He has been the man beside the bed, and he has been the man who put a child in it. I want nothing more than to not think about that, here, now, but I know I must. Know I can't let myself put it out of my mind.

A man in scrubs passes our table with a tray of food, nods to Asa. He lifts a couple fingers from his coffee cup in a stunted wave. "They all know me now," he says. "They didn't at first. I was down here a few days after the bombing—it was the first time I'd left Em's side—and I sat right over there"—he nods toward a table across the room—"and I was picking at a sandwich and heard this group of nurses talking about Emily. They didn't call her that. 'The girl from the church,' they said. They all agreed she'd never wake up."

"They were wrong," I say immediately. "I hope you reported them."

Asa shrugs. "People gossip. There's a reason there are so many verses about it in scripture."

I take a sip of my coffee. I've missed the window to drink it: scalding at first, it's already passed through hot into lukewarm.

"I was angry at the time," Asa continues. "Furious. But now there's part of me that's almost glad they said it. I can't admit it's a possibility. Not out loud. Not to anyone. I won't even admit it to myself most of the time."

"She's going to be fine, Asa."

He jerks his eyes away from his coffee, to me. "Let me say what I need to say. I know you know it's a possibility, Jo. I see the fear that she won't wake up all over your face whenever you mention her." The words are sharp, but I almost welcome their sting; Asa's anger feels safer than his despair. "I keep having these thoughts I don't want to have. Not the obvious ones, not just, *My God, what if she dies?* But other thoughts, things like, *I'm glad she still has Sunday school faith.*"

I shake my head. "I'm not sure I understand."

"She's right at that age where she's going to start asking questions," he says. "She's going to notice the apparent contradictions in the stories she's heard, start paying attention to the harsh tales as well as the beautiful ones, wonder about all the things most of us wonder about if we think about God. Most of which ultimately amount to: If He loves us, why does He allow terrible things to happen?"

Because he does not exist. Asa glances at me as though I've spoken aloud.

"They're good questions," he says. "People should ask them as they mature in their faith. They should think about them, talk about them. I want Em to do that. I don't want her to be afraid of doubt. I want her to know it's okay to wrestle with it. But she hasn't gotten there yet, and while I hope—so much—she still gets the chance to get there, I'm glad she hasn't yet." He pulls the stir-stick from his coffee; it leaves a trail of droplets across the tabletop before he sets it on a napkin and the liquid soaks and puckers the paper. More stains. "In the church . . . after the bombing, after she got hurt . . . when she was bleeding—so much—she was afraid she might die. I know she was; I could see it." He looks at me again, and I am struck, suddenly, by how young Asa must have been when Emily was born. No older than me, probably, and maybe younger. "I hope you never know what it's like to see your child fear her own death, Jo. No one should know what that's like." He pauses, clasps his hands on the table. Maybe I should put my own hand out, offer a comforting touch, but I don't know if he would welcome it, and I don't want to interrupt him if he's praying. When he speaks again, he does so without lifting his eyes. "I told her she was okay, and I think she believed me. She has always believed me before. But if she didn't . . . and if she's aware now, if she's able to think the way . . . the way she is now . . . I'm glad she believes in Heaven, a literal Heaven. I'm glad she believes she'll see her mother again. I'm glad she believes that if she dies, Jesus will be there to meet her." His voice has lost the steadiness it gained from anger; the words tremble as they rise from his tongue.

"You believe those things, too, don't you?"

"I believe there is an afterlife," Asa says carefully. "And I believe we will be united with or separated from God after our deaths. Most days I believe that. I want to." More quietly: "I used to." He picks up his coffee, puts it back down without drinking. "Maybe I'm kidding myself. Maybe there's nothing."

"But you healed that boy," I remind him. I worry the words might sound false coming from my lips, but he seemed so sure when he told me about it, and I try to remember his quiet confidence.

"You don't think I did," Asa says flatly. "And maybe you're right. I was still a kid myself when it happened. Come on, Jo, I spent my entire childhood at revivals. My father might have been a fraud, but I believed it. Real or not, what other frame of reference did I have? I laid on hands, the boy lived, I must have healed him, right? What would you have thought in that situation?"

"I don't know."

"Of course you do." He laughs once, an unpleasant light in his eye. "A coincidence. An injury that must not have been as bad as it looked. Maybe you would have even thought of it as a miracle, but not a real, capital-M miracle, just something you couldn't explain, but who cares because it all worked out for the best."

I take a deliberate sip of my coffee. Cold, but it buys me a few seconds. Asa doesn't shift his eyes from mine, and I see anger there, a fury fueled by a dwindling faith. "I don't know what really happened with that boy," I finally say. "But I know you believed you healed him. You believed it so strongly it changed your entire life. It made you reject your father's charlatanism. It made you become a pastor. Whatever happened, it was powerful. I don't think you should give that up. Not if you can help it. Not right now."

Asa stares at me for several long seconds, and I watch the fire fade from his eyes. The weariness returns, and with it a sort of disappointment. He nods, but it's an automatic gesture, meant to placate. Another thing to worry about. Another harm I hadn't imagined when I first heard about the bombing. The specter of physical death is alarming enough; I don't want to think about spiritual death, too.

"I know there probably isn't," I say, "but is there anything I can do?"

Asa is silent for a long time, and I let myself hope he won't speak at all. There is nothing I can do; I know that. The only thing I think he might ask is for me to pray with him, and I do not want to do that. I want to avoid it so badly I almost didn't ask. It's one thing to scrawl, *Our prayers are with you*, on the bottom of a get-well card, or even to promise prayers the way I did in the statement I wrote after the bombing, but it's another entirely to agree to pray with a man who has formed his life around the church, believes the laying on of hands can heal, and is praying to save the life of his only child.

When he finally speaks, his words are very quiet, but very hard. "You can come upstairs," he says, "and see—really see—what your brother has done to my daughter."

I have not known what to say to Asa before, but never like this. Never have I been speechless in this way; never have I been faced with such a void in my mind when I search for words.

Asa seems to expect it. I think I see a hint of reluctance in his expression, some slight acknowledgment that this anger is not really for me, but his eyes betray no sympathy.

"I saw her," I start.

"You looked at her," he corrects. He glances away for a moment, returns his gaze to mine with a bolstered resolve. "I know you aren't your brother, Jo. I know that. But I don't think you fully understand what he's done. I don't think you've really let yourself understand it."

I open my mouth to protest, but he cuts me off, and after a moment I realize I'm glad; after a moment I realize he's right.

"I know you aren't your brother," he repeats, and I wonder if he's trying to persuade himself. "But he's not here." The words hardly contain his anger, and the syllables strain and snap beneath the hoarse burden of emotion. "I don't know where he is. No one does, they've told me." His voice drops. "I wonder. You've said nothing about it. But I wonder."

I wince at the implied accusation, try to reassure myself. *I don't know where he is.* It doesn't work as well as in the past;

the semantics are failing me, the distinctions between *know* and *suspect* and *guess* beginning to lose their significance. But I can't tell Asa about the mountains now. I don't know what he would do if I told him now.

So again I have nothing to say. I can't take on Samuel's sins for him. Even if I wanted to—and I might, if only because it would give Asa a target, one he doesn't need to feel reluctant for hating, if only because then he could seek from me whatever it is he needs to seek from my brother—even if I wanted to, I can't. It's not possible.

"I will look—*see*—her again, if it's what you want," I tell him. "But I can't be him. I can't stand in his stead."

Asa's jaw works, and he looks down at his cold coffee, back at me. When he speaks the words come so quietly, so deliberately, so calmly and without any trace of anger, that I know he did see me wince earlier. I know he no longer trusts me, if he ever did. And I know his words are for me, not my brother. "He must face what he's done."

———

I pull off the road halfway home, in a dirt semicircle carved into the bank above a narrow, sharply curving river. I did go back up to Emily's room with Asa. I tried first to see her as she might have been before the bombing, but I had *not* known her before, and I could not. I felt the kind of sympathy for her I would feel for any injured child, with whatever extra poignancy my guilt might add, and with a visceral understanding of what it is to be a little girl in a hospital bed. But I did not see Emily as Asa wanted me to.

So I spent the next minutes seeing her as a painter—an artist—might. I looked for shapes and shades and shadows. I saw curves and lines, darkness and light. It sounds abstract, but it's the deepest way I know how to see. And I will remember what I saw in those moments, will be able to recall Emily's face forever, to imagine how it might look wearing different expressions, or at different ages. But that is not what Asa meant me to see.

I tried again, and I still don't think I saw Emily the way her father intended me to, but what I did see was that there was no way to undo what had been done. No way to go back and say whatever I should have said to Samuel, to see what he had planned, to stop him. To save her. To save him.

And that, I think, is close to what Asa wanted.

I watch the river now. It is dappled, low sunlight filtering through evergreens to the water's surface, lighting patches of the water and leaving others in darkness. The sunny spots look backlit, the light penetrating rather than reflecting, and I watch those spots, so much water passing through them, yet looking like it isn't moving at all.

I wonder if this water comes from the mountains. If it originated near my brother, has sustained him these last weeks. If it flowed past the house in my creek, where I blended it with its sediment and dipped my brush into it. If it carries the weight of those places and their people in its currents. How I wish I could get down the steep bank to the river's side to trail my hand in the frigid water, feel the force of it. How I wish I could borrow its strength.

———

A week until the eviction. I'm beginning to realize part of me still hadn't thought it was real. Hadn't thought it was final. Some part of me thought it would turn out to be a misunderstanding. The state would change its mind, realize the road was better placed elsewhere, or not needed at all. The lawyer would call and say he'd found a way to stall the seizure of the property, that there were more options. Samuel would find a solution, as he always did.

He must have accepted the truth before I had. The bombing was no attempt at a solution. Even if it had gone the way I suspect he intended—no injuries, no cameras, a week out of town and back to the house with no one the wiser—it wouldn't have changed the outcome. We would still have lost the house, the land. What he did wasn't an attempt to change anything, save anything. It was an outburst, anger, revenge. Thought of that way, it seems a strangely futile gesture, a particularly violent tantrum. An admission of helplessness I never expected to see from my brother.

I thought we would leave together. Hard now not to feel I'm being cast out for my brother's sin, sent away from my Eden for what someone else has done. I know it's not truth. I know Samuel's actions were at least in part a response to having our home stolen, and in no way its cause. But he is somewhere else, and I am here, and I am alone.

I call the Elk Fork apartment complexes with accessible units, put my name on the waiting lists. Neither will have a unit available by the time I have to be off the property, but the second complex expects a vacancy the following month, and I can afford a cheap motel that long if I have to. It feels like surrender.

I set up my painting outside. I ought to finish the house. Only a few more days, a few more opportunities. Still I leave the mud cakes untouched, the brushes dry. The painted house's final window remains blank.

I keep thinking of Emily. I find myself tracing the outline of her face on my palm with my empty brush, those curves and lines I memorized when I went back to her hospital room with Asa. It would be a quick painting. I would use my painting knives, my thick acrylics. Exchange the large paper with the painting of the house for a small, square canvas. Outline the broadest shapes of the portrait with a soft pencil. Head and shoulders only, a pose not quite like the one in her school photo. I'd squeeze my paints onto my palette, a rainbow of hues, choosing those that would suit the longest, warmest of summer evenings, to suggest a life lived under the most brilliant sunlight.

Then I would trade the pencil for my knives. I'd work quickly, the paints blending into each other at some points, butting sharply up against each other elsewhere. I'd soften some places with the pad of my thumb, wipe it clean on my jeans. The colors would build swiftly into the shape of a face, a girl's face, Emily's face. Eyes the color of May grass, gold rings around the pupils; youthfully rounded features highlighted by pink cheeks; auburn hair streaked with sunny oranges and yellows.

Painting that way is familiar and comforting, and I will never do it again. Not for a portrait of Emily, and not for any other reason. So tempting to paint only the brightest vision of things. To hide damage and decay beneath thick layers of vivid pigment, to depict life as it might be in a dream. It's the closest I can come to magic, to healing, and it isn't nearly enough.

———

I don't understand why I can't leave. I don't mean right now; I mean at all. Why can't I leave Prospect? This place has never offered us much, Jo, certainly not since the mines closed, but even now I'm guarding it, circling it as I write, protecting it from the inky weight of my words.

If I were another kind of man I might've seen the government's theft of the house as an opportunity. An escape. I tried to escape when I was younger, and I think I might have done it then. (Don't think I'm blaming you. Blame Archer. Blame the impotent piece of paper telling him he couldn't come into our lives anymore.)

You've always loved our home in a different way than me. You love it for what it is, and I envy you that. I love it because it's all I have left. Because those forty acres to my name are all I still have of Mom and Dad and the Fabers who came before them. Because our home is the one dream that didn't evaporate that night.

Do you think things would have been different somewhere else? I know they would have if we'd left after Dad died—Mom could've found better work, and maybe better men, too—but would it have been different if you and I left after she died? What if we'd really gone to South Dakota? Or to Denver, or Seattle? Say we'd woken up to cornfields rather than mountains, to asphalt instead of gravel, salt water instead of sandstone.

I did ask you once. Do you remember? You were twelve. I asked where you would live if you could live anywhere. I even said it twice: anywhere. *You thought about it for just long enough, Jo. If you'd answered immediately, I could have told myself,* She didn't think; *if you'd waited too long to answer I could have said,* She isn't sure. *But you thought about it just long enough, and then you said,* Here. *Only here.*

(I'm still not blaming you, Jo. Do you really think I would have gone?)

Maybe I should have made you choose anyway. Maybe I should've handed you a map like this one, but with all the states on it. Maybe I should've told you to pick somewhere, anywhere.

Maybe it was already too late.

———

I spot Devin's car coming up the drive late Saturday morning. I open the door as he climbs the stairs to the porch, don't even have to ask before he shakes his head and says, "No news." Inside, I watch him take in the neatly stacked boxes, the unadorned walls and bare bookcases. He turns a chair so it faces away from the kitchen table, sits without waiting for an invitation. I wearily position myself a few feet from him. These visits have become almost routine far more quickly than I would have guessed possible, and while knowing Devin considers me untrustworthy at best and hostile at worst simplifies things, I still feel deeply uneasy with this role. I wonder how much longer I'll have to play it. How much longer these visits will continue, if there is a point at which Samuel will have stayed gone so long they'll turn their attention to other things.

You could stop the visits now if you tell him about the mountains. There's still part of me that wants to. I can't hold this question in my mind forever. I can't keep pretending Samuel hasn't hidden before. But what Asa said to me at the hospital has led me to understand that while I might not be my brother, and might not be responsible for what he has done, he is still *my* brother. Mine and mine alone. I can't simply hand that truth, or the burdens that come with it, to someone else.

Devin doesn't immediately speak. I'm impatient with his tactics and manipulations. I've said everything I mean to say to him before today, and now I just want him gone. I wait, but he still doesn't speak. I wait some more, and then I nod to his pristine boots. "You still need to scuff those up."

He glances down, flexes an ankle to get a better look at the leather. "I give the shoeshine guy a good tip every Monday to make sure they don't look scuffed."

"Makes you look like you belong on a dude ranch."

"This might shock you," Devin says, "since I get the distinct impression you think I'm from somewhere terribly pedestrian like Pennsylvania or New Jersey, but I was born in Helena."

It does surprise me, but I try not to let it show.

He leans toward me. "There are ways to be a Montanan without being a mountain man."

We've crossed into dangerous territory. Devin has somehow led us to this point, though I'm the one who started the conversation, and I can't quite see how he's done it. "Don't know any mountain men," I say carefully.

There's a long silence, but I vow not to speak again until Devin does.

"You look ready to go," he says finally, nodding toward the boxes.

"Don't see I've got much of a choice."

"Where will you be moving?"

"I don't know." He raises an eyebrow, and I tighten my jaw. "I'm on a waiting list for an apartment in Elk Fork, but it's not going to be ready in time. I don't know where I'll go until it is."

Devin looks at me for a few more seconds, then nods minutely. "Let me know when you figure it out."

Silence again. For all his tendency toward speechmaking and ranting, Samuel has always been comfortable with silence, willing to wait others out, to let his words stand without further explanation or adornment. That kind of silence makes me uncomfortable, but I try to emulate him now. To remember that there aren't always words, and what words there are might better be left unspoken.

The silence won't have much power over Devin; I'm sure he was taught its usefulness if he didn't recognize it instinctively. He lets it stretch between us, but in the end he's the one to break it. "I did come to ask you about something," he admits. "I've been stalling because it will probably hurt you to hear it. And whatever you think of me, Jo, I don't want to hurt you." I bite back a scoff. Has he already forgotten his threat during his last visit? "I don't think you're a bad person," he continues. "I think you're stunned by what Samuel did, but you're also deeply loyal to him, and that's left you unsure what to do in this situation." He's got the profile spot-on again.

"Ask."

"The night your mother died—"

"Was a long time ago." I wish I hadn't interrupted. Might as well put my hands over my ears and start humming.

"The report says Sheriff Hawkins responded to the emergency call."

"This has nothing to do with anything," I insist. "This has nothing to do with the bombing."

"Sheriff Hawkins responded to the emergency call," he repeats. Waits until I reluctantly nod. "It says he killed Benjamin Archer."

"In the hallway." I point, and Devin turns, as though he might see Archer's ghost there. I don't look; even now a small, childlike piece of my soul is afraid there might be a ghost to see.

"Hawkins's gun jammed." Another nod. "He used a baseball bat."

"Samuel played in high school," I say. Hear my own voice getting quieter with each word. "His bat was by the door."

"There were other guns in the house," Devin says, his head cocked just slightly. "A couple rifles, a shotgun."

"There was no time to open the safe." I close my eyes. I don't want to remember this now. "Everything was so fast. It probably seems slower written in a report, but it was very fast. There was no time. He was coming down the hallway."

"Archer was."

"He had a gun. He heard me."

"You were in the bedroom closet."

"I didn't see it." I open my eyes. "I didn't see anything." Firmer. Louder.

"You must have heard."

"I was in shock."

"Your mother had already been . . . had already died?"

I reach down beside my chair, throw back the corner of the rug. The stain. Faded but not gone. Could be anything: a pet stain, water damage. Just a dark blotch that might be any of a dozen things other than the blood it is. "Samuel sanded it down," I tell Devin. "Too much, actually. There's a little dip in the floor if you run your hand over it. He should've ripped out the boards, replaced them. That's what he had to do in the hall-way. But he never got around to it. Couldn't bring himself to do it, I guess. Hawkins bought us the rug."

Devin stares at the spot a couple seconds too long, and I take a dark satisfaction in having surprised him. He seems to anticipate all my answers before I give them, and finding something that isn't in that damned report, isn't already part of Devin's theories and conjectures, is almost a relief. He recovers quickly, though, straightens, looks back at me.

I flip the rug down.

"Archer was hit more than once," he says, and his voice is steady as ever. "The investigation . . . let's just say it wasn't con-ducted the way I would have conducted it. But based on what was done, on the blood spatter and the coroner's report, he wasn't only hit more than once, he was hit more than a dozen times."

He waits, and I finally say, "That's not a question."

"Where was Samuel when Archer was in the hallway?"

"I was in the closet."

"Where was he, Jo?"

"I was in the closet," I repeat.

"Where—"

"You tell me." I force down memories of that night, the dark, the sounds. Look Devin in the eye. "You're the one who read the report."

I heard eleven shots. One, solitary. My mother, I understood, because her voice was suddenly gone. Her murderer's name the last thing she said. Then a second shot. Aimed at my brother, I learned later, but it found me through the wall. And despite the pain, despite my scream, I heard the third—Samuel's voice gone, and I thought he was dead, too, because I heard him fall—and then the rest all at once. Nine bullets in my mother altogether. And then the footsteps coming down the hall.

I still hear the sound of the shots sometimes. A wrenching Morse code, a staccato pattern I hear inside my skull, sometimes over and over, sometimes just once, when I've stopped expecting it. As a child I thought people were haunted by ghosts, but I understand now that the senses can haunt. Louder there in the darkness of the closet, louder now when I close my eyes at night.

One.

Two.

Three.

Four five six seven eight nine ten eleven.

I push a slice of carrot around the frozen dinner tray in front of me. Some of the gravy from the turkey has spilled into the carrot compartment, and I use the carrot as a crude brush, swirling the gravy across the black plastic.

"Not good?" Hawkins asks, watching me.

I quickly lift the fork to my mouth. "It's fine."

We spent the afternoon moving nearly everything from the

house to the storage unit I rented in Split Creek. (I tried and failed not to think of Samuel's unit, Samuel's bomb.) The house is almost empty now. My bed is still there, and my easel and a few brushes, the unfinished mud painting. A few toiletries in the bathroom, some paper plates and plastic forks in the kitchen, the handful of unimportant odds and ends I've abandoned upstairs for the bulldozers.

Another cop show is wrapping up on Hawkins's television. The kidnapped woman is rescued. The criminal arrested. The cops share a reflective beer. Hawkins switches the set off. "I'm not running for reelection this year."

I turn to him, but he's staring at the black screen.

"I've had enough of it. Enough. I get called to Hank Branson's place at least once a week and I take him in to sober up, but I know I'm gonna be right back out there again next week. I toss Ren Wallace in jail for hitting Macy and then she comes to pick him up. And at least that's doing something. It's some kind of action, even if it don't mean nothing in the long run. I spend most of my time sitting on my ass in my truck waiting for speeding tourists, but when they build that damn road I ain't even gonna be able to do that. I'm tired of not mattering, Jo. I'm tired of not being able to do any good."

"You do good," I protest. The words come out hollow, like a line read by a middling actor.

"God knows I've tried," Hawkins says. Tips his soda can up, finds it empty. He crumples it in his fist. "I did a great job helping your brother, didn't I?"

"Hawkins . . ." I start, but he waves me off.

"Maybe I just don't want to be the sheriff of a dying town anymore."

"Where will you go?" I wonder if I he wants me to try to talk him out of it. Not really his style. He's probably been stewing about it for a while, has only said it aloud now that he's finally decided.

"Somewhere I don't know nobody." He looks at me, shrugs. "And somewhere it don't snow."

I offer a small smile, because he wants me to. I should have stronger feelings about Hawkins's decision, probably. Next to Samuel, he's been the most consistent figure in my life these last few years. With Samuel . . . gone . . . losing Hawkins will be tough. But things have shattered so wholly, so spectacularly, that this registers as minor, an aftershock. And I think he might be making the right decision. I can't forget those pills, even if Hawkins wishes I would.

"I thought about asking if you wanted to go with me," he says. "We could find a nice town somewhere, set you up in an apartment. A fresh start, you know? We could both use that. But you won't leave Prospect." He leaves a pause long enough for me to fill, if I wanted to. "I'll be selling the house." It takes a moment to register what he's saying, what it means, and then I experience a little spark of excitement. Feels foreign, like something almost forgotten. "I got nowhere to put the mule, and I'm sorry about that, but there's the ramp."

"How much you asking for it?"

"Not that I think you ought to stay, understand. I mean it when I say this place is dying, Jo, and that road's only gonna kill it faster."

"Hawkins."

He names a price that's half what the place is worth.

I didn't count the footsteps. Too much pain, too much fear. I heard them, though, and the breaths, heavy, winded. I didn't hear anything from the living room, no groans or cries, and no second set of footsteps. So the first swing, when it came, was a surprise. A crack as sudden as any hit in a ballpark, but not so sharp, not so clean. A brittle sound, shattering. It changed over the next few seconds, became duller and wetter, though no quieter.

I didn't count swings, either. More than a dozen, Devin told me. I suppose that's right, but I didn't count. I only knew it was enough.

Hawkins takes the empty trays to the kitchen and I cross the living room to the mantel, study the portrait of Kev. I remember him only a little. He came to the house sometimes, but mostly he and Samuel spent their time in town, or the mountains. Kev was nice to me, in the way you might be nice to your friend's cute puppy. "Hey, Kid," he used to say when he saw me. I try to recall if he ever used my name, but I don't think so.

"You'll take him a Dr Pepper once in a while?" Hawkins asks.

He's in the doorway, watching. I nod, turn back to the portrait. Kev is in uniform, the stark colors of the flag behind him. So much sterner than I remember. He smiled a lot. More than Samuel ever did. "Do you think Kev ever killed anyone?" I ask quietly.

"I know he did." Hawkins shoves his hands into his pockets. "Last time he was home on leave he told me about it. It was when he was stationed near Baghdad. A man approached the base, wouldn't stop when Kev ordered him to. They found all kinds of weapons on the man after." Hawkins slumps onto the couch. "Kev knew it was the right thing, but it shook him up pretty bad. I could tell right away when he came home. Wasn't himself. When he finally told me, he asked me how you cope with it. Killing a man." Hawkins meets my eyes. "He thought I'd be able to help him, see? Because of Ben Archer."

"Devin asked me about the report," I whisper. "This morning."

"I know." Hawkins sighs. "He asked me about it, too."

"What did you tell him?"

"I told him I knew it was a hell of a story but it was God's honest truth." The words come slowly, like they weigh more than most. "I lied about it this long, Jo. Don't see how it would help to stop now."

So many secrets.

"Hawkins?"

He looks at me.

"Have you ever killed anyone?"

He shakes his head.

Later, when that staccato sound memory wouldn't leave me—one, two, three, four five six seven eight nine ten eleven—when it circled in my head, over and over, so loudly and incessantly I couldn't eat, couldn't sleep, couldn't hardly breathe, Samuel was there. He spent so many nights in the hallway outside my bedroom, slumped lengthwise across the hall, head propped on a folded pillow, one hand draped over our father's rifle. And I would look over and see him there, guarding me, and the sound would quiet, subtly at first, a little at a time, until the memory of those gunshots faded to an echo, fainter and fainter until I couldn't even imagine their sound anymore, and finally I could sleep. Because I knew Samuel was there. Because I knew he would protect me. Because he had done it before.

———

Something I have never told you, Jo. Something I have never told a soul. Something I hesitate to write even here, so I cross the words atop one another until they build to a heavy, thatched black along the backs of Eden and Gethsemane. Sometimes I wish I hadn't got up from the floor that night. Sometimes I wish I hadn't stopped him. Sometimes I wish I had let him kill us all.

———

A beautiful morning. The sky above the eastern ridgeline is like a clear, deep lake, such a pure blue I think if I look long enough I might be able to see through it to the stars. When I go to feed Lockjaw, I'm greeted by a gentle breeze, absent the lingering chill of winter, the lightest of touches against my face. There will be only a handful of days like this all spring, and I'm not sure I'm glad they have arrived now. Rain would make it easier to leave the place behind.

Two days left. I try not to calculate the hours, the minutes, but the figures run constantly in my mind against my will. How do you leave a place knowing you will be someone else without it?

Inside, I spend an hour in my bedroom, sketching the ridgeline of Eden and Gethsemane from memory, then going to the window to test my recollections. Every sketch is identical. Accurate enough for a map.

I hear a car pull up late morning, watch Asa walk toward the house. I'm surprised to see him. We didn't part at the hospital on bad terms, exactly, but I left with the sense that Asa would never be able to fully separate me from my brother. That maybe he was right not to.

"I should have called," he says, when I open the door.

"No need." He steps past me into the empty living room, hesitates when he sees that the couch, table, and chairs are missing. "I put the things in storage yesterday."

He settles himself slowly on the brick of the hearth, bending one joint at a time, like an old man. Asa seems even more exhausted than at the hospital, and it crosses my mind that the lines on his face—new lines that weren't there when I first met him, too deep for the heavy stubble on his face to hide—might be permanent. Despite the temperate weather, I have a sudden urge to wrap a blanket around his shoulders.

"I hope you don't mind that I came," he says. "After we last spoke . . ."

"It's fine, Asa."

"I didn't want to go home. And I didn't want to be alone."

"I understand." He looks at me, and I'm afraid I've offended him—I only meant that I know homes feel wrong when they're missing one of their usual occupants—but he nods, then puts his hands to his face and rubs his eyes. I consider asking about Emily, but the memory of his anger at the hospital stops me. Asking after her would be the right thing to do if I were anyone else, but I'm not, and I suspect Asa can no longer pretend I am. "You haven't slept," I say instead.

"I know I look like shit." The profanity startles me, and I'm embarrassed by my own surprise; Asa is a preacher, not a monk. He's heard all the same words I have.

"I have coffee," I offer. "Not real coffee. Instant. But it's better than nothing."

His eyes are closed when I come back from the kitchen, but he opens them at my approach. I hand him one of the mugs I've balanced on the tray across my knees, and he takes a cautious sip, then a greedier one. I move my chair back a few feet, stopping short of where the desk used to be. An automatic accommodation of absent furniture.

"What I can't understand," Asa says suddenly, as though continuing a conversation we've already started, "is why I would be given this ability to heal if I can't use it when I need it most. When the people close to me need it most."

I look down at my mug. My hands are pressed tightly around the hot ceramic, welcoming the overload of sensation. "I don't know what to say about that kind of thing, Asa. Theology, the whys and wherefores . . ."

"I already know all the answers you could offer," he says. "I've been to seminary. I've read books on theodicy and the will of God and spiritual gifts. God knows I've prayed about it." He sets his own mug beside him on the hearth, holds his hands in front of his face. Long fingers, prominent knuckles. "But still I'm left with the memory of healing that boy on the road, and the knowledge that I have not done a thing like that since. And I'm left with a belief—or a remnant of belief, a memory of belief—that God does have a plan. That things happen for a purpose, even if it's a purpose that serves God's interests rather than my own. And I can accept—try to accept—that it might be a purpose I can't fathom. That I see through a glass, darkly." Something weary in the words. "That's what I'm meant to say, isn't it? I know what I'm meant to say. I know what I'm meant to believe. I know I'm meant to trust. But I can't help looking for that purpose." He lowers his hands to chest level, turns them palms-up, and I am reminded of Samuel praying in church all those years ago, how ready he seemed to receive whatever it was he thought or hoped God had to offer. "I can heal," Asa recites. "I've done it. It's possible. My daughter was caught in your brother's bombing. There must be a purpose. A reason. And if there's a reason, it must be one I can see, understand. Maybe it's arrogant to think so, maybe I lack humility, but surely in this case it's a reason I can understand? Otherwise where's the purpose in it? If I can't heal her, then whom am I meant to heal?"

Asa looks at me then, and though nothing obvious changes on his features, I see that he thinks he's worked it out. That he came here today for a reason. I see that he has to grab on to something, that his faith is evaporating and he might want to let it, that this is a last attempt to contain it. I back my chair a few inches without meaning to, invading the space where the desk used to be. "It's not me," I tell him. "Asa, it's not." I don't want to be harsh with him, but I force an edge into my voice and emphasize each word. "I do not need to be healed."

"It's not a judgment," he says quietly. And then the anger rises suddenly, the steel in my voice matched in his. "You have to let me try."

Hard not to yell at him, throw him out. But he's desperate, and I don't want to be unkind. My family has hurt him enough. And it isn't that I never had those kinds of thoughts in the early days. The *Maybe someday I'll walk again no matter what the doctors say* thoughts. The daydreams—yes, some of them even populated by a benevolent Jesus who looked very much like the one in the illustrated children's Bibles used in Sunday school—in which someone fixed me with a touch, undid everything Ben Archer's bullet had done, and just as quickly. But those were fantasies, nothing more, and I left them behind long ago.

"I'm fine the way I am," I say, as gently as I can. "I really am, Asa. I've been paralyzed a long time. Longer than not. This is who I am, and I'm okay."

Already the anger has bled away. Its absence leaves him hollowed out, his voice thin. "I could just try . . ."

"Asa, no." Might be a kindness to let him. What would it really cost me, a minute or two to let him lay on hands and say a prayer? It would do me no harm; I didn't believe it would work, so it wouldn't hurt me when it didn't. But it would disappoint him at best, devastate him at worst. I don't want to be responsible for dashing the last of his hopes. "I don't know if there's an answer out there or not. A person you're supposed to heal. But I do know it's not me." He's staring into his coffee mug, and if he hears me, he gives no indication. "Just try to forget about all this for now, Asa. Stay focused on Emily."

"Em's gone."

I hear the word *NO* tumbling through my mind, but it doesn't make its way to my tongue. I close my hands tightly on the handrims of my chair, watch my knuckles go white.

"She's dead." The word seems forced through Asa's throat, razor-edged and longer than its single terrible syllable, and I know it's the first time he's said it aloud.

I should say something. Must say something. But I'm afraid that if I open my mouth I'll vomit and I cannot do that, cannot do anything that will make this moment worse. Finally I fight it all down and say, "I'm so sorry, Asa. I'm so sorry." And it is grotesquely inadequate, but it is all I have to offer, and it is long overdue, so I say it twice more and am quiet.

Then words are spilling from Asa, too softly and quickly for me to catch most of them, but I hear *neurologic* and *brain stem reflexes* and *apnea* and others like them, and I hear the way the grief makes every word strange and painful, and ultimately I hear enough to understand that whatever happened in the early morning hours in that hospital room, Asa watched his daughter die.

And all the while I'm listening to Asa, I'm hearing another voice in my head, and though it is silent it tries to overpower Asa's spoken words. It says *Samuel has killed.* It says *Again.* It says *This time everyone will know,* and *This time no one will understand, because there is nothing to understand.* It says *Emily is dead and your brother killed her.*

She's gone. She's gone. How can I know it with such wrench-ing certainty and disbelieve it all at once? Twice tonight I've driven myself nearly mad thinking about where she is now, what cold room she's lying in, whether she feels alone, whether she feels frightened. And then I remember she can't feel. She is not. There is no she anymore.

They are the most familiar words: *For God so loved the world, that he gave his only begotten Son . . .* I've spoken them aloud, heard them spoken aloud, perhaps more than any of the other words in Your book. They were the first I taught my daughter. My only child.

You sacrificed Your only child for the world. I would never do such a thing—I would sacrifice the world to save her, yes, but never the other way around—and I don't know whether the fact that You did makes You unfathomably benevolent or unfathom-ably cruel. I don't know if it makes Your love greater or lesser than my own.

But You knew there was a reason. Thousands of reasons, millions. Whatever Your pain at losing Your child, You knew His death would save the rest. But what of us down here, the ones You supposedly *so loved*? What reasons do we have when we lose our children? What purpose does my beloved daughter's death serve? She is gone and for nothing. You've taken her and left me without even the meager salve of meaning.

I know I am to believe she is with You now—and I hope she is, and I must believe it, and You will care for her, won't You?—but she is lost to me, and in this grief a moment is an eternity.

And in these endless moments, in this blackest loss, I cannot help but fear that if she is no longer here with me, then perhaps You are lost to me as well.

Asa cries for a long time. I sit near him and stay mostly quiet. There are no words of comfort, and I know better than to search for them. It is not okay. It will not be all right. I wonder if rage might chase the grief, and try to be prepared to weather it if that is what he needs me to do, but there are only the tears, and then silence. The sun dips behind the western mountains and slowly the light leaches from the room, and I let it. At dusk I feed Lockjaw. I offer Asa dinner when I come back inside, but he declines, and I am glad because it means I don't have to eat, either. Eventually I turn on the lights. I wonder if Devin will contact me about Emily, but no car comes. My phone vibrates once; when I look later there is a missed call from Hawkins, but no message.

Whether my presence is any comfort to Asa, I don't know. I hope it is. I hope, at the very least, it is not a burden. He leaves just before midnight. I try to convince him to stay the night—he could use my old bed upstairs—but he insists he wants to go home. When he is gone, I brush my teeth and change into pajamas and transfer from my chair to the bed. I lie in the dark and try to weave sleep from the threads of fatigue and sorrow. But there is only the dark. No sleep.

The strangest thing is that Samuel will not know. I barely register my certainty. Not long ago—even this morning—I would have reminded myself he could be anywhere, could be somewhere with radio, television, Internet. But now I am sure he does not know, and maybe I have always been sure, and tonight, in the dark, it seems deeply unfair. He's the one who conceived of that bomb, built it, detonated it. He shouldn't avoid full knowledge of the consequences. That heavy comprehension shouldn't fall only on me.

I knew Emily might die. Maybe even expected it, as much as I tried not to. But now Emily is gone and the finality of it weighs on me even as part of my mind tries to deny it, tries with a frantic urgency to figure out what needs to be done to undo this, go back, fix it.

I can't even grieve properly. I try to summon tears, and muster a few, but I can't swear they're for Emily and not for Asa or Samuel or myself. Because I never had the chance to know Emily. I prayed for her at the community service, sat beside her hospital bed, heard her father say her name with such desperate love the memory of it hurts. But what do I really know of her? That she liked horses with coats the color of the sun. That she still believed in heaven. That her father loved her, maybe even more than he loves his God. It's a sketch, not a portrait, and as much as I yearn for a purer grief, the one I feel is weak and muddled and no less terrible for it.

———

In the morning the break of aspens along the front of the property glitters again: the cars are back. Mostly press, I imagine, but at least one must be FBI. Not a surprise; my phone started ringing again last night. Not so many cars as before, not so many calls.

A blip is all Emily's death amounts to. An excuse to check back in with that story in Montana—*Remember? That crazy militiaman or whatever who bombed that building last month?*—during a slow news cycle.

I'm scheduled to work at Fuel Stop, but I don't put on my uniform and don't call in. One Bear stocks the papers; he'll figure it out. Instead, I call the man who came with his son to look at Lockjaw. I ask if he's still interested in buying the mule; he is, can pick her up this afternoon. Better make it tomorrow, I tell him. Then I take my painting supplies out beneath the pine one last time. I glance over my shoulder once I'm set up, see the bright glimmer through the trees. They can probably spot me if they look hard enough. Might even be able to get a picture with the right lens. It wouldn't look good—"Terrorist's Sister Paints in Wake of Child's Death"—but the only person who could truly be hurt by it is Asa, and I think he would understand.

I open the Bible I brought outside; it falls, as always, to the Twenty-Second Psalm. Carefully, I razor half of a single verse from the thin page: *my heart is like wax / it is melted within my breast.* I thought slicing apart a Bible might feel blasphemous, but if it does, the feeling is too subtle to rise above the other emotions of the day. I put the narrow strip of paper in a shallow metal bowl, place a stone on top so it won't blow away. I turn to the front of the Bible, find the papers I've tucked there. I cut again: the headline: "Prospect Woman Killed," and the drop-head below: "Two Children Wounded by Gunfire." And lastly, I hold the photograph of my father in my hands. I don't want to damage it, though there are a handful of others in the albums sealed in a box in the storage unit. Finally I cut just a corner of the picture away: a few blades of grass, the toe of my father's boot. I add the bits of newspaper and photo to the bowl, remove the stone, add a lit match. The onionskin-thin Bible paper burns quickest, the aged newspaper only a moment behind. The slick photo paper takes a few seconds longer, but soon it, too, is reduced to ash.

A breeze picks up, and I cup one hand over the top of the bowl; when it dies down, I add a tiny amount of powdered silver ore our father brought out of Gethsemane for Samuel, mix it all together with a few drops of water from the creek. The result is a thimbleful of smooth color that is nearly—but not quite—black, like the night sky seconds after the darkest point of night, with the barest hint of a shimmer that sparks beneath the eye and dims almost as soon as it's spotted.

I've thought about including my family in the painting. They are so much of what I want to remember about this place, so much of what makes it hard to leave. But I haven't been able to imagine how to do it. I don't remember my father but could never exclude him, so I'd have to paint him as I've seen him in photographs. But I would want to paint my mother as she looked when she smiled and called me Josie, and then my parents would not match one another—my father younger than my mother in image when he was in fact two years older—and it seems cruel to separate them that way when the mountain has already stolen enough. And Samuel, how would he appear if I painted him now, with love and fury and disappointment battling in my heart? So they will be represented in my composition not by their forms and faces but by these scraps and bits, these papers and photos, and I alone will know what gives this paint its darkness, and its points of light.

I dip my brush into the ash paint. Hesitate. Still afraid of the dark. I remind myself that this is the virtue of the mud paint. Even this, the deepest pigment I'll use, is not as void of light as the bone black from my tubes of acrylic. Though my eye can scarcely discern a difference, this is still a shade of gray.

I begin with a line of shade beneath the jut of rock on the slope behind the house, a touch along the ridgeline that is last to escape shadow in the morning and first to succumb to it in the evening, move to the curve of creek that remains hidden from sun even at noon. And then the eave of the barn, the edge of the window that was once my mother's and is now mine, the sill of the big picture window in the living room my mother looked through one afternoon to see the mining officials driving toward the house, the same window Samuel looked through that awful night to find Ben Archer's truck barreling up the drive.

And last of all—the thimble's worth of paint nearly gone—Samuel's window, tucked beneath the northern gable. Last of all and darkest of all. I dip my brush and paint, thinking of the history of this place. Trying to work out when the boy who looked out of that window with hope became the man who looked out of it with hate. Somehow everything that ever happened on this land—the optimism of a new home, cattle grazing and then dying, a burning light so dark might never come, a promise to never sell, a death beneath the mountains, two killings on a pleasant spring evening, a decision about a road—all of it led to this. To me, painting the house I am thirty hours from losing. To Samuel, a brother I love but do not recognize, hidden but so close—I'm now certain—I could almost include him in the painting. To a grieving father and a child awaiting burial.

There's no color to spare, but I lay it down firmly, refusing to fear the darkness. I start in the lower right corner of Samuel's window and work my way to the upper left, using small, layered strokes. I don't have enough paint. I know it when I've covered only half the window, but try to make it last, adding another drop of creek water, swirling my brush along the edges of the shallow bowl to pull the pigment into the bristles. When I finish, the upper corner of the window is just starting to fade to light, just slightly less dark than the rest. I look at it for a long time. Think about trying to make more of the ash paint so I don't renege on my resolve to paint darkness where darkness is due. But it is the barest fade, the window still quite black, and in the end I leave it, grateful for that subtle promise of light.

That afternoon, I curry Lockjaw and brush her first with a stiff bristle brush and then with a soft one. The mule rarely shows much love of grooming, but when I reach high to run the brush along her crest, she arches her neck and leans into the touch. She raises each hoof obediently when I tap each leg, and lowers her head to my lap so I can guide the small goat-hair brush over the contours of her face, around each swirl and curve. I try to draw out the routine even as I do my best to pretend it isn't the last time. Samuel roached Lockjaw's mane a month ago and it still looks all right, but when I finish the rest of the grooming, I carefully bell her tail. I make three cuts into the hair so the tail appears to have three tiers; it's an old military tradition I read about in one of my books: Mules broke to pack have one bell, those broke to pack and ride have two, and only those broke to pack, ride, and drive get three. When I was a kid I always belled Lockjaw's tail before the Silver Days show, proud to have such a well-trained mule. I make a note to tell the boy about it when he and his father come to pick up Lockjaw so he can be proud, too.

I'm sorry I haven't taken the time to give my tack more than a cursory cleaning recently; dust has collected in the curved petals of the floral tooling on the saddle, and the shanks of the bit are marred by green flecks of chewed, hardened hay. I bat as much of the dust off the saddle as possible, scrape the worst of the hay from the bit with a fingernail.

At the top of the mounting ramp, I check my saddlebag:

water, granola bar, hoof pick, Vetrap, poncho, cell phone. As I mount, I wonder whether I'll ride again. Probably not anytime soon, not like this. Not so independently. Samuel worked patiently to teach Lockjaw to tolerate my flopping legs, my imprecise seat. He taught her never to move at the ramp, no matter what. He taught her to stop the moment she felt her rider becoming unbalanced. These things could be taught to another mule or horse, but not every animal would be as receptive or reliable. None will be Lockjaw.

I guide her onto the trail that leads northeast over the ridge. It's narrow, but not as steep as some we'll ride later. The trail switchbacks lazily along the face of the slope, and though we aren't yet far above the valley floor, I imagine that as we ride higher into the hills the sun becomes brighter and warmer. The air seems thinner, each breath not doing the job as well as the one before, but that's anxiety, not altitude. I try to notice everything: the magpies swooping from the trees closest to the meadow, the sound of the small rocks sent skittering down the hillside by Lockjaw's hooves, the way the heights of the pines sway degrees at a time while the bases remain still. All things I have seen or heard before, but I focus on them anew to forestall the inevitable forgetting, the coming fade of memory. And because it's easier to look at what I'm leaving than to consider where I'm going.

Like most riders, I fear the unseen gopher hole, the den or burrow that might swallow my mount's limb and snap it. But I long ago extrapolated that rational worry into a torturous fantasy in which the entire mountainside gives way, sending me and Lockjaw plummeting into the depths of the mines. I imagine sudden darkness, still air clotted with dust, and bones. They would be bones, wouldn't they? Surely after all this time? Or might there still be flesh of some sort clinging to the bodies?

Sometimes I worry that I would see my father, sometimes that I would not.

A child's nightmare, nothing more. I'm not even over Gethsemane on this hill; Eden sprawls beneath us now.

I cross the ridgeline, taking one last glance down at the house that seems very small indeed from this vantage point. The trail is steeper on the far side, and I lean slightly backward as Lockjaw descends, gripping the saddle horn with one hand. I resisted this during my first few solo rides after becoming paralyzed—in my mind, only beginners and babies held the horn—until Samuel went through an issue of *Western Horseman* and circled every picture of a professional barrel racer hanging on to the horn as she rounded the barrels. "And they can feel their legs," he said.

He brought me here on Lockjaw's back. He rode in front, pulled me up behind him so I could put my arms around his midsection. I still had pain then, and the ride sent it jarring through me with each hoofstep. I didn't tell Samuel, because I was afraid he would take me back to the rehab center. Might have been the first time I kept a secret from him. I thought he'd catch me at it, but he hadn't, and it was a power I'd found less intoxicating than frightening.

The journey seemed to take a long time that day. Hours, certainly, maybe enough to fill an afternoon. I haven't been back since, and I don't quite remember the way.

Still I ride on.

Samuel knew about the cabin, he told me, because our father showed it to him when they took their first and last hunting trip together, when Samuel was seven. Like most of the mines in this part of the country, Eden started as a placer mine, established by men seeking gold. There was only a little gold to be had in these mountains, and then only in the very early days, but plenty of people came looking for it. The cabin dated from that time, our father guessed, which meant it was almost a hundred and fifty years old. One room, a simple rectangle. One window, also a rectangle, no glass. The rusted remnants of what had once been a woodstove, a hole in the roof where the pipe had gone when it still existed.

I suppose people had stayed in it now and then before Samuel and I briefly made it our home. The occasional hunter or backpacker, maybe, or one of the handful of men who chose to live in the mountains, alone and at least a little crazy, not quite homeless but something like it. But probably not that many people ever bothered. The roof had more than just the one hole in it, the floorboards were warped and in some cases missing, the door had at some point been torn down, most likely by a bear, according to Samuel, and a variety of small animals and insects had taken up residence over the years, leaving copious evidence of their presence behind.

By the time Samuel brought me to the cabin, it was clear he had already been there many times. A heavy green tarp was fastened over the roof, a sheet of screen stapled over the window. A new campfire ring had been built from stones on a flat patch of dirt, a tripod with a cooking pot positioned above. The interior of the cabin was not only impeccably swept, it bore the scent of what I finally recognized as the oil soap our mother had used to clean the floors at the house. Inside, Samuel had arranged two cots—mine in the back corner of the cabin, bolstered with a heavy pad, his below the window, where it could be easily pulled across the closed door every night—as well as a camp toilet behind a dark shower curtain hanging from the ceiling. He'd brought plenty of food, sealed it all in bear canisters, and piled it beneath a lean-to he'd built fifty yards from the cabin. He'd even bought me a pair of all-terrain tires for my wheelchair, had them waiting when we arrived.

It was, in retrospect, a ridiculous plan. But Samuel formulated it so carefully, with such attention to detail, that we encountered few problems. He approached the entire endeavor with the earnestness and determination of the Eagle Scout he had recently become. He tried to imagine every possible obstacle we might encounter—from rainstorms to bears to pressure sores—and made plans to avoid or overcome it. I needed very clean hands to use my catheters? He brought bottled water, boiled creek water when it ran out, and packed in a huge container of alcohol-based hand sanitizer, which he insisted I use after washing my hands. Rain might come through the screened-in window? He cut a piece of tarp to cover it, mounted it along the top edge of the window, then rolled the tarp and tied it so it could be pulled down like a shade if it rained.

Samuel made it seem like an adventure, linked it to the books we both loved, separately, as children, he reading them first, me inheriting them years later: *Little House on the Prairie* and *The Swiss Family Robinson* and *My Side of the Mountain*. It had not been an easy place to learn to cope with my body's new limitations and demands, but it ensured I learned work-arounds, didn't dally mastering floor transfers, didn't fear trying new things with my chair, and when we finally left to go back home, everything there seemed simpler by comparison. My memories of the place, considering the circumstances, are peculiarly fond.

These last weeks, I've wondered when a thought becomes a suspicion, a suspicion a certainty. I still can't pinpoint when one changed to another, but I know now I'm riding toward my brother. What I still don't know is why he's there. It makes so little sense. Why the cabin? There are better places to go, dozens, hundreds of them. So many more places to hide, to disappear. So many places I don't know about.

Lockjaw stops and flicks a long ear backward, and I realize I'm gripping the reins in my fist. I take a breath, relax my hand, and cluck to Lockjaw. She walks on toward the cabin.

The shadows of the pines stretch down the side of the mountain, each tree shading those below. In another couple hours the sun will be low enough the mountains will cast their own eastern slopes into darkness. The effect is amplified by the clouds building in the sky overhead. They were thin at first, almost wispy, but have become more substantial as the day wears on. I should turn back. Even now there's no way I'll make it home in daylight, and though I trust Lockjaw to carry me out of the mountains safely, the wilderness is often unkind to those who underestimate it.

I do not turn back.

I have no plan beyond getting to the cabin. Have not allowed myself to think beyond that point. I don't know what I will do when I get there. What I will say. I'm not even sure why I've come now. Because of Emily, of course, but—harsh as it sounds—what difference does it really make? I can't bring her back, and neither can my brother.

There's something selfish in it, I acknowledge. I miss him.

I don't see the mountain lion arrive; it is simply in front of me on the trail. Lockjaw halts abruptly, aims her ears sharply forward, and blows a lungful of air hard through her nostrils. I tighten my grip on the reins but am careful not to pull. I saw a mountain lion once before, in the hills west of Kalispell, but I was in my car then, the lion a tawny blur that flashed across the road in front of me and then was gone.

This cat has frozen mid-step, no more than three yards ahead, its gold eyes fixed unblinkingly on us, intent the way even a housecat's gaze can be, but with the honest threat of power and ruthlessness behind them. One large forepaw remains lifted. A breeze kicks up, and the mountain lion's whiskers move with it, and I see the rise of breath beneath the curve of ribs, but the animal is otherwise utterly still. Oddly, what I notice most is its tail, held in a graceful curve behind its body. There's an undeniable muscular strength even there, in something so inconsequential as its *tail*, and that is perhaps the most menacing detail of all.

Make yourself small for a bear, big for a lion. The thought comes automatically. I learned it so long ago I can't remember who taught me. Probably Samuel. I unzip my jacket with my free hand, catch the hem and raise it above my head with my dressage whip, steel myself with a deep breath, and yell, "Get on, now. Get!" I wave my arm over my head, banging the whip against the nearest tree branch, and at the same time I carefully ask Lockjaw to take a single step backward, then another. "Go on," I holler again, and suddenly the mountain lion obeys, springing off the trail in a single leap, but I feel only a split second of relief before Lockjaw rears and spins sideways. I still have my hand above my head, and I fall to the left, over Lockjaw's shoulder as her forefeet touch earth again, and then I'm on the ground and Lockjaw is galloping ahead down the trail, stirrups slapping her ribs, reins over her head, slowing only to flatten her ears and snap her jaws at the place the lion had been. I try to call to her, but the wind has been knocked out of me and all I manage is a whisper, followed by a pained wheeze. In moments the mule is out of sight.

I lie on my back for several seconds. Panic waits in the wings of my consciousness, but I evaluate the parts of my body I can feel—I'll have a bruised shoulder, and when I touch my cheek my fingers come away bloody, but not very—and then I slowly sit up and examine the parts I can't feel for unnoticed fractures or blood. I can't be sure, but I don't think I've injured anything seriously. I unbuckle my helmet, find a small but sharp dent in its side. So I've been lucky, but only to a point. The cell phone wouldn't have worked here, but now I can't even try because it's still in the saddlebag attached to Lockjaw. The water is gone, too, and the poncho. As I think it, I feel the first raindrop.

It's taken me almost three hours to ride to this point. I'm not sure how close I am to the cabin, but guess it's still at least an hour's ride away. I wish, for the first time, that the FBI people were watching me more closely, but I've gone riding in the hills so many times—and I was trying to normalize it, wasn't I, whether I fully realized it or not; I was discouraging them from following me in anticipation of this very journey—and I doubt anyone has paid much attention. They might notice I'm missing at some point—certainly after 5:00 p.m. tomorrow, when I'm to be off the property for good—but they won't know where to look. Hawkins will notice, too, but he won't know where to look, either. South Dakota, I told him.

The rain is soft but steady. I've propped myself against the nearest tree, which makes the drops less frequent but larger. I zip my coat and put my damaged helmet back on my head, but rain seeps below the coat's collar and through the helmet's vents. I'm not cold yet, but will be when it gets dark.

Feels foolish to stay here. Ought to at least try to save

myself. A pervasive thought, though I know it's wrong. I have no hope of making it either to the cabin or back home on my own; I'd exhaust myself in short order and be worse off than I am now. Even the able-bodied are told to stay put, though I imagine that works better if people are actually looking for you. I wonder if I should move to the center of the trail, out from beneath the tree, in case someone does notice I'm missing, in case they send a helicopter. I decide that's unlikely to happen anytime soon. I stay where I am.

The second time in my life I expect to die. It's more peaceful this time. I was so terrified in the closet, so panicked. Here in the woods I worry about the mountain lion coming back—I can hear the narrators of those nature shows I used to watch before Samuel destroyed the television intoning, *The predators seek out prey that is injured or infirm*—but I think it's long gone, and here, at least, there are no guns, no shots, only the steady rhythm of rain on branches and pine needles and stone. I close my eyes and listen to the rain and realize I am not frightened to be alone.

I try to quiet my mind, but it keeps turning to Emily, to Asa's insistence that there has to be a reason for what happened to his daughter. He seems to have concluded that there's someone he is meant to heal, that if that person is not, could not be, his daughter, then it must be someone else, because otherwise it's all for nothing. He wants—needs—something good to come of it all. But suppose God, or the universe, or fate, isn't so high-minded. Suppose it's simpler. Emily's death was unjustified, unjustifiable. It must be balanced. Maybe I'm the balancing weight.

I do not believe in things like that, I remind myself. There is no fate, perhaps no God.

But the thoughts do not leave me.

The sun disappeared some time earlier, but it's not yet dark. There's a break in the rain, though there looks to be more coming. Through a broken patch in the cloud cover I glimpse the bare sky. It's a deeply fading blue, like water coalescing below a steep waterfall. I pass a few minutes contemplating how I would mix the color on my palette. Cobalt blue, I decide, with a dab of titanium white and maybe a swipe of ultramarine or even violet.

The blue patch passes, the clouds come overhead, the rain returns. It's heavier now, louder, and at first the hoofsteps blend with the rainfall. *Lockjaw*, I think, when the sound becomes distinct, and I crane my neck to look down the trail but can't see her yet. I'm glad the mule hasn't become lion fodder or tumbled down the side of the mountain and broken a leg or her neck, but I can't muster relief. I might be able to reach the bottom of a stirrup, but that won't do anything but put me in a good position to get kicked. I can't get back into the saddle from the ground. Lockjaw can't save me.

And then there is another sound. More steps. Footsteps, not hoofsteps. I squint into the darkening evening, convinced I'm beginning to experience auditory hallucinations or some kind of sound-mirage. But then, moments later, he is there, just a few steps away, leading Lockjaw by the reins, rifle slung over his back, bearded and skinnier than when I last saw him, but definitely there, definitely real.

Samuel.

"I wondered if you'd come," my brother says, stopping in front of me. The words are soft, almost overcome by the rain. He crouches beside me, takes one of my wrists in his hands, bends it this way and that.

"I'd know if my wrist was broken." He drops my wrist, moves to my legs. He feels for the bones, moves toward my feet a few inches, feels again. I can't register the touch, but I see it is firm but gentle, and I think again of how he would have made a good vet. "I checked myself after I fell," I say. "I don't think I'm hurt." He nods a brief acknowledgment, but still squeezes each ankle through my boots before he stands.

"Lockjaw's okay, too," he tells me, giving the mule a single pat on the neck. "Scraped up a knee, but she's sound."

"There was a mountain lion."

"I've seen him a couple times."

I wait for Samuel to chastise me for riding so far alone, but he says nothing. Maybe he figures it's self-evident; maybe he's waiting for me to volley far more righteous anger at him over the things he's done. And during the last weeks I've thought of so many things to say to my brother, so many questions to ask, but here in the darkening wilderness they all seem too remote to speak aloud. What has already been done is so much worse than anything I can say about it; I understand that. But I also know if I put voice to my thoughts, neither I nor Samuel will ever again be able to pretend that he didn't do those things, that I didn't say those words. I know, too, that silence won't last forever. That this is delay, not avoidance, but for the moment I keep the words in check.

Samuel reaches for me, and I wrap my arms around his neck; he lifts me into the saddle. While I adjust my position and place my feet into the stirrups, he takes off the rifle, then his coat, hands the coat to me. The outer canvas is sodden and heavy, but the interior flannel lining has stayed dry, and when I put it on it's warm and I'm grateful for it. Samuel has a red plaid shirt on, and I've washed it enough to know it's near-threadbare. "There's a poncho in the saddlebag," I tell him.

He pulls it out, puts it on. Opens the water bottle, takes a long swig, passes it to me along with the granola bar. When I give the water bottle back he has my cell phone in his hand. An ordinary enough thing to have on the trail—spotty reception or not, it's foolish not to carry it; you could get lucky and have your emergency happen in line with a cell tower, after all—but I did not bring it for emergencies, I understand that now, and I see in the tightening of my brother's features that he understands it, too.

He glances at me—there and gone, a motion too quick for me to read what's in his eyes—then puts the phone in his pocket. He slings the rifle back over his shoulder, outside the poncho, then loops the reins over Lockjaw's head and hands them to me. He keeps hold of the near rein below the bit. We start toward home.

"How did you find me?" I ask.

"Lockjaw turned up at the cabin." Samuel looks over his shoulder. "You believe that? She ain't been up there in more than ten years, and I hear something in the clearing and look over and there she is, standing in that same spot where I used to picket her." He pauses, and then something almost like levity creeps into his voice. "She's practically Lassie."

I want to let the small joke hang there, pretend I'm just a sister being kidded by her big brother, nothing more. Out here in the woods, in this place where we found refuge before, it seems a viable fantasy. But the unspoken things are still there between us. "I'm selling her."

Samuel doesn't say anything, but there's a single hesitation in his step. The rain seems louder, but I don't think it's falling harder than before.

"What did you think I was going to do, Samuel?" I lift the reins and Lockjaw obediently stops; Samuel stops with her, takes a breath, turns to face me. "They're taking the house tomorrow. I don't know if I'm still getting the government's money for it or not; the deed's in your name, and I don't know what happens now that you've . . . done what you did. Even if I managed to find a piece of land to keep her on, I can't take care of her myself. I work thirty hours a week at a gas station that's closing down and your paycheck's gone; I can't afford to board her. Forget the mule; I don't even know where I'm going to sleep tomorrow night. Damn it, what did you think was going to happen?" I hear my voice rising until the last line comes out a yell, and I listen for an echo but the rain dampens the sound and nothing comes back. My pulse is going hard in my chest, I don't know whether to scream or cry, and I haven't said half of what I want to, mean to.

It would be a good moment for an apology, or at least an explanation, but I know my brother too well to expect either. Samuel puts a hand on my lower leg, but if that's intended as a comfort, it's a meaningless one. "Why did you come out here today?" he asks. "Why now?"

A sudden flash of a memory that can't possibly be my own: I'm sitting on the couch, our mother beside me, and I know bad news is coming; I'm doing everything I can to avoid hearing it: studying the embroidery on the throw pillows, talking over our mother every time she begins to speak, finally clapping my hands over my ears until she pries them away and tells me that my father is trapped in the mine. But I was only a year old. It isn't my memory. Isn't me on that couch.

"I told you," I say, and the anger has bled from me, only weariness left. "They're taking the house tomorrow."

Samuel says, "Josie." Hasn't called me that in years.

I close my eyes. See the school picture. The hospital bed. "There was a girl."

"In the church." The words a sigh. I look at him. He's wrapped an arm around Lockjaw's neck, speaks as though to the mule, his head pressed against her wet coat. "I listened to the radio those first few days."

He knows. As soon as I mentioned Emily he knew. Still I hesitate.

"Tell me."

"She's gone." I echo Asa's words. "She died."

Samuel closes his eyes, tightens his jaw the way he does if he cuts himself, waiting for that first wave of pain to rise, crest, pass. I wonder whether the pain of this will pass. Whether I should wish it to.

When I've almost decided to say his name, Samuel straightens. He doesn't look at me, but turns around and clucks to Lockjaw, leading her into a walk. He stays alongside her head, his back to me. This non-response shouldn't surprise me. How rarely has Samuel shared his feelings with me. How easily has he become someone who follows a logic I don't understand, who has been shaped by memories and worries he won't confide. This is what Samuel does. He keeps things to himself, or at least keeps them from me. He listens, analyzes, accepts, reacts, all in his head. He goes silent. Sure, sometimes he rages, repeats the talking points of whatever crackpot ideology he's most recently latched on to, but his own thoughts? His emotions? Those he doesn't share. I know this about him, have known it almost as long as I've known him, but I still expected something more from him upon learning that Emily had died. That she died because of him. That he killed her.

Part of me wants to scream it, over and over again, if necessary, louder and louder until he has to listen, has to react: *You killed a child, Samuel!*

I don't only because I already know he won't answer. Doesn't matter how loud I get, how furious I am, how distraught. He won't get angry, won't cry, won't do anything at all but keep his eyes on the trail ahead. So I gather my anger, my thoughts twisting darkly, sharp and heavy inside my head, rising and building to a new potency now that I've released them from the bonds of doubt and denial. So I cry, the tears swift and plentiful and endless, washed away by rain as soon as they fall. I get angry. I cry. Let Samuel worry about the damn trail.

"We don't have to go home," I say, some time later. I hear my voice as though it is someone else's, the voice of a sleepy child, exhausted and ready to yield to dream.

Samuel keeps walking, his stride no shorter than an hour ago, no less steady. "You want to live in the woods again?"

"We did it before. We could do it again." I might as well say, *We could go to the moon, Samuel. It doesn't seem so far away.*

True dark now. Still almost an hour back to the house, by my guess. Samuel has let go of Lockjaw's bridle and I've given the mule free rein to choose her path. Samuel walks behind us, out of kicking distance, following in the mule's tracks. He carries a flashlight but refuses to turn it on. He isn't so far back, but in the dark I can barely see him, glimpse him only in movement, the edge of a shoulder, a boot sole, a hint of a face. I keep twisting in the saddle to look for him, and every time I turn he knows, and calls, "I'm here, Jo."

Turn. "I'm here."

"I'm here."

We come to the crest of the ridgeline above the house. Samuel stops just short of the height of it, and Lockjaw stops, too. "There's probably a car by the gate." I suppose I shouldn't warn him, but it's automatic, instinct.

"There's probably more than that." Samuel looks at me. "Can you make it to the barn on your own? Put up Lockjaw?"

"Yes."

He runs a hand down Lockjaw's long face, scratches her crest behind her ears. He seems reluctant to leave the mule, and I hear the sibilant sound of him whispering to her but can't make out the words. At last he steps away, lets his hand slide off her neck like water. "I'll see you at the house." He's down the steep hill and out of sight before I can say anything.

I hear the first thunder just as I come off the mountain, a low growl in the dark over the western slopes. Lockjaw tenses beneath me, breaks into an uncomfortable jig. "Easy." I look for lightning, but there is nothing but black. The moon would be nearly full, but the clouds block it with remarkable totality; I can't even distinguish the ridgeline from the sky. Then there's a flash, distant, a burst that lights a length of cloud from within, and for an instant I see the contours of the valley, the silhouette of the mountains visible for a blink before it vanishes again. I'm prepared for the thunder when it comes, several seconds later than I guess, and Lockjaw dances but does not unseat me.

It feels good to be back in my wheelchair after so long in the saddle—and after being unceremoniously reminded of how limited I can be without it. I hurry in the barn, but still take time to rub liniment into Lockjaw's legs; it was a long ride for an old mule. I put ointment on her scraped knee, toss some extra hay into the stall, shut the rear door so she can't tear around the pasture in a repeat of the last thunderstorm, and turn off all but the exterior security lights.

I'm startled to see that the house is dark, and I wheel quickly across the creek and to the porch. The door locked. He could have come in the back, I tell myself, shoving down the panic rising in my chest. But there are no lights in the living room, the kitchen, nothing but darkness through the picture window. *I'll never find him again.* I didn't believe he'd do this. Despite everything else he's done, I never thought he'd leave me this way. I fumble for the key, find the lock, open the door. Flick on the living room light: empty. But then I hear the rush of water in the pipes, the twinning of the downpour of the upstairs shower with the rain on the roof.

Of course. I'm supposed to be alone. If anyone were watching, they would have seen me in the barn. Light in the house could have aroused suspicion. Samuel is better at this than I could ever be. I wonder if it's a trait to be proud of.

I'd like to make coffee, but the kitchen is almost empty. A single bottle of cola, warm on the counter, but Samuel doesn't drink soda. I run the tap until it's cold, fill two plastic cups, and set them on the counter. No table, either. The water shuts off upstairs. I pull the shades on the kitchen windows. I do most nights, don't I? Nothing unusual in it.

I glance around the kitchen for my cell phone. No. He'll have taken it upstairs. Nothing significant in that, necessarily. It was in his pocket. Probably forgot about it.

Creaking floorboards above. He's in his bedroom. Not a lot left there. The bed, the jeans and sweatshirt I loaned Asa. I found the clothes a few days ago in the laundry room when Hawkins hauled out the washer and dryer. Too late to donate them, so I had him put them upstairs with the other things left behind.

Samuel comes downstairs cautiously, moves quickly past

the living room—no curtains there anymore—and enters the kitchen. He carries the rifle with him, sets it in a corner. He looks more like himself. He shaved in the shower; there's a bead of blood on his jaw. His hair is longer than he likes, but he's finger-combed it into place. The jeans hang lower on his hips than before he went into the mountains for a month, but otherwise he might have come back from that trip to Wyoming he told me he was taking. The sweatshirt is in his hand, and he wears a ratty T-shirt that has faded to something less than white. The tattoo black on his skin.

Samuel sees me looking. "I'm warm," he says, "and it ain't like you don't know it's there."

I hand him one of the cups of water. "I wish you wouldn't do this."

"What?"

"Act like you've become this irredeemable person. Like you're not Samuel anymore but 'Samuel Henry Faber,' public enemy." I nod to the tattoo. It's faded a bit over the years, and the edges have blurred, but it hasn't lost its power. I still recoil from the sight of it. "You believed in that shit for like five minutes and you've been embarrassed about it ever since. Don't try to convince me you're a neo-Nazi."

"People *would* be better off keeping to their own kind."

"Ben Archer was our own kind." Familiar words. Reciting lines we long ago memorized. "I guarantee the people involved in taking this house from us are mostly 'our kind,' as you define it." He opens his mouth, but I cut him off before he can speak. "I swear to God, Samuel, if you're about to say something about 'the Jews,' I'm going straight out the front door." I hate that I have to say those words. What does it matter that he keeps his tattoo covered in public if he still voices the sentiments it represents in private? What does it matter if he's put a more rational, respectable veneer on the old radicalism? I've let him—let myself—believe it does matter, but that bomb has shown me how wrong I was.

Samuel says nothing, which is confirmation enough. But he puts the sweatshirt on.

I thought I would have so much more to say, so much more to ask. These last weeks I've wanted answers to so many questions. I wanted to know why. I wanted to know whether he was sorry. But the bomb has exploded. Emily is dead. Nothing can change that, and nothing Samuel might say about the subject can justify it. I don't want to hear him try.

Thunder, closer.

"You lose the tree in that storm a few weeks back?"

I nod. He doesn't ask who cut it up for me. Probably assumes it was Hawkins.

"It clobbered me up in the hills. Hail like you've never seen." He takes a sip of the water, sets the cup on the counter. Crosses his arms. "Didn't trust the roof on that old cabin, so I rode out the storm down the old East Shaft. I'd already been down it twice." He looks at me. "In the early days I heard helicopters a couple times. Don't know if they were for me or if they belonged to one of the logging companies or what. Didn't stick around to find out. They've got infrared on those, you know. The government."

I don't want to talk about the government with Samuel. "I thought they sealed up those old shafts."

"They did. This one's so old they sealed it with wood, not concrete. About rotted away." He shrugs. "Dad told me about it when he took me up there. Ain't even that deep. Never found the vein they sank it for, abandoned it pretty quick."

I try not to think too hard about the shaft. When I was in high school there were some weekend parties at one of the adits that had been busted open a long time ago. I was always relieved to have my wheelchair as an excuse not to go. Wasn't the parties or what went on at them that bothered me, but the dark. Lanterns and flashlights are nothing against the black of a mine, the consuming depth, the sense that such a descent might not be reversed.

"When I was down that shaft I started thinking about what if none of it happened. Not just Archer and Mom, but Dad, the mine collapse, all of it. What if none of it ever happened. Great, right? But I realized if we took it back that far, if Eden and Gethsemane never closed, I'd probably have grown up and spent my whole life down shafts like that."

"You would've still had the baseball scholarship. Or the Army." *If you hadn't given them up for me.*

"Maybe. Or maybe it would've been, 'Oh, just one summer. Just one year.' The mines aren't so easy to avoid in a town like this. I know you were too young, Jo, but I wish you could remember when Dad used to come home after his shift. He'd already showered at the locker rooms, washed the tunnels off him, but he'd come home and smile at us and try so hard to be happy, but you looked in his eyes and it was like all that dark was still clinging to him, like there was no relief in it because he knew he'd have to go right back down tomorrow." He looks at me. "I got plenty of complaints about the sawmill, Jo, but at least I can see the sun."

I watch him, but as usual can't make any sense of his solid expression, his guarded eyes. It's not like him to ruminate this way, and I'm not sure what he wants me to say. "The mines closed," I remind him. "You never had to go down them. You never will."

"I know. And I never wanted anything to happen to Dad, or Mom, or you. Never wanted to see this town die. I'm not saying I'm glad those things happened; I'm not. But if you think about changing the past, where do you stop? How far back do you go? Let's say Dad hadn't died but instead the mines wore him down and turned him mean. Or I joined up with Kev after all and was on that Humvee with him." Samuel isn't looking at me as he talks. His gaze roves across the empty kitchen, lingers over the uncovered hole he punched in the wall all those years ago, pauses at the back door Archer kicked in. "I've spent a long time thinking that everything that happened to our family was pure curse, that our lives would've been so much different—better—if all those things hadn't happened. But these last few weeks I've been thinking a lot about how we get where we are, how we become who we are. About how things lead to other things, and how they change a life."

I recognize this tone, its earnestness and urgency, its hint of mania. And I recognize the logic, too, such as it is, with its holes Samuel ignores and the connections only he sees. The particular forcefulness behind the words I hear only when he's still trying to banish doubts. This is the way he talks when he's trying on a new conspiracy theory. A new philosophy he's decided explains the world, *his* world. A new justification for beliefs and actions others condemn.

"Maybe it's just because I was down in that dark alone—you know how the dark is, Jo, how it twists your thoughts—but that day in the shaft I started thinking about whether I really should have spent so long wishing for a changed past. Whether I might've been wrong. Whether it really would have been better if all those things never happened."

It would have been better for Emily.

I think I've kept the words in my head, silent. But then I look at Samuel and see that he's gone pale, that I might as well have slapped him across the face with all the force I could muster, and I realize I've spoken aloud.

He passes a hand over his face, closes his eyes. The bead of blood smears across his jaw. Cadmium red. Stain on skin.

I have no idea what time it is. The clock packed away in the storage unit. The microwave with its glowing display, too. It's late, or, more likely, very early. I am tired, both in body and mind, and I yearn for sleep but resist. Go to sleep and it will be morning. And I do not know what morning will bring.

Samuel sits on the floor below the kitchen sink, his back against the cupboards. He turns his plastic cup of water in place on the floor beside him, like a bar patron nursing a beer he has no intention of finishing. An excuse for his presence. An excuse to stay. "How's your face?"

I look at him, confused, and he puts a hand to his cheekbone. I touch my own cheek, feel the scab forming over the scrape I got falling from Lockjaw. "Oh," I say. "It's fine."

He looks toward the dark hallway, so suddenly I think he must have heard something, and I feel my pulse accelerate. "You know Hawkins didn't kill Archer, right?"

Have Samuel and I really never spoken of it? "Of course I know," I say. "I was there."

"I know, but with the shock and all . . . I've never been sure how much you remember about that night."

"Everything." Still he stares toward the hall. "I've always known it was you, Samuel."

"Were you afraid of me?"

My brother turns toward me, and for once I can see what's in his eyes, what he's hidden from me for twelve years: the horror of what he did, and how its weight has bent and burdened him. "No," I say. "Samuel, no. I was never afraid of you. You saved me. I felt safe because of what you did. I knew you would always protect me."

He looks at me several seconds longer, as though searching my face for any betrayal of a kindhearted lie. Finally he nods. "I'm glad."

It's never occurred to me Samuel might think I was afraid of him. Surely he remembers all those nights afterward, when I couldn't fall asleep unless he guarded the entrance to my bedroom. Surely he understands that my own fears were never about him, that I managed them—even conquered them, mostly, in time—only because of him. "I know Hawkins meant well," I say, "but I wish he'd never come up with the idea of taking the"—I almost say *blame*, reject the word just in time—"credit for Archer's death. It's made you think it was shameful."

Samuel looks at me, something almost like a wistful smile crossing his lips for the briefest moment. "That wasn't Hawkins's idea," he says. "It was mine."

I almost ask why, but before I can form the question, I know the answer. Me. Samuel wasn't concerned for himself. Wasn't concerned with what people might think of him. He worried they would think it meant he couldn't care for me, that he was too damaged, maybe even too dangerous. Suddenly I'm angry with Hawkins. I can picture my brother making the proposal, maybe that night, maybe sometime the next day. Samuel could have done that, could have ordered his thoughts even in those moments, seen the coming days and weeks and months, anticipated the thoughts and judgments of the counselors and social workers: *trauma, damage, responsibility, anger, rage*. It would have been framed as being for our own good. Hell, maybe it *would* have been for our own good—I cringe at the thought, but force myself to acknowledge it—maybe Samuel and I would have been better off if we had been separated. Samuel, at least, might have been better off if he had been allowed to process what he had done, grieve, recover. Leave my care and problems to someone professional, someone more equipped to deal with them. Move on with his life. And if I can see all that now, why wasn't Hawkins able to see it then? Why did he allow himself to be talked into a cover-up by a traumatized teenager? And I know the answer to that, too: guilt that he didn't get there in time to stop Archer, to save Samuel from having to do it himself.

"Don't be angry with Hawkins," Samuel says. I scowl at him. Unfair that he can read me so easily, when I so rarely know what thoughts pass through his head.

"It wasn't necessary," I say. "It was self-defense."

"The first hit knocked him down," Samuel says. "The second knocked him out. The third killed him. I hit him twelve times after that."

More than a dozen times, Devin said.

"People would have understood," I insist. Hear the doubt in my own words.

Lightning again, bright enough to wash the room white, the thunder coming while the memory of the flash still burns my eyes. The kitchen lights flicker, die. I feel my breath catch, force it back to its regular rhythm. *Only the dark.*

Samuel turns on his flashlight, sets it upturned on the floor beside him. It casts a distorted circle on the ceiling, reflects enough light into the room to bring us both out of the shadows. "Thank you," I say, and Samuel nods.

"Battery won't last," he warns.

More thunder. I look at Samuel, to see if the sound still troubles him the way the dark troubles me. But he doesn't move, his face still as a portrait, and if the thunder makes him feel anything at all, it doesn't show.

He is not like Archer. Archer was evil.

"Jo?"

"What is it, Samuel?" Already the light in the kitchen has begun to dim.

"Are you afraid of me now?"

I watch the filament as the light fades, see the glowing wire soften from a hot yellow to a brilliant orange to something closer to the color of cooling embers. The darkness encroaches again.

I let the silence stretch until it has lasted so long no answer I could give would matter.

I don't remember nodding off, but then Samuel is waking me, and I'm slumped in my chair. Still dark. "Go to bed," Samuel says. "I'll still be here in the morning."

I stifle the urge to ask him to promise. If he says it, he means it. I was able to trust that before the bombing. Now I won't be able to trust him whether he promises or not.

"Does the flashlight have anything left?"

Samuel switches it on; it glows weakly. Off again. "Might get a minute or two out of it." He hands it to me.

I move down the dark hallway to the bedroom. The cloud cover heavily veils any moonlight there might be, and with the security lights out along with the rest of the electricity, I see nothing through the uncovered windows. Too dark even for shadows. I close the curtains anyway, then transfer to the bed. Don't bother undressing, just stretch out atop the quilt. My eyelids already dropping. "Samuel?"

I hear his footsteps in the hall, and then he's in the doorway. His gaze lands on the painting of the house, propped on an easel near the window. He crosses the room, bends to look closely at it, though it's so dark I doubt he can make out much. "Is this blood?"

It's such a startling question I gasp, try to cover it with a scoff. "Of course not."

"Looks like it."

"It's earth," I insist. "Soil from the meadow. Ore from the mines. Water from the creek. Ash and earth. Ash and Eden."

Samuel continues to stare at the canvas, raises two fingers as though to touch it, skims them through the air a millimeter or two over the painting. "You think about all that's happened in this place," he says, "and you realize maybe blood and earth aren't so different."

I don't particularly want to consider the possibility. It sounds thoughtful, to some extent, but also a bit unhinged. "Just dirt, really."

He straightens, starts toward the door.

"Samuel," I say again. He stops, and I remind myself that I vowed not to ask. That it won't matter if I do.

"I'll be here," he says softly. "I promise."

He goes upstairs. I take the flashlight off the table, clutch it in my fist. I'm tempted to turn it back on, let it provide enough dying glow that I might fall asleep—if I can sleep until the sun comes up, who cares if the flashlight burns itself out for good in the night?—but I don't trust myself not to wake in the dark, so I hold it tightly, hold tightly to its promise, and let exhaustion do its work.

The usual nightmare wakes me: sounds in the darkness, shots, footsteps, strikes. I open my eyes to the blackness of night, fumble for the flashlight, hear it clatter to the floor. I try to catch my breath. No way to know how much time has passed, but it can't have been long. The previous day seems like a dream itself: the mountain lion in the woods, Samuel finding me, talking in the kitchen. I scan the floor, trying to make out the flashlight, but there is nothing.

I am trying to decide whether to call for Samuel when I hear his step on the floorboards. I almost don't believe he's really here—a dream after all—until I see his form in the doorway. There is something both comforting and unsettling in his knowing to come before I called. He doesn't ask what woke me—I never told him about my dreams, even as a child, though of course he must have guessed what they contained—just says, "Upstairs?"

He wraps me in my quilt, carries me easily up the stairs, sets me gently on the bed in my old room. "I'll get your chair." It doesn't seem to have surprised him that I've had a nightmare this night, and I wonder if he thought about it while he was at the cabin, if he knew I would have nightmares and be left to weather them alone.

Samuel comes back upstairs, sets my chair beside the bed. "Found this," he says, and presses the flashlight into my hands. "Careful if you use it. I know it's dim, but anyone sees it is gonna wonder how you got up here by yourself."

I look out the window. There's the barest hint of dawn in the southeast, a thin band of gray encroaching on the black. "I'll be okay." I put a hand to my cheek, feel the dried tears there. "I need to wash my face."

I move to my chair, go down the short hall to the upstairs bathroom, mindful of the open top of the staircase. I close the door behind me—there are no windows in this bathroom, so the darkness seems more ordinary here, less threatening—and turn on the tap. The water is cool, and I feel my head clearing as I splash it on my face. I turn my chair back toward the door, feel the tire catch on something.

Samuel's clothes on the floor. I pick them up automatically—he the slob, I the neatnik, a dynamic unchanged since childhood—and as I fold his jeans, my cell phone falls from one of the pockets into my lap. I pick it up, glance involuntarily toward the door. Part of me thinks it might be a trap, a test, though that isn't like him. And besides, Samuel didn't expect me to be upstairs. Did he? I should be relieved to have the phone back, but realize instead that I've been relieved to have it out of my possession, to have a reprieve from the responsibility it brings. I cup a hand over the screen to minimize the glow, touch the power button, not sure whether to hope for the battery to be drained or not. The screen lights up.

Seconds to decide. Though that's not really true, is it? I've had more than a month. Every day I let pass I didn't ride over the ridge was a decision. Every time I didn't tell Hawkins about the cabin was a decision. And I know I could put the clothes back on the floor. I could pretend I didn't find the phone. But I can't pretend that wouldn't be a decision, too.

Hawkins keeps his cell off at night—*Dispatch knows how to reach me at home,*he says—turns it on at 9:00 a.m. and not a minute before. I type quickly. When I'm done I let my thumb hover over the delete button, but I made this final decision when I rode into the mountains, didn't I? I made this final decision the minute Asa told me Emily was gone. I give myself a moment more to change my mind, then press send.

He is here.

———

I wake to knocking on the front door. Glance at the bedroom doorway: empty. Samuel was there when I fell asleep, propped against the hallway wall, eyes closed, breathing even, one hand cradled in his lap, the other resting on the rifle beside him. I thought he was asleep but couldn't be sure. For the first time, the familiar sight made me uneasy, and I hadn't meant to let myself sleep.

I hear the knocking again, and I remember the text message

I sent in the night, and I see that it's morning, and I hadn't meant to sleep and it's too soon and I'm not ready. "Samuel," I call, but the name comes out more quietly than I intend and instead of calling again I transfer to my chair. I make it to the landing in time to see Samuel crossing the living room on the first floor, rifle still in his hand. "Samuel, no," I say, and I know he hears this time but he ignores me. Hawkins will know he'll have the rifle, right? Hawkins knows him well enough to expect that. But suppose it isn't Hawkins, suppose it's Devin or some faceless, anonymous SWAT-type people, but they wouldn't knock, would they, so it has to be Hawkins.

Samuel pulls open the front door without even a pause to peer through the peephole—is he so eager for confrontation?— the rifle at a forty-five-degree angle, aimed toward neither the floor nor the person at the door. And Asa stands there on the porch. My impulse is to go to him, but I stop myself with my tires inches shy of the top step, feel the frustration build to something like a growl deep in my throat. I watch Asa blink, stare at my brother. He is very still, like a mouse frozen beneath the gaze of a cat, or perhaps like a cat that has spotted a mouse; he seems poised between retreat and attack, fear and fury equally plain on his face. I can't see Samuel's features, but I see the tension sharpen his shoulders, and before Asa can make his decision, Samuel lunges forward and grabs him by the collar, pulls him into the house, kicks the door shut, raises the rifle.

"No!" I am startled to hear the word come out not as plea but command. Startled again to see my brother obey me. The rifle lowers only a couple inches at first, and then he lets its muzzle drop toward the floor.

I try another command. "Let him go," I say. "Just let him go, Samuel."

He hesitates, considering it, maybe, then shakes his head.

"Your phone," he says, and holds his free hand out. Asa reaches into his pocket, surrenders the device. "Upstairs," my brother orders. His demeanor disconcerts me—how gently he'd said the same word last night after I woke from my nightmare—but Asa seems to expect it.

When Asa reaches the landing he doesn't meet my eyes. Hardly looks at me at all, except to step around my chair. He turns carefully to Samuel, who nods toward my room. I follow the two men. "Stay," Samuel orders, and the word seems directed to both me and Asa. He leaves the room, and I hear his tread on the stairs, the front door locking, shutters being yanked shut.

Asa stands in the center of the room, his expression still and unreadable. He looks oddly rested, and I wonder whether he's finally slept now that he has no one to stay awake for, or if his grief has stripped the exhaustion out of him, so thoroughly transformed him he's transcended any yearning for rest. He clutches something small in one hand: the plastic palomino. He sets it on the bedside table. "I wanted to bring this back."

I almost tell him he didn't need to do that, but of course he knows that already; it was an excuse, a reason to come see me. I realize in that moment that this man has become a friend. That in these strangest, harshest circumstances I have made a friend. Or might have, were it not for Samuel. "I found him yesterday," I say. "I told him about Emily."

Asa closes his eyes, not quite a wince, something deeper.

"I didn't know where he was before," I say. "I promise I didn't. I tried not to. And I didn't know for sure until I found him. Or he found me. I didn't—"

"It's okay, Jo." It's a reflexive sort of forgiveness, and it means nothing.

"I went because of Emily," I say, and that sounds true, finally, and he looks at me for a long moment and then nods.

Samuel comes back up the stairs, his boots hitting hard on each riser, purposeful but not rushed. He goes first into his room, latches the shutters, comes back into my room and does the same. Dark again. Samuel sets a glass-sheathed votive on the table beside the palomino—his eyes glide over the model like it's nothing—and lights the candle with a match. "Found this under the bathroom sink," he says. "There's one more, but that's it, Jo. Sorry it's not brighter."

"I'm fine." I'm not. I feel the panic of the darkness pressing in already, and knowing there's daylight beyond these walls barely helps. My father died in daylight hours, and the sun was hidden from him as surely as it is from me now. The room is as airless as the closet was, as close. But I can't say any of that in front of Asa. What's the absence of light compared to the absence he endures?

Samuel faces Asa. Wrecked as he is, Asa still carries himself with the upright authority and presence I first noticed at the prayer service. But it's a quiet authority, gentle, and that hardly seems enough now. My brother is a head shorter than Asa, but he stands with his feet apart and shoulders squared, giving the impression he is simultaneously grounded and coiled. I don't like to think it, but it's a predatory stance, and even without the rifle, Samuel would be the more imposing of the two. "You are?"

Asa looks him up and down. He must be trying to align what I told him, what he read in the newspapers, with the person standing before him. Is Samuel as Asa imagined him? Does he see the answers he's searched for in Samuel's eyes? "Asa Truth." I expect him to offer his name tentatively, but he almost seems to savor it, carving the syllables sharply.

"The pastor." Samuel waits for Asa's nod. And then he shifts his grip to the center of the rifle, holds it at arm's length, horizontally, so it hovers there between the two men, pointed at neither, ready to be plucked from his hand. Its strap swings beneath it, the only movement in the room.

Asa looks at the rifle, at Samuel, at the rifle again. I think he understands Samuel's offer—Samuel's challenge—a moment before I do. He blinks but doesn't betray his thoughts with his features. Then I understand, and before I can gasp or object or plead I see Asa's right hand flex. See the impulse. The yearning.

I can't even blame him. I'm furious with Samuel, not Asa; what right does my brother have to lay his life before another this way? Maybe he thinks Asa won't take the rifle because he's a pastor, but Samuel wasn't there when Asa cried for his daughter. He hasn't watched him be whittled down by diminishing hope and grief. He doesn't realize what temptation he's placed before the other man. Or maybe Samuel thinks Asa *will* take the rifle; that's worse. Does Samuel believe that's atonement? Does he think it's that easy, that simple? He knows what it would do to Asa to take a life. He knows what he's offering isn't peace.

Words feel dangerous, as though they might entice a finger to curl around a trigger. I can see what Asa wants, feel how much he wants it. What would lead Asa from this temptation? An appeal to his daughter's memory? To his God? Either could backfire. Either could release him from the control I see him battling to hold on to. Does he care enough about me that he'd listen if I begged him not to make me watch my brother die?

I don't think I move, but Asa glances at me then, meets my eyes for the first time. If the pain and fire in his own soften, I don't see it, but he looks back at Samuel and after several more seconds—long seconds—relaxes his hand. He takes a single step backward and shakes his head ever so slightly, and with a grimace, like the movement causes him pain.

Samuel drops the rifle to his side. I study his face for relief, anger, contempt, see none of those. His features are closed, set into an expression I've become regrettably familiar with over the years. It looks hard, steely, but I know it shields doubt. It's the expression he wears when he's made a decision I disagree with, when he expects to have to fight for something he doesn't entirely believe in himself.

I move my chair toward him. "Samuel," I say. Wait until he looks at me. "You should let him go."

"You know I can't." His voice is soft, almost tender. The voice of an adult denying the impossible, innocently fanciful request of a child.

"There's no reason to make him stay." I take a breath, meet his eyes. "Samuel, I told Hawkins you're here."

"I know." My stomach lurches, and then again when I realize it's from fear, that I'm afraid of my own brother. Of Samuel. "I found the phone last night."

He might be saying, *I found these candles. I found some granola bars.* Like it doesn't matter. Like he isn't angry. But I don't trust that tone, the calm it implies. Can't. I didn't know about the bomb. Don't know what he's going to do now, next. "Why didn't you leave?" I ask. "If you knew, why are you still here?"

"Because I told you I'd be here in the morning," he says. "I promised."

A little while later a phone rings, and Samuel pulls it out of his pocket: mine. He squints at the screen, holds it toward me: just a number, no name. "Will Devin," I tell him. Never wanted to put his name into the phone, make it seem like a permanent relationship. "He's FBI."

Samuel taps the answer key, says, "This is Samuel Faber. I have my sister and the preacher with me." Hangs up without listening for a response.

I wonder what Devin makes of that, if being hung up on angers or concerns him. Maybe it just fits the profile. I wish I knew whether he's in charge now, or if they call in someone else for situations like this. I can't say I like Devin, and I worry about him making a miscalculation with Samuel like he made when he threatened to charge me, but he is at least familiar.

Asa doesn't seem to have paid any attention to the phone call. He's taken a seat on the edge of my bed, elbows on his knees. I wonder if he regrets refusing the rifle; his eyes are on it. I notice his shirt is studded with fading damp spots, and I listen and hear the rain again. Asa glances at Samuel, looks away when he sees my brother watching him.

"What's the plan here, Samuel?" I try to keep the words casual, but the situation makes the lightness in my voice sound like a lie.

He hesitates, a pause so slight I doubt Asa will notice it. "They have no right to take this house."

"That's not even a losing battle, Samuel; it's lost."

"You don't have anywhere to go."

"There are lots of places to go." The phone rings again, and I wait, but Samuel ignores it. I try to figure out how to handle this. Usually my brother is the one insisting there's always another plan, always more to be done. The one asserting facts must be faced, solutions found. It worries me to hear him mired in these stale concerns. "Hawkins is leaving town. Offered his house to me for a song."

"You're going to live on thirty hours a week at Fuel Stop."

I take care to keep my expression and voice calm. "It's closing. I told you that."

His hand tight around the rifle. Something in his eyes that will look cold to Asa but looks desperate to me. Just as dangerous. A chill centers itself in my chest, spreads outward. Surely Samuel knows I can take care of myself; he's the one who taught me how. But what did he say when I asked about his plan? He had no real answer. Just a grievance. There's no good way out of this situation, and that means it isn't safe to be in this situation with him. It's never occurred to me before today that he might hurt me. He's spent his entire life protecting me; it seems unfathomable he could become the danger. But if he feels there are no options. If he feels leaving me alone is the worst thing he could do.

"I'll find something else," I tell him. Try not to rush the words. To sound afraid. "Or if I don't I'll go to Split Creek. Maybe Elk Fork. Martha asked if I'd teach a class at the art supply shop a couple times a week. My last painting sold for more than I earn at Fuel Stop in a month. And a gallery in Whitefish offered me a show." I don't tell him I turned it down, or why. "I'll be okay, Samuel."

"You don't need me." Challenge more than question. Here a new danger. Abandon me, reject me. Lose himself along the way.

"You're her family," Asa says quietly. "Of course she needs you."

The phone rings again, and Samuel lets it. He stares at Asa, and I fervently wish my brother's face would soften, even break, that he would apologize for what he has done, or if not apologize at least acknowledge. I wish I could take his desperation and reshape it into regret, sorrow, grief. All the things one should feel when one has caused a child's death. It would hurt him—he deserves to have it hurt him—but it would be better than this hard-edged despair. But I can't compel him to apologize, and even if I could, I couldn't make it mean anything. I can't force him to feel what he doesn't feel.

He's still looking at Asa, and this time the other man doesn't look away. "Do you still believe in God, Preacher?" It could have been a goading question, but it comes out genuine. Almost gentle, had the words issued from someone else's lips.

"I don't know." A bewildered, brutal honesty.

The phone again. Samuel taps it. Silence.

"I think it's easy to believe when life is comfortable," Samuel says. "It was easy when I was young. Even after our father died—Jo was too young to remember, but I was eight, and that's a hard age for a boy to lose his father—it still seemed possible. You expect to lose your parents. Not so early, but it doesn't upset the order of things." I think of Asa's mother, her illness, the father it left him with. "He died in the mines. There was hope they might be alive at first. A rescue mission that went on too long, a second collapse, a couple rescuers dead. They had to give up then. And as I got older I started thinking about all that time we were hoping, because I came to understand that while I was hoping, my father was dying. Maybe he was dead already, maybe he died in the collapse, but he might have been trapped and waiting, and I wonder when he realized no one was coming. At the memorial service the pastor said God had been with the men. That he had waited with them, comforted them. It was a nice idea, one I clung to for a long time. But then Ben Archer killed my mother and there was no time for God to be with her. There were only a few seconds of terror and then she was dead. And there was no time for God to comfort me, because Archer had shot my sister and was going to kill her unless I killed him first, so I did." He pauses, and I see his eyes flick toward the door, the hall, all that lies below. So quick I almost miss it. His gaze already back on Asa. "And it's not just us, is it? There are people who have suffered worse and suffered longer, and they're not rare. I'm not an idiot, Preacher. I didn't throw away faith on a whim. But—"

"But you don't understand how a loving Father could allow such things to happen to His children if He had the power to spare them." Asa recites the words as though they are as familiar to him as scripture. He clasps his hands, leans over his knees in a stance I would say looked like prayer if he didn't seem so crushed beneath a weight I cannot see. "And so you decided there is no loving Father."

Samuel tugs at the cuffs of his shirt. A nervous gesture I remember from childhood. "If you care to change my mind."

A long silence. Long enough I think maybe this is it, maybe this is the moment it will be okay. Maybe this is when Asa will reach out, and Samuel will reach back, and things will work out, somehow.

"A month ago I might have tried," Asa says at last. He looks toward the shuttered window, stares at it as though he can see what lies beyond. "Now I don't know what you think I have left to offer."

I've been hearing sirens all morning, and vehicles crunching gravel near the house, and now the unmistakable chop of a helicopter, the sound of its rotors rebounding off the mountain slopes.

"You should talk to them," I say, when the phone rings again. Asa's had started ringing, too, and Samuel shut it off, but he's left mine on. "At least talk to Hawkins. Tell them you'll only speak to him. That's what I did."

Samuel glances at me, something like approval crossing his face for the briefest moment. "What would I say?"

"I don't think it really matters, as long as you say something." I pause, weigh the urgency of the situation against that frightening desperation. "They're not going to wait forever."

"I thought they'd have used tear gas or something by now." A contribution from Asa. I'm relieved to hear it; in the hours since his conversation with Samuel, he's remained hunched on the edge of my bed, head bowed.

"They won't want to use gas with Jo in here if they can help it." I frown at my brother. Hate to think he planned on taking advantage of the fact that they'll worry about my inability to walk and whether my injury has compromised my lung function. "Also," he adds plainly, casting a glance at Asa, "they're afraid I'll shoot you." Asa doesn't react.

I want again to ask Samuel how he thinks this can possibly end, but bite back the words. No good will come of highlighting the circumstances. "Is this what you wanted?" I ask instead. The words could sound like a challenge, but I think he'll hear that the question is sincere.

"I wanted them to leave us alone," Samuel says, but then he shakes his head, closes his eyes. I glance at the rifle, but his hand is still closed tightly over the stock. He sits silently for several seconds. "I wanted . . ." Eyes still shut. The phone again, muted before it finishes sounding a single ring. Another several seconds. They slide by more slowly than usual, and I have time to notice the things that usually slip by too quickly on ordinary days: the way Samuel's eyes move feverishly beneath their fragile lids; the hard arch of the tendons in his neck; the color of a candle flame, *colors*, really, because like all light it contains all of them at once; the groan of the building wind against the eaves, the way it sounds just as I once imagined ghosts did.

I wait. Listen to the rain on the roof. Wait some more. After a while Samuel opens his eyes, but he keeps them cast toward the floor. He does not speak.

I tell him to go downstairs to my room. I tell him there is a painting there, on paper, not canvas. Not the house, another one. Smaller. I tell him to bring it here.

Samuel looks closely at me—I've never been the type to give

commands, always more willing to discuss, to edge into a topic sideways—but he stands. Stares hard at Asa. "You're going to stay." Asa nods, a single dip of his head.

"Thank you for not taking the rifle when he offered," I say quietly, when he has gone.

"I wanted to."

"I know you did." The candle on the table hasn't burned down as much as I would have guessed. Not so much time gone by as it seems. Those slow seconds again. I feel a sudden impulse to push it over, let its flames lick at the bedding, the curtains, consume the room. Burn the house and settle it once and for all. It seems a melodramatic thought even in these circumstances, and I let the candle be. "I think he would have let you."

Asa pushes both hands through his hair but doesn't say anything.

Samuel's footsteps come back along the downstairs hall. He was a long time in my room, and hardly anything in it. The painting stopped him, then.

He appears in the doorway. He's slung the rifle over his shoulder again, cradles the sheet of paper in his upturned palms. He looks at me first. "It's for Asa," I tell him.

Samuel presents the painting to him carefully, still balanced flat on his hands. I almost tell him he doesn't need to be so careful; it's heavyweight paper, the pigment safe beneath a fixative, but of course it isn't the painting itself he regards as fragile, but its subject. Asa takes the sheet, his hands folding possessively around its edges. He tips it toward himself so Samuel and I can't see it. I watch as he studies the portrait I painted of his daughter. The way his own eyes soften when he looks at hers, the way his mouth so briefly curves to match her smile.

He angles the paper toward the candle, holds it at a protective distance that would be safe for its living subject. She is happy in the portrait, because I could not give her to her father any other way, but there are shadows in the painting, too, the shadows I've learned can't be denied if they are to cast the light into brightest relief. I painted it after the hospital, after he wanted me to *see* her. I wanted to show him I had.

And I wanted Samuel to see what he had not been there to see. I wanted him to look upon that which I witnessed on his behalf.

"Created from mud," Asa says at last, lowering the paper.

I hear the wonder in his voice, hear it break through the numbness and grief and fury, for just a moment. I used soil from the base of the fallen tree, water from the rain barrel. Mud made from the dust of the earth, blended and brought to life with the water of the heavens. "From Eden," I tell him, because whatever crisis of faith he might be experiencing, I think it will still matter to him.

He mouths the words after me.

Hardly ever rains like this here. Usually it's a downpour that lasts five minutes, ten at most, or maybe a slow drizzle that peters out over the course of a few hours. Must be a chain of those spring storms, one after another rolling in off the solid ocean of the western slopes. The wind has kicked up again, pushing more thunderclouds through the valley, and rain comes against the side of the house in waves, steady most of the time but then suddenly battering before backing off again.

The people outside have a bullhorn, and every so often they call Samuel's name, ask him to answer the phone, pick it up, just for a minute. Twice they call my name—they call me Josephine the first time, Jo the second, and I wonder who corrected them, Devin or Hawkins—and once Asa's.

Every second that passes seems to carry weight, and the

weight builds with the elapsed minutes and hours to a mounting pressure I'm finding harder and harder to bear. Part of it's the uncertainty, yes, and the worry, but part of it's the odd pairing of tension and tedium, waiting in this dark room listening to wind and rain, to the audible breaths of Samuel and Asa.

The phone rings again, and Samuel glances at the screen. "Says it's Hawkins," he announces. Holds the phone in my direction, but offers no further instructions. I take my cell from him, my hands shaking. Hunger, probably. Or adrenaline. Adrenaline doesn't have to mean fear. I glance once more at Samuel, who is seated on the floor against the opposite wall—his expression doesn't change—and accept the call. "Hawkins?"

I thought it might be someone else using Hawkins's phone, but it's him. "Jo? Thank God." I feel a rush of relief at hearing Hawkins's voice. I'm so glad someone who knows Samuel is on the other side of these walls. "What's going on in there?"

"We're fine." *Fine.* An insipid enough word even in casual conversation, and virtually meaningless here, but it seems less inflammatory than *None of us are dead.* Hawkins won't be the only one listening.

"Truth is there with you? He's fine, too?"

"Yes, Asa's here," I say, glancing at him. "Asa, I told you about Hawkins; say hi." My own voice sounds strange to my ears, like that of a mother coaxing a child to speak to Grandma and Grandpa.

I hold the phone up, and Asa leans toward it and says, "I'm here. I'm . . . fine."

I put the phone back to my ear. "Someone needs to feed Lockjaw."

"I fed her," Hawkins says, and I can't tell if he's exasperated or amused by my thinking about the mule at a time like this. "Think Samuel would maybe let Truth go? That would really help. Calm these guys down out here, you know? You all have been in there awhile and they're getting kind of antsy." He's kept his tone casual, but I hear the warning beneath the words.

I keep the phone at my ear, look at Samuel. "They want you to let Asa go. You really should, Samuel. I'll stay with you."

He shakes his head.

"I know you don't want to, but I'd really—"

He shifts his hand forward on the rifle's stock.

"I don't think that's gonna work right now," I tell Hawkins, as steadily as I can manage. "We need maybe a little more time." God, I wish there were a script for this. All I want is to not make it worse.

"Damn it, Samuel." Hawkins sighs hard. "Look, the FBI has a guy here who wants to talk to Samuel. A negotiator. He ought to talk to him. They know how to handle these things."

I look at Samuel again. "They want you to talk to the FBI negotiator."

Again he shakes his head.

"He doesn't want to, Hawkins."

There's a long silence on the line, and for a minute I think Hawkins is handing the phone to someone else, but then he speaks again, louder than before, and there's a clarity to his voice I haven't heard in a long time, an iron intensity I'd forgotten. "You tell Samuel I'm doing my best out here, Jo. And he'd better believe it's a fight to get these folks to listen to me. He don't got a lot of friends out here, okay? You tell him I know I wasn't there when he needed me, once. But I'm here now. I'm trying real hard, and I'd sure appreciate it if he didn't muck it up any more than he already has. So you tell him all that and then you ask him right now: Will he talk to me?"

I cup a hand over the phone's mic. "Hawkins says—"

"I heard him." But he doesn't reach for the phone.

"Please talk to him, Samuel." He watches me. Says nothing.

But doesn't shake his head, either. "That first day . . . the day of the bomb—" I look quickly at Asa, but he doesn't flinch. "The FBI man, Devin, he came to the house and asked me what was the one thing he should know about you. One thing. Do you know what I said?"

Samuel's gaze is steady.

"I said you would do anything for me." And nothing changes on his face, nothing shifts in his expression, but still he is listening. "Was I right, Samuel?" I hold the phone out to him. "Will you do this for me?"

At first my brother doesn't move. Doesn't speak, doesn't nod. And I start to think I have gotten it wrong, and if I have gotten it wrong then I have nothing else to say, no other appeals, no more gambits. Then he pushes himself off the floor. Extends his hand. The wind rises up again; the rain slaps the house. He takes a step toward me. The shutter, the damned broken shutter, flies open and flattens itself against the outside of the house with a crack like a gunshot. And then Samuel is back against the wall—I hardly saw him move—and he slides back to the floor and his hand is at his chest and there is blood, blood on the wall and blood on his shirt and blood spilling over his hand and through his fingers.

So much blood. So fast.

I don't scream. The air has stilled itself in my lungs, frozen in my windpipe, no movement, no inhale or exhale. There is light in the room now, and I see the window glass shattered on the bed and Asa ducking with a hand over his head and his eyes wide and his mouth moving—*He's saying something; why don't I hear him?*—and the colors all seem leached to gray except the red, the blood.

Samuel looks at his red-slicked hand, blinks, grimaces. He

ungrits his teeth, opens his mouth, starts to say something but it comes out a grunt—I don't hear that, either, but I see the shape of the pain—and he sucks in air and it seems to remind me how to breathe, too, and when he opens his mouth again I hear the words. "Close the shutter."

Asa looks at him, only looks—what must he see in this blood?—and Samuel lunges for the rifle with his free hand, lifts it so its muzzle stares at Asa. "Do it."

"Don't," I say, but I don't have the rifle, so Asa rises carefully, leans across the bed, moves in slow motion. I think of those stories Samuel has told me about other standoffs, about the wrong people being shot because federal law enforcement doesn't care about citizens. But Asa reaches through the shattered window for the broken shutter with one hand, keeps his other open, raised—he must have learned it from television, must hope that what works in prime time will work here—and he draws it closed, latches it as well as it can be latched.

The candle has blown out, and the brief wash of daylight has ruined my eyes for the dark.

"I meant to fix that," Samuel says, a pause between every other word. "God, it hurts worse than before, Jo."

He has something to compare it to. The old scar is halfway down his side, but Archer's bullet tore only flesh, and did so cleanly; this bullet has struck more solidly. I get out of my chair, onto the floor, pull myself to the wall beside my brother. I move his hand away from his chest—it isn't quite his chest, I realize, but his shoulder, below his left collarbone—and I feel the slickness of blood, yes, but also the movement of it, the flow of it over my hands as his heart ushers it from his body.

"Here." Asa's voice, a bundle of cloth pressed into my hand. His shirt. I press it hard to Samuel's wound, hear the choke of a suppressed groan. My eyes have started to adjust, and I can make out shapes, lights and darks. See the stain spreading in the fabric beneath my hand. I try to remember what Samuel said when he found me in the closet afterward. "It's okay," I say, but that's not quite right. "*You're* okay. You're okay. You're okay." I know now the words were as much for him as me.

The cell phone rings again, and I reach for it but Samuel snatches it first. Puts it to his ear, growls, "I'm not dead," and hangs up. Throws the device into the hall; it skids on the hardwood and clatters down the stairs. I hear it ring again from somewhere in the living room, distance rendering the chiming melody weak and forlorn.

"That's too much blood," Asa says hollowly. He would know.

"We have to go, Samuel. We have to get you out of here." He shakes his head, and I expected nothing less.

"Not as bad as it looks," he insists. Would be more convincing if he didn't need a new breath for each word. If I didn't feel the shirt go soft and sodden beneath my palm.

"You need a doctor," I say. "A doctor can fix you."

Samuel laughs, short and ugly. "Fix me for what, Jo?"

He's let his hand slip off the rifle. I reach for it; he grabs my wrist before I get close. "No," he says. Firm, sharp. I would have thought his grip would be weak, but I can't pull free. Get my hand back only when he lets me go.

And still the blood.

I glance at Asa; he's looking at the burned-out candle, the blackened wick. His jaw is taut, his hands clasped so firmly the knuckles have gone white. "It's him," I say.

Asa turns to me. I can see his eyes just well enough to know he already understands what I mean.

"It's him," I say again. "It's Samuel. He's the one you heal."

"He's not." The words a whisper.

Samuel watching us, bewildered.

"He's *not*," Asa repeats, louder this time, a fire kindling beneath the words.

"Please, Asa. Try. You can heal him. You've done it before; you told me."

Asa looks at me, his hands, Samuel. "I was wrong," he says. "I was a kid. I remembered it wrong."

"Jo." Samuel, looking at me like I'm the one on the edge of delirium. "The hell?"

"Asa's a healer," I say, hearing the desperation in the words. I know how this must sound to Samuel, so I chase all traces of skepticism from my voice, channel the calm certainty I heard in Asa's words the day he told me the story. "He lays on hands. He healed a boy once who was worse off than you." I say it like I was there. Like I believe it.

"It can't be him," Asa insists. Rises to his feet in an instant, looms above us both. A solidity in his voice I've only heard hints of before, an unyielding strength that's new. Takes me a moment to realize it's fury, so hot I don't feel it at first. "If I couldn't heal Em, he can't expect me to heal him." At first I think he means Samuel can't expect Asa to heal him. But then he says it again—screams it, spittle flying with the words—*He can't expect me to heal him*—and I hear the capital *H*, understand that this is anger not only at my brother. Asa's hand lunges out, sweeps the useless lamp from the bedside table; it crashes to the floor, its porcelain pieces mixing with the shards of window glass. He paces through the mess and the slivers shatter under his feet. This sudden rage is without lull; Asa ruins whatever he can reach with strangely fluid movements, like a violent but rehearsed dance. He takes the candle in his hand, throws it to the floor. Pulls the drawer from the table and dashes it against the wall; wood splinters.

Samuel's hand closes around the rifle again.

Asa scans the room for more; there's little left. He spots the plastic palomino, lifts it from the table and hurls it toward the floor in one furious gesture. A leg breaks, and one ear snaps off, skitters across the hardwood.

Samuel draws the rifle onto his lap, moves his finger to the trigger.

As suddenly as he started, Asa stops. He doesn't look at Samuel. Doesn't move. Doesn't speak. There are no more angry words. No raging at God. No heaving chest. Nothing. He stands silently over the little yellow horse, head bowed, staring down at a broken toy his daughter never played with, never saw.

And then he falls to his knees at my brother's side. Raises his hands before him. No longer in fists but open, fingertips up, palms out. He meets Samuel's eyes once, for only an instant, and closes his own.

I take my hand from Samuel's shoulder, reluctant to pull away the soaked shirt, to let blood spill unimpeded, but I expect Asa will need to reach the wound.

But he ignores the blood, the bullet. He lays one hand on Samuel's forehead, gently, like a mother comforting a feverish child, rests the other on his chest, over his heart. His lips move but he does not speak, not aloud. Samuel has closed his eyes; I watch to see that he still breathes.

Time passes, but very little of it. Seconds only. Asa takes his hands away, the one that touched Samuel's chest now stained red. He lets out a slow breath, rocks back on his heels, opens his eyes. There is weariness in the slump of his shoulders.

It seems too quick. I lean closer to Samuel, squint in the dark. What do I expect? A miracle I've insisted over and over again I don't believe in? A magical stanching of blood, a knitting of flesh? Foolishness. Desperation. But I watch, wait. Even offer a short, awkward silent prayer of my own, a frantic *Please* issued to a deity I doubt is there. But I see no change. The hole still there in my brother's shoulder, his blood still seeping from it raw and bright. I press the wadded shirt back over the wound, angry with myself for asking Asa to do this, angry with him for failing. Angry with myself for wanting to believe it might work.

Samuel's eyes are still closed. He sighs heavily, such a release in the sound that I'm afraid it is his last breath, that he intends not to take another. He opens his eyes, looks not at me but at Asa. "Preacher," he says hoarsely. Licks his lips. "Asa."

Asa stays in his crouch, watches him warily.

"I'm sorry," Samuel says. "For what I did." Another long pause. He closes his eyes again, forces them open. Lets go of the rifle, reaches for the other man's hand. "I'm sorry I killed your little girl."

He lets Asa go. Actually I tell Asa to go and Samuel doesn't stop him. I tell him to find the phone downstairs if he can, call Hawkins and tell him he's coming out. He does, then brings the phone back upstairs. Offers to stay, and says it like he means it, but I say, no, go, and finally he does, the painting of Emily in his hand. I hear the door, and the shuffling and stamping of a lot of feet, and I brace for them to burst inside, charge upstairs, but instead they retreat and then it is quiet. Even the helicopter has gone.

It is very dark still, so dark, but I'm close to my brother and I can see the damp of his hair, the sweat on his forehead, the color of his skin, which is not a color his skin should be. The blood on the floor and his shirt looks almost black in the dim light, in such quantities, and I consider what it would be like to paint blood that way, to paint not a brilliant shock of red but that saturated threat of black. I will never try it.

"We should go, too."

Samuel doesn't deny it. "Where will you go?"

"Hawkins's house," I say, because it's the answer he wants and because it's true.

"Where will I go?"

"You know." I try to remember what he always told me. Okay not to like what was, not okay to pretend it wasn't. "To prison somewhere. I'll visit."

"They could kill me anyway." He doesn't have to pause between every word anymore, and I think that should be reassuring, but it isn't, because there seems so little breath at all, each so shallow there's little to separate it from not breathing. "Execute me."

"That won't happen," I tell him. "And if it does, I'll come to be with you."

He grimaces, the flash of teeth. "I wouldn't want that."

"Then I would do what you wanted. Please, Samuel. We will deal with what we need to deal with. I will. But please don't make me watch you die here and now, in this house." I tug at his arm, but he resists, doesn't even let me move him a few inches. He looks at me, a hint of an apology in his expression, but I see there is something keeping him here, something appealing about it, the idea of dying here in this house, in the shadow of Eden. I feel it pulling at him. Our father in the mountain. Our mother downstairs. Now Samuel here, a delayed fulfillment of that horrific night so many years ago.

"I didn't mean to become this," he says.

"I know."

The phone has been silent a long time. Asa talked to them, explained Samuel and I needed more time. Or they're planning to move in soon. Or the battery is dead. In any case it stays dark.

"I wish I could go back," he says. Doesn't say to when. Doesn't have to. Back to the cabin. To the moments before the bomb, the idea of the bomb. Before the militia meetings, the pamphlets and tracts. Before the tattoo. The hallway. Gethsemane.

"You can go forward," I tell him. "You can't go back. People hurt us. You hurt people. Those things can't be undone, and they can't be escaped. But your life is not over."

A long silence. Broken by her name. "Emily's is."

"Yes." She is waiting for me in the darkness when I close my eyes, smiling in her school picture, lying in her hospital bed. I suppose she always will be. I open my eyes. Emily is gone, Samuel is there. "And that's your fault, Samuel. Maybe . . . maybe it would be fairer if your life were over. Maybe it's fairer that you have to live with what you've done. Fair or not, your life is not over. No, you can't be who you used to be. But you can change again."

He looks at me, ashen and weak. I have never thought of that word in conjunction with my brother, *weak*. It makes him look frightened, and I know Samuel must have been frightened in his life, probably many times, but he has never let me know it, has never let it show. Maybe that's what frightens him most of all: Being afraid. Being weak. But now he puts his bloodied hand on my cheek, turns my face and brings it low to his so he can see my eyes, so I can see his.

"What if I can't change?" His voice is fading, quieting to something lower and starker than a whisper. "What if this is all I am?"

"Oh, Samuel," I say, "you're so much more."

And he looks at me, and looks at me, and after a long time I see something shift in his face, and I know he has finally remembered how to believe in something good.

I have been thinking a lot about what I say at the beginning of every prayer I lead with my congregation: Gracious and Heavenly Father. Not *Lord*. Not *God*. Father.

Perhaps I haven't been fair to You. It is not possible for any being to love another more than I loved Emily. And still I could not protect her. So I have allowed myself to consider the possibility that You could not protect her, either. Is that blasphemy? All-knowing, I have preached, all-powerful. But isn't love the greatest power of all, haven't I preached that, too? *The greatest of these is.* So maybe the fact that You didn't protect Emily doesn't mean You didn't love her. Doesn't mean You aren't there.

But it hurts, Father. I have a thought I can't seem to rid myself of. It says: If I believed she was with You, it would not hurt this much.

I keep remembering my own father praying the psalms outside my window at night. So many of those songs, even the ones that begin with blackest despair, have a turn. Somewhere before the end there is a revelation. A resurgence. Faith restored, emboldened. Jubilation replaces anguish; joy banishes sorrow. It seems impossible to imagine I might ever have faith so robust again. Lamentation resonates; elation does not. I am still in the desert, and I can't imagine ever returning to the ocean of faith I dove headlong into as a young man on the side of a road. But perhaps one day I will make my way to a small oasis. Maybe I will have to content myself with a quieter faith than I am used to. A faith of still waters.

You have promised that faith as small as a mustard seed can move mountains. And that is all I have left, Father: a mustard seed, and an especially tiny, fragile one.

But I am surrounded by mountains.

*Y*ou will start reading here, won't you, Jo? It's where I've finished, the place I've avoided and worked relentlessly toward all the same. Home.

So. A first thing to say, and a last. The obvious would be that I love you, but that is simultaneously too trite and too profound. I was thinking today, walking down the mountain with you, that Mom used to say it all the time. When we woke up, when we went to school, when we came home, before bed. Like she knew she'd have to work them all in before it was too late. I never said it much, did I? I hope it was plain enough anyway.

You will tell them I'm here, if you haven't already. Your phone in the bathroom. I forgot it in there, but only for a few minutes. After that I left it on purpose. Not because I want to be caught. If I wanted to be caught I could have hiked out of the mountains anytime; I didn't have to wait for you. It's not a test, Jo. You'll turn me in. I knew it as soon as I saw Lockjaw outside the cabin, maybe before. And this isn't blame, either. Lots of places I could have gone. Lots of opportunities for me to leave, had I wanted to. (I don't know if I'll let them take me when they come. Forgive me if I didn't.)

So how to explain it? Why did I go to the cabin, stay there until you came, leave the phone for you to find? Why am I here in the hall *outside your old room, watching you sleep, instead of vanishing into the night? I've lost myself, Jo. Didn't realize it until you told me the girl had died. (I can hardly make myself write it. Can you tell? Does it show in the way I ink the words?) I can't understand how I became someone who could be responsible for that. I can't see how it happened, or what to do next.*

It's an unfair thing to lay at your feet. Something else I hope you can forgive me for. But I have made so many choices for you over the years, little Josie, hard ones, sometimes. Make just this one for me.

In the end, maybe there is only this, Jo. Not as heartwarming as "I love you," perhaps, but because you are my sister and you have known me all your life, you'll realize it might mean more: I trust you.

I tape the map to a piece of board propped on my easel. Run my hand over the river of words along the Missouri, the smudges where Samuel's hand crossed his own words over the Continental Divide, the thumbprint of blood near Prospect that he left when he handed me the map in the old house, made me promise to hide it from Hawkins and the rest. One last secret.

I tilt the easel toward the southern window. This had been Kev's bedroom, and its view is the best on the ground floor. Windows on two walls, south toward Elk Fork and the sun, and east toward the mines. No room for both my easels and my bed, so I sleep in the living room. Hawkins has called a couple times, says one of these days he'll come up from Arizona to build an addition onto the back for me, or maybe an elevator. (He always forces a laugh here, and I can never tell him Samuel and I joked about the same thing in the old house.) But Hawkins is never coming back here; I know that even if he doesn't.

I've been to see Samuel twice. They're keeping him in Great Falls for the trial, but it's looking like he'll end up at the supermax in Colorado. Won't see him so often then. It will be letters, mostly. At least the map assures me he knows how to write one.

I turn back to it now. Thin paper, already some small tears along the creases where Samuel folded and refolded it. I'll have to take care not to get my paint too wet. This new house is higher on the hill than the one I shared with my brother, and farther south. The outline of the mountains is slightly different than I'm used to, the peaks over Eden and Gethsemane in equal balance through the window. I tilt my easel again, position my chair so I'm looking north, until the meadows and mountains that were once mine fill the frame.

I dampen my brush, load it with the clay and ore and silt that flowed out of the mines, out of the mountains, the years of earth and labor and struggle that made this sullied, beautiful valley what it is. I brush it across the map, where it mingles with my brother's words, his blood, blurs them all to a smooth wash that gentles the rivers and mountains and plains beneath. I angle the brush, move my wrist, my fingertips, and the paint obeys me, forms the familiar ridgeline along the top of the paper. Subtly different, yes—the perspective, the light—but familiar nonetheless, in a way that is both comforting and maddening.

I return my brush to the water, the mud. Bring Eden into creation once again.

ACKNOWLEDGMENTS

[TK; allow 2 pages]

A Note About the Author

S. M. Hulse's debut novel, *Black River*, was a PEN/Hemingway Award for First Fiction finalist, an Amazon Best Book of the Month, an ALA Notable Book, an ABA Indies Introduce title, an Indie Next pick, and winner of the Reading the West Book Award. She received her MFA from the University of Oregon and was a fiction fellow at the University of Wisconsin–Madison. An avid horsewoman, she has lived throughout the American West.